Praise God From Whom All Blessings Flow

To: [handwritten inscription] Many blessings to you! Amy Shelor Dye

This book is a work of fiction. Names, characters, businesses, organizations, places, events, and incidents either are the product of the author's imagination or are used fictitiously. Any resemblance to actual persons, living or dead, events, or locales is entirely coincidental.

Cataloging-in-Publication Data
Dye, Amy Shelor
1.Young Adult—Fiction 2. Paranormal—Fiction 1 3. Science—Fiction/Fantasy
4. Self-awareness—Fiction

ISBN 978-1494856953
1494856956

Cover design by Amy Shelor Dye

Printed in the United States of America
Charleston, SC

First Edition

Moonshine Serenade

AMY SHELOR DYE

Chapter One
Do You Want To Know A Secret

I am an unwilling participant in someone else's dream.

And in this living nightmare, I have been dragged to Boones Mill - a single stoplight town with a police force of one and a so-called downtown area that includes a post office the size of a postage stamp and a farm supply store which in addition to the vegetable seeds and bags of fertilizer also sells the only apparel available within a ten mile radius: work gloves, bib overalls, and barn boots. Unless you count the *Moonshine Capital of the World* t-shirts displayed proudly for sale in the local convenience stores.

It's all because my mom has a *feeling* about this place, deciding to buy our new dwelling before stepping one foot inside the front door. She calls it her dream home, having admired it from afar for the many years she passed by it while growing up on a nearby farm.

My parents broke the news to my little sister, Samantha, and me that we would be relocating from the city of Springfield, Virginia, near Washington, D.C., further south to this rural town in Franklin County one evening over supper. Their reasoning: to help my aging grandparents, but mainly for - as Dad had put it – the betterment of our family. They had grown tired of the hustle-and-bustle of the city that had excited them when they were first married. Their forties had brought on a yen for the calm and quiet of the country life.

Much moaning, groaning and gnashing of teeth had ensued on my part.

And I call my best friend, Kaye, the drama queen.

Since our arrival I'd only managed to send one measly text to Kaye because we were so busy: unloading boxes, telling the movers where to place boxes, unpacking boxes – boxes, boxes, boxes. After this I hoped to never see another of those square brown things for a very long time.

Unless it meant we were moving back home.

Back home.

It was easy to forget that Springfield is not my home anymore, that Kaye is not down the street – but two hundred or so miles away, that another family with two children will be moving into the home that bears my pencil marked growth chart on the bedroom door frame. Though we had primed and painted every square inch of that house to prepare for the sale, those crude memories were the one thing I couldn't erase. It would almost be as if I had never existed there.

Mocking my dark thoughts, the summer sunlight streamed through my bedroom window and hit me square in the face as I rolled over to check out the clock. It was almost 11:00 o'clock in the morning. I'd been sulking in my room, but now I had been summoned by a voice from down below.

After a brief search I discovered a pair of jean shorts and a t-shirt that I unpacked yesterday. I pulled my hair back into a ponytail – why bother with a shower and makeup, I'd be working all day and who would I be seeing around here anyway? Instead I took my time making the bed, a four poster hand-me-down that I love - especially covered in my vintage ivory chenille bedspread. Kaye finds my preference for old things odd. I get it from Mom – her idea of weekend fun is dragging my little sister and me on her antiquing adventures.

The bed making done, I sat on the edge and fiddled with the photos on my bedside table. Dawdling – as my Grandma Ellen would say.

She'd be right.

I still wasn't ready to head down the stairs per Mom's bidding. But the second time her three name call proclaimed that Sallie Beth Songer better get down here right now; I decided that my dawdling time had ended.

I trudged down the creaky stairs to face my mom and the tasks she had laid out for me today. Before rounding the corner that led into the kitchen I heard my name – not as another call to duty, but as part of a conversation. Samantha and Mom must be talking about me. I knew Dad was gone; it was Monday morning, and even though we had just relocated over the weekend he had started the first day of his new job as a manager at a manufacturing company in the nearby town of Rocky Mount.

"I still don't understand why Sallie is upset about moving," I overheard Samantha chattering. "I think living in the country will be a lot more fun than our old neighborhood where I couldn't even ride my bike without old Mr. Cundiff complaining that the noise bothers his dog. And this house is way better – it's bigger and so old that it's kind of spooky."

I prefer not to admit that my sister is right about anything, but she is spot on about our new residence. The realtor told us it was built in the 1820's and has been renovated over the years to include electricity and indoor plumbing. It is two stories of solid brick with large windows and a small front porch topped by an enclosed Romeo and Juliet balcony.

My biggest complaint about the house (other than the fact that we are now living in it) is that the closets are too small, so my parents let me pick out a beautiful antique armoire for my bedroom.

My room is at the back of the top floor and from my windows I can see mountains that rise up behind the house like stately Confederate generals and an old apple orchard with spiky, green-leafed trees that line up as if they are rifle bearing soldiers standing at attention before their commanders. Dividing the orchard and the mountains is a forest thick with pines, oaks and maples. A glance to my right reveals an expanse of fields and in the distance is a large red barn with the biggest American flag I have ever seen painted on its side. With the windows open I can hear the nearby creek babbling as it splashes over rocks that it will smooth over time. It is so peaceful and quiet here that I had found it hard to fall asleep the last two nights.

"I can hear you talking about me, Sam," I grumbled to my sister as I walked into the kitchen. "You may think this house is cool, but I hardly have any closet space."

"And she's alive!" Mom attempted some humor with a Dr. Frankenstein voice. "Speaking of closets," she ignored my scowl. "Here's a box that I need you to take up to the closet in our computer room."

"But I just got down here," I groaned.

"It will only take a couple of minutes, Sallie. I want to get it off this island so I can start unpacking my roosters."

Mom is a rooster fanatic. She has rooster plates, a rooster teapot, cookie jar, salt and pepper shakers - the list goes on and on.

"May I please have some breakfast first?" I was being snarky on purpose. Mom doesn't particularly care for snarky.

"Don't you mean brunch?" When my only response was a hard stare she waved her hands around the disaster of a room. "Sure, if you can find something to eat on."

I rummaged through a few boxes and found a Styrofoam bowl and plastic spoon. Mom and I had made a quick grocery store run our first night here, picking up the essentials: milk, cereal and bread. We also grabbed some stuff to make sandwiches, hot dogs and hamburgers. Of course the grill was one of the first things my dad had ready to roll.

I fixed myself a bowl of granola, sat down at the kitchen table and noticed that Samantha's attention had been turned to her latest mystery novel. When we had starting packing up to come here she had run across Mom's collection of Nancy Drew books from her own girlhood days and had been devouring them ever since. Today's title: *The Mystery at Lilac Inn.*

Mom busied herself around the kitchen. Even after the last couple of weeks with little sleep, late night packing, and preparing for the move, she appears as beautiful as ever. Her auburn hair bounced about her shoulders as she dug into a box and pulled out some rooster stuff. She looked slim in her yoga pants and tank top; she must have already finished her bit of morning exercise. Maybe I could go for a run this evening after the air has cooled down; the thought cheered me up a bit. It was mid-June - not too hot and humid yet for an early evening jaunt.

Along with music – which I tend to devour - running is my salvation. It helps me to think clearly. The sound of my paced breathing is calming and the patter of my shoes hitting the pavement is almost melodious. Back in Springfield I was on the track team at my high school. I shoved another spoonful of cereal in my mouth and crunched hard, wondering if the Podunk high school I would be attending for my junior and senior years even has a team.

With my belly full and my mood slightly improved, I was ready to get to work. "So, where's this box you need out of your way?"

"It's right here." Mom started to hand the box to me; then, as if having a second thought, she sat it down on the table and instead wrapped her arms around me in a warm hug.

"I hope you realize how happy it makes me to be back where I grew up; living in the home I've dreamed about for years." She whispered in my ear. "You could have made this move a lot harder on us than you have. Thank you for that. This is a special place to me; I hope it becomes that way for you as well."

I hugged her back. The last thing I want is for her to feel guilty about ruining my life - even if I'm the only one who thinks my life is being ruined.

"You grew up here and you turned out great, so I guess it can't be so bad," I gave her my most convincing fake smile as I grabbed the box from the table.

As I headed toward the stairs I could hear my mom's laughter - actually more of a "Ha, Ha, Ha," at my last remark. It felt nice to be jovial with her. In the last few weeks there had been some tense moments; we'd had a huge yard sale in Springfield, and I had accidentally sold my dad's favorite golf clubs for a mere pittance of their worth. They had both expressed their suspicions that it was not indeed, accidental.

And realizing that she was the primary catalyst for our move, I know my mom felt guilty as she watched my tearful goodbye with Kaye.

I walked into the small bedroom that we would be using as an office and opened the door to the tiny closet. Without thinking I threw the box down on the floor a little too eagerly, causing a floorboard to pop into the air like the light end of a see-saw.

Perfect, Sallie. You've broken something already. Won't it be delightful informing your parents about the damage to the new house?

Well, new to us anyway.

I knelt down and pushed the box away. Where it had dropped one of the boards had lifted and was now lying partially on top of the one next to it. Even in the dark closet I could tell there was something underneath where the floorboard once was. I stood up and pulled the overhead light chain so I could get a better view of what was inside the hole – hoping like the dickens it wasn't a mouse, spider or something else creepy. But with the closet lit up I could see clearly that it was no living creature.

"It's a book," I said out loud.

I pulled it from beneath the floor and blew off the dust to reveal a cover made of worn brown leather. Inside were pages yellowed with age – putting me in the mind of one of the old maps that Grandpa Jesse has hanging up on the wall above his desk. As I carefully turned the fragile pages, a photo fell into my lap. It was black and white school portrait of a teenage girl wearing a collared buttoned-down dress. Her wide eyes were expressive and her shoulder length dark hair was held back by a barrette. But it was her smile that captured my attention; I felt as if at any second her lips would move and begin a conversation with me.

I flipped the picture over.

The name Letitia Holley was printed across the back.

Plopping onto the floor, I thumbed back to the beginning of the book; it was handwritten in a cursive script, the first page dated May 30, 1939.

That's interesting. May 30 is also my parents wedding anniversary, but not the 1939 part; that was more than seventy years ago. A quick glance at the first few words and a shiver ran down my spine.

My name is Letitia Holley and today I saw a murder!

I was compelled to read more, but felt somewhat akin to a voyeur for reading what certainly appeared to be the diary of the girl in the photograph. If I had taken the time to write a private journal, I certainly would not want anyone reading it; but this one was from the 1930's and there was a chance that she might not be alive anymore. And if a murder did happen around here then surely it was in the news at the time, so this information wouldn't have been totally private.

I had made myself a convincing argument to keep reading without any guilt.

I've never written in this book before. It was a birthday gift from my parents when I turned sixteen last winter and here it is spring already, but I had to write down what I saw today because nobody believes me when I tell them I saw somebody get killed. I was walking in the woods today because it is lady slipper season. I love those flowers because they resemble a dainty pink slipper. They are rare and can be hard to find. And even though it is further out than I'm allowed to go alone, I know the best place to look for them. I took off this morning in search of some and had just spotted a patch when I heard the voices of two men arguing. The sound frightened me, so I crouched down behind an old tree as the two men came into sight. One of the men had his back to me, but I could see that he had dark, curly hair and wore blue pants with suspenders. The other man was dressed as if he'd been farming. He wore a wide-brimmed straw hat that was pulled down so low it hid his face.

I heard him tell the other man, "I told you what I'd do to you if you came 'round here again." Then he hit him hard on the head with a big tree branch, and the man fell to the ground with a loud thump. The man in the hat knelt down. He must have been listening to see if the man on the ground was still breathing. Then he grabbed him up by the arms and started dragging him off further into the woods.

I waited until I could not see them anymore, and then I ran home as fast as my shoes would carry me. I found Mama in the kitchen and told her that I had witnessed a murder. Turning away from the pot she was stirring on the stove, she told me to calm down and asked me to tell her exactly what I had seen. I told her everything as I've written it here, and then she asked me if I was sure about that.

I said, "Yes, Mama, I swear it!"

Then she scolded me for swearing and said that she'd ask Daddy to take a look after supper.

"Sallie, how long does it take to put a box in a closet?" Mom was nothing if not relentless in her quest to get this house in order. "The rest of these boxes down here aren't going to get unpacked on their own!"

"I'll be down in a minute," I shouted back. "I was… um… reading something!"

I leafed through the pages of the diary to make sure there was more written there and was excited to see pages filled with Letitia's pretty lettering. I held the book in my hands while I debated if I should show it to my mom.

Being the history buff that she is, I was afraid if I did that she would want to donate it to a local historical society or insist that I find the owner or her living family.

Selfishly, I wanted the opportunity to read the rest of Letitia's diary and find out more about what happened – more about her life. There were so many questions running through my head. Had she lived in this house? And most importantly, did she really witness a murder? For some reason I felt as if I had found an old friend in this new place - a friend who was already sharing her secrets with me.

"Letitia," I whispered to the snapshot, "You can be my secret for a little while."

After being imprisoned in the house all day, I was able to escape for a run in the early evening. Mom suggested the route she had taken that morning, and it was pleasantly refreshing compared to the many runs I had made amid the stench of SUV fumes and invisibly-fenced, barking dogs in my old neighborhood.

With freshly harvested hay and tilled dirt, the air here smells like a scratch and sniff of the colors green and brown, and only once did a car pass by on my side forcing me to retreat to the knee high grass on the far shoulder of the road – it felt itchy and scratchy up against my bare legs.

I enjoyed the run. It was the most fun I'd had since our arrival and gave me the chance to forget about the move for a while – meditating instead on the sound of my breathing and pounding feet. I found that I missed Will, Kaye's big brother and my running buddy as of late, less than I thought I would.

When I got back home, I took a shower and then spent some time organizing my room. The disarray was making me mucho loco, and I had hoped that if I found a place for all my belongings the room would feel more as if it belonged to me instead of a stranger. To my disappointment, even with posters on the walls and photos displayed on my dresser, the room still didn't feel quite like it was mine.

I was exhausted by the time I felt organized enough to go to bed and decided that I was not up for reading more of Letitia's diary. I wanted to be able to concentrate on what she had to say, and tonight was not the night for focused reading.

Instead I sat on my bed and stared at the picture of Kaye, Will, and me framed and parked in pole position on my nightstand. Their mother, Mrs. Landry, had taken the photo a couple of weeks before I moved. The three of us were sitting on their patio laughing about Will's first foray into coaching a little league soccer team. He got a little too close to one of the kids as she was practicing her goal shot; she missed the soccer ball, and ended up kicking Will in a sensitive location instead. Mrs. Landry must have heard our giggles and jokes about Will's future ability to father children because she ended up outside with her camera. I tried to hide how thrilled I was when she asked me to stand in the middle; I knew that Will would have no choice but to put his arm around me. We all had large smiles on our faces, despite the fact that we knew my leaving was the reason she was taking this photo.

I held the picture in my hand and ran my fingers over Will's face. Will is the masculine version of Kaye with wavy black hair so unruly that he is constantly brushing a stray lock away from eyes that twinkle brighter than the sapphires in my Mom's birthstone ring.

It was close to midnight, and not knowing if Kaye would still be awake, I punched her number on my cell anyway. I had to talk to Kaye - it wasn't even an option really. I wondered if this is how a recovering addict feels when going through withdrawal. If so, I wasn't the type that was going to stay on the wagon. It was the most difficult thing I had ever done - to go from speaking with my best friend almost every day for the last eleven years to barely speaking to her at all for the last few.

Kaye answered on the first ring. "Hey! I wasn't expecting to hear from you again so soon, not that I'm complaining. Is everything okay there?"

"Yeah," I could feel tears start to sting my eyes as I tried to talk. Stupid emotions – can't I carry on a conversation without getting all weepy? "I miss you. I miss Will. It's so different here."

I managed to choke out. "Have you talked to him since I left?"

"Yes, I have. He called from soccer camp to see if I'd talked to you, and he finally 'fessed up that he has a thing for you."

So, Will was thinking of me. *Yay* - an imaginary cheering section hurrahed in my head.

"Do me a favor, Kaye."

"What is it?" I could tell she was curious.

"The next time Will calls you to ask about me, give him my number and tell him to call and ask me himself."

"Sure. I promise to do that," she said with a giggle. "Now let me tell you what happened here today."

And then Kaye was off faster than a champion horse sprinting around the track; rambling on about how Mr. Cundiff's Chihuahua got out and snapped at one of the Mason twins (who probably deserved it – I had babysat those kids many times, and they were hellions) and how Mrs. Mason freaked out and called 911, which sent an ambulance, police cruiser and dog catcher into the neighborhood. Kaye would have gone on and on, and I would have listened happily and contentedly reliving my old neighborhood.

After chatting with Kaye, I knew that I could fall asleep easily. It was a relatively cool night, and my parents had turned off the air conditioning. With the windows open, I could hear the chirping of crickets, the croaking of bullfrogs and the low hooting of an owl – sounds of a summer night in the country. If not for the regular visits with my grandparents, I'm not sure that I would have recognized them. For the first time since moving into this room, they were a gentle lullaby coaxing me to sleep.

I drifted away, the soothing music of the night interwove with my dream. I was walking through shadowy woods. The stars were concealed by mist and leafy branches; the pale yellow moon barely visible as it rose behind the trees. Ahead of me, a man stood in bibbed overalls with a battered straw hat pulled down over his brow. His bearded face bore a scowl and then, upon spotting me in the shadows, contorted into a pleased sneer. He lunged at me like a stalking cat about to strike. My instincts told me to turn and run, but before I could move, the man disappeared in a vapor before my eyes. It was then that I heard a faint sound – someone calling out a name that I couldn't quite make out.

Was it...mine?

I tore through branches pushing them aside as I searched for the source of the voice. I stumbled, falling to my knees. As I pushed myself up, a hand grabbed my elbow. Panicked, I tried to shove it away, but then I saw him – a different man. This one was young with dark curly hair and dressed in suspenders. His dark eyes pleading, he released my arm and beckoned for me to follow. I felt no fear, rather a sense of responsibility to follow him.

A thud and a crash jerked me back to reality. I sat up straight in my bed and scanned the dark room. One glance at the clock revealed I had only been asleep for about an hour. What could the noise have been that woke me?

Then I noticed that the photo of Kaye, Will, and me was no longer sitting next to the clock. My eyes dropped to the hardwood floor – it was laying there… the glass cracked. Had someone been in my room? But how could someone escape so quickly and why on earth would anyone be in here to begin with? The strange dream and abrupt awakening must be creating these delusional thoughts. I must have hit the picture with my hand during the dream and knocked it from the table. I reached down, picked up the photograph, and set it gingerly next to my clock.

Relaxed now that I had solved my own mystery, I yawned and laid my head back on the pillow. Just before closing my eyes, I noticed the broken glass had formed a perfect zigzag line between Will's head and mine.

Chapter Two
Crazy

The small stream meandering through our property is lined with weeds, bright orange wildflowers, and gnarled trees with exposed roots that remind me of the snakes on the mythical Medusa's head. Miniature white caps rush over the rocks, bright green leaves and twigs ride them like white water rafters bobbing and lurching before plunging over the side.

Samantha was standing barefoot and ankle-deep in the creek. Her red ponytail swung back and forth as she splashed her hands into the water attempting to catch the darting minnows and crawfish that would slip quickly under rocks to peer out at her with beady little eyes.

I watched from a loamy spot along the bank with my own bare toes sunk in the sandy red mud mixture and tossed the occasional pebble into the tiny rapids – always away from Samantha who otherwise would complain that it was me who was scaring the little creatures away.

She's persistent, I'll give her that - a miniature replica of my mother in both appearance and personality, though Samantha's hair is a much brighter shade of red that Mom often compares to the setting sun. They're both strong-willed and hot-headed with tempers that come in quick bursts and then diffuse quickly – similar to a firecracker my fair-haired dad has always said which is ironic since I'm the one who was born on the Fourth of July.

My personality is a mix between my parents. Dad tends to be more laid back than the rest of us, although if you get him riled up, as Mom would say, he would be quick to let you know his opinion on a subject. If I'm passionate about something, I can get fired up too, allowing my emotions to get the best of me; but, most of the time, I try to think about something before jumping to conclusions and saying something I might regret.

Mom claims I'm the spitting image of my namesake, her grandmother. Having only seen her in black and white pictures, I've noticed the resemblance. Even without being able to see the strawberry blonde hair and green eyes, I could be looking at a photo of myself during a time when women wore hats, gloves, and bobby-pin curled tresses on a daily basis.

My great-grandmother, Sallie, was quite the rebel in her

time. She had a secret love affair and ran away from home at seventeen, returning a few months later married and pregnant, but without a husband. She kept her maiden name, and refused to say who her husband was and why he didn't return with her. She never married again and died from pneumonia when my grandmother was only nine years old. Sallie's parents raised Grandma Ellen from that point and left her the farmstead that she and Grandpa Jesse still own today.

Though similar in appearance, I'm not sure how much of my great-grandmother's personality I inherited. I'll be seventeen soon and can't imagine acting rashly and running off to get married. I rarely act impulsively; although I have on the occasion when I'm thinking with my heart instead of my head. Maybe that's what my great-grandmother had been doing – thinking with her heart.

Today, I don't know what I had been thinking when I had volunteered to take my twelve-year-old firecracker of a sister out to investigate our new environment. Samantha's half-hour of determination had paid off with a loud splash and a squeal of triumph as she held up a squirming crawfish between her thumb and pointer-finger.

"Check this out, Sallie!" She shouted, "It looks like a little lobster."

"Be careful, or it will pinch you," The words had barely left my mouth before Samantha yelped and launched it off her finger.

"See, I told you!" I couldn't help laughing despite her pained expression. A few minutes outside had made me realize how glad I was to be out of the house today and I was hoping the sweet smell of victory Samantha had achieved would make her willing to venture on to something new.

I washed my feet off in the creek and pulled on the ratty tennis shoes that matched my equally as old t-shirt and cut-off jean shorts. "Didn't you say that you wanted to find that old cemetery," I knew this would be just the thing to arouse her interest.

"Yeah!" She climbed out of the creek enthusiastically - wiping her muddy, wet hands against her shorts. "Do you think ghosts only come out at night?" She asked expectantly as she donned her own shoes.

I smiled at my sister's adventurous spirit. "Samantha, you know I don't believe in ghosts."

"Why not?" Her smile flipped to a frown. "Don't you think

any of the stories Grandma has told us are true?"

"I think people who claim to have seen a ghost probably think that they did see something unnatural, but I tend to believe that there's a rational explanation behind what they think they saw." Samantha's expression was perplexed; I didn't want to ruin this adventure for her like the time I had accidently revealed to her that the tooth fairy isn't real. I linked my arm with hers. "But Grandma's stories are fun, and I enjoy hearing them too."

Grandma Ellen's most recent supernatural tale was about an old graveyard on our property that held graves from as early as the 1860's. It was also rumored to be haunted.

"The people that lived in this house before you let the local historical society stop here to explore the cemetery as part of its Halloween ghost tour," explained Grandma Ellen as she sat at the kitchen table on the Saturday afternoon of our move. She and my grandfather had stopped by with lemonade and homemade snacks for us and the movers.

"Mom," Mom scolded with a smile. "Stop trying to spook the girls."

"I'm not spooked," chimed in Samantha with wide eyes. "I hope it's true!"

Following the directions our grandmother had given us, it didn't take long to top the grassy hill that led down to that cemetery. It was located a few yards from the edge of the forest. A rutted road which hadn't been used in years ended almost directly in front of the gate. A wrought iron fence with jagged metal spires encircled the burial area; gravestones in various heights, sizes and colors jutted chaotically from the ground toward the sky.

I surveyed the cemetery from my perch on the knoll and noticed some movement among the cemetery stones. A sudden discomfort came over me, a sort of sixth sense that left me feeling as though bugs were slithering across my skin; it was urging me that whatever was down there was up to no good.

"Crouch down!" I hissed at Samantha, shoving her to the ground and dropping down beside her.

"What's wrong?" She whimpered, sounding a lot less brave than she had a few minutes ago.

As we lay with our chins on the grass, a man rose up from a bent position in front of one of the gravestones. I sucked in my breath as I took stock of the man's appearance - he was wearing a battered straw hat, pulled low and shielding his face.

"I *said* what is going on?" I could tell that Samantha was expecting some guidance from me, but I wasn't about to take my eyes off the man to offer her some comfort.

"Be quiet, and don't move until he leaves." I instructed.

"Until who leaves?" She questioned again, looking around us.

"The man...down there...in the cemetery." At this point I did dare to turn away from him long enough to question my sister. "Don't you see him?"

Samantha struggled to get up. "No, I don't see him! What's wrong with you, Sallie? Quit trying to scare me, this isn't funny at all!" I pushed her back down again because I could see a man standing amongst the graves and the bad feeling about him had not dissipated whatsoever.

"Stop it!" She yelled at me.

As if hearing Samantha's shout, the man turned toward us, cocking his head like he was listening for another sound. Thankfully, Samantha remained quiet, and he began to move in the opposite direction of where we were hiding. He passed through the cemetery gate without even opening it and disappeared at the woods' edge.

I couldn't move. My legs had turned to concrete blocks and the air had been knocked out of my lungs.

How could I see the man and Samantha not?

What was this place doing to me? First, I had imagined that someone was in my bedroom last night, now I was seeing people that possibly did not exist.

Samantha was growing fidgety next to me. She had sat up with her legs crossed and was staring me down. "Can we go now?" Her voice was angry, "If you are done trying to be funny."

I realized I had two options.

I could let Samantha think that I was totally insane by trying to convince her that, although she couldn't see him, I did see a man standing in the cemetery that walked through a gate and vaporized in the air.

Or, I could take a cue from what she really thought was going on and pretend that this was all a joke at her expense. I quickly chose the second option.

Hoping that some of Kaye's acting skills had rubbed off on me, I gave Samantha the best *aw shucks* expression I could muster and then stood up, pulling her up with me. "You got me." I shrugged my shoulders, pretending to admit a farce, "I thought you would be much easier to scare than that."

She rolled her eyes, "Of course I wasn't scared. Actually, I'm more disappointed. I would love to see a ghost." With those parting words, she took off down the hill toward the cemetery.

It took me less than a second to comprehend the term that had so casually rolled off her tongue.

Ghost? Ghost!

I wasn't ready to admit to myself that that was what I had seen. There had to be another, better, more plausible explanation - maybe the man had been obscured from Samantha's view...which might be conceivable if we had not been in the exact same location with the exact same line of vision. Plus, there was no quick excuse that I could come up with to explain away how he had plainly vanished at the edge of the woods and with him that strange foreboding feeling.

"Are you coming?" Samantha called.

She had a head start on me, I had to walk fast to catch up with her. We entered the cemetery through a rusted metal gate that hung by one twisted hinge and squeaked as we pulled it open. I felt surprisingly calm, for which I was thankful; I did not want to cause Samantha any further excitement with my anxious behavior.

We wandered in opposite directions amongst the graves. This place was old. It hadn't been used as a location for new burials in some time. It even smelled old, reminding me of funeral flowers left to decay on the graves like the bodies that lay under the dirt beneath them.

Some of the headstones were covered with a spotty, greenish moss and many of the engravings were so weathered that it was difficult to make out names or dates. I found some that were readable: Isaac Renick, 1834-1891; Bessie Renick, beloved wife of Isaac, deceased 1839-1903; infant son of Isaac and Bessie Renick, died 1853. I sadly noticed that it was not unusual to see the graves of infants - most of them marked only by a flat stone. One stood out - a small concrete marker adorned by an angel statuette with empty eyes that stared at me. Its broken wings lay crumbled across the ground.

As I moved about the stones reading names, I thought about the living people they represented. Had they led happy lives? Did they laugh out loud at funny jokes, or chuckle quietly to themselves? What was their favorite meal? Had they lived nearby?

It was then that it occurred to me that Letitia's family may be buried here. What was her last name? It was on the tip of my tongue but wouldn't come to me - something with an H – Haley, Harley, Hall?

I walked around searching for a name that sounded familiar and realized I was standing in about the same location where I saw the mysterious man.

I read the markers in front of me: Elsie Wertz, died April 15, 1927; Nathan Wertz, died October 22, 1925; Beauregard Jones, died May 30, 1939.

Wait a minute…May 30… my parents' anniversary.

But the date was familiar to me for another reason - something I remembered seeing recently. It hit me so suddenly I spoke out loud. "That's the day Letitia saw the murder!"

"Who's Letitia?" Samantha's voice caused me to almost jump out of my skin. I didn't notice she had come to stand beside me.

"Geez, Sam! You nearly gave me a heart attack!" My words were too harsh as I turned toward her.

Samantha's face began to flush, and her eyes turned a deep shade of emerald. "Well, you're the one yelling about a murder!" She retorted with hands-on-hips. I had unintentionally upset her. Again.

"I'm sorry," I wrapped my arm around her and gave her a half-hug. "I guess this graveyard is making me jumpy."

My apology did the trick because her eyes and skin began to fade back to their normal colors. "So, are you going to answer my question?" she prodded, "Who's Letitia?"

I had to think fast. I didn't really want her to really know who Letitia was, or how I knew about her. Samantha wouldn't be able to leave me alone until she got her hands on that diary too. "Oh, that's the name of a girl in a…um…book I'm reading."

I didn't feel too bad. That wasn't really a lie.

"Well, that's a dumb reason to yell," she scolded. "I thought you were talking about a real murder."

For all I knew, I could be talking about a real murder. From the little I had read of Letitia's diary, she sure seemed convinced. Suddenly, I felt eager to get back home and read more of what she had written. I wondered if Beauregard Jones was the man she saw killed, or was it was a coincidence that he died the same day.

The return trip was uneventful, mostly a straight path of meadow between the cemetery and the house. Samantha chattered endlessly. I hardly paid attention; answering yes and no when appropriate. I was too busy trying to decipher the encounter I'd had, at moments questioning my own sanity.

When we rounded the corner of our house, I saw a black Jeep parked in our driveway. A male figure was leaning up against it, his back to us.

And he was wearing a straw hat.

Samantha, who had been too busy talking and not paying attention, jerked her head up to see what had caused me to stop dead in my tracks. Her eyes lit up excitedly. "Now, that guy I see. Come on. Let's find out who it is." She started walking faster, and so did I just to keep up.

"Hey there!" Samantha heralded as we approached.

The guy standing against the Jeep turned around. One glance at his face left me with no doubt. He was definitely not a ghost, but an absolute vision clad in faded jeans, flip-flops, and a t-shirt that fit snugly across his lean, muscular chest.

He seemed to be around my age, maybe a bit older and was movie star gorgeous in a rugged sort of way – this guy could be a modern day cowboy. When he saw us, he smiled widely, revealing a row of perfect white teeth gleaming against tanned skin that harbored a couple days growth of scruff. As we got closer he removed what turned out to be a straw western-style hat with curled edges and ran his hand through sandy blonde hair that was styled in shaggy layers with the back grazing the top of his shirt.

"Hey yourself," he waved his hat in our direction. "I'm Zeke." The greeting flowed warm from his mouth like melted butter oozing down one of my grandmothers hot biscuits. It was the most beautiful southern drawl I had ever heard. I immediately felt at ease with him.

"Hi. I'm Sallie, and this is my sister, Samantha."

"Sallie. Now that's a name you don't hear much anymore," Zeke's voice was teasing.

I'd never really thought about it, but I guess it was true. I had been the only Sallie in a high school of over 2,000 students. "Well, Zeke's not exactly a name you run across every day either," I countered, my eyebrows raised.

He smiled that big, perfect smile and laughed. "I guess you're right. It's a Bible name, short for Ezekiel." Then he shrugged. "My dad's a minister."

Zeke placed the hat back on his head, and the movement brought my attention to his eyes. I had never before seen a pair that color before. Or, should I say colors. They were a fusion of green, gold and gray. They reminded me of a marble – swirled with color, but clear and bright. I realized I had been staring when he tilted his face toward the door of my house, breaking the spell his eyes had temporarily put me under.

"Can I help you with something?" I didn't know what this guy was doing here. Zeke had said that his dad was a minister, but I didn't get the impression he was out recruiting members for a church - though, he would certainly give me a reason to attend every Sunday.

"Oh, I stopped by here with my mom." He shifted his gaze to me again. "Our mothers were good friends in high school, and since we live down the road, she wanted to welcome your family personally."

"If they're inside, then why are you standing out here," blurted Samantha.

I elbowed her in the side; leave it to my little sister to be so rude.

But Zeke looked down at her and smiled, clearly entertained by my sister's poor manners. "Well, Little Red," he drawled.

"Samantha," she corrected.

"Oh, excuse me, Samantha," Zeke exaggerated her name.

I stifled a giggle. Maybe my sister had met her match.

"Mom can be a bit long winded, so I thought if I waited for her out here that she might not prolong her visit. Not that I would mind visiting with you lovely ladies for much longer," he took a second to glance at his watch, "but I need to be somewhere in about half-an-hour."

Normally I might have considered that last comment coming from someone who cut such a fine figure to be arrogant, but not Zeke. He seemed sincere – I could see that he truly was sorry that he had to rush off.

As if on cue, the front door of our house opened and out-stepped our mothers. They were laughing as if they had shared a good joke. I noticed that Zeke's mom has the same sandy blonde hair as he, cut in a bob similar to one I wore last summer.

Seeing the two women together gave me a sudden mental picture of my mom in high school – younger, but much the same as she appears now. I could see her chatting with friends as she leaned against her locker, laughing as she sat at a lunch table, and cheering on the football team from the stands. In that vision, my face could easily replace hers; those were all scenes from my own happy high school experience in Springfield.

"Sallie…Samantha - you may have heard me talk about Mrs. Marlow," Mom made the introduction as they neared us. "I see the three of you have already met."

"Please, call me Sara," she offered as she hugged both me and Samantha. "It's so good to see both of you. I hope you enjoy your new home." Sara paused to think for a moment. "Actually, Beth, this is not the first time that Sallie and Zeke have met. Remember that weekend we camped at the lake when they were toddlers?"

Zeke and I perused each other both searching for something that might reveal that memory from our past.

My mom burst out in laughter. "How could I forget that? We swore we'd never take kids that age camping again. They were cute, though. Do you still have those photos of them running around naked?"

"Mom!" I shouted, blushing. As I ducked my head down to hide my embarrassment, I caught Zeke's face out of the corner of my eye; his lips were twitching. I could tell that he was trying his best to hold something back.

But…obviously could not. "Yeah, she still has them," he snickered with a gleam in his eye. "Mom, didn't you pull them out for us to look at the other day?"

My head snapped back up with that comment; I narrowed my eyes and gave him the most evil of all the evil expressions I can give. I'm good at giving them too; Mom says I can shoot someone down with one glance. She says that talent will come in handy when I'm a parent.

Sara adjusted the handbag on her shoulder and gave me a sympathetic look. "No, I did not. Ignore my son."

"But if you really want to see them, Sallie, I'm sure we could dig them up for you." If we had been kids standing on a playground, Zeke would have reached over and yanked my hair.

"Ezekiel James Marlow!" Sara Marlow admonished. "Let's get out of here before you cause more trouble."

"Yeah, didn't you say you had to be somewhere in a half-hour, five minutes ago?" I added, not out of concern for his lateness but because I certainly didn't want him getting the last word.

"Yes, Ma'am." Zeke hopped into the Jeep. "Thanks for the reminder." Then with a wink he added, "I'll see *you* later."

With that last comment, they headed down the driveway amidst the waves and shouts of goodbye from Mom and

Samantha while I stood there staring after them with a gaping mouth not sure what to make of Zeke Marlow, but finding myself fascinated by him.

Though I trailed behind them as we walked back toward the house, I could hear Mom and Samantha discussing our morning's activities. I was surprised that Samantha made no mention of the incident at the cemetery. It must not have made a lasting impression on her; unfortunately, I was still going to have to deal with the fact that what I saw today was not explainable – at least not yet.

I grabbed a quick peanut butter and jelly sandwich and a cold glass of milk for lunch before I headed up to my bedroom, and shut the door behind me. I did a belly flop onto my bed, reached over to my nightstand, and opened the top drawer where I had hidden Letitia's diary.

Propping myself up against the headboard with pillows, I turned to the page dated May 31, 1939.

It was dark when Daddy came in from working on the farm last night. He does most of the work alone now since my older brother Charles joined the Navy. Mama and I pitch in as much as we can, and we have one hired hand that helps out during our small apple harvest, but Daddy doesn't know if we'll be able to pay him this year.

Daddy sat down at the table, and Mama explained to him about what I had seen in the woods while he was trying to enjoy his beans and cornbread. That's been our dinner almost every night for the last few years. I shouldn't complain. We are blessed. I have friends who've lost their homes, and some whose fathers have been carted off to jail for making a living the best way they could. Some of those men have helped to keep us in business, buying our apples to make their homemade liquor. Mama doesn't approve of it, but Daddy figures he'll do about anything to keep a roof over our heads and food in our bellies.

When Daddy finally got home , he was flat worn out and told me it was too dark for him to take a look right then, but that he would go out there first thing in the morning. After that, I washed up his dishes, kissed them both goodnight and got ready for bed.

I hadn't fallen asleep yet when I heard Mama and Daddy talking quietly outside my bedroom door.

"Do you really think he came back?" I heard Mama ask Daddy in a whisper.

Then I heard Daddy say, "It sure sounds like it by the

description Letitia gave you."

"Brave man," Mama replied.

I couldn't hear anymore after that. Their voices turned to mumbles as they went into their bedroom and closed the door. I tossed and turned trying to fall asleep. Finally, after counting sheep after sheep, I fell asleep only to see the man with a hat hitting the other man over and over again in my dreams.

I was caught up in my reading and barely heard the knock at my door. I quickly shoved the diary under my pillow and grabbed a paperback that was sitting on my nightstand.

"Come in," I opened the book, pretending that I had been engrossed in its pages.

Mom sat down on the edge of my bed. "Hey, Sweetie."

"What's up?" I replied.

"Sara Marlow called and invited us over for a cook-out on Friday."

I wondered if my eyes gave away the uncertainty I felt about spending more time with Zeke. On the one hand, he seemed incredibly charming, on the other -incredibly annoying. "That's fine with me. It's not as if my social calendar is full." My irritation with Zeke today was seeping into my conversation with my mother, "unless you all have planned to drag out those naked pictures of me and put them on display."

"No, definitely not for display," she assured me. "Party favors, maybe."

I groaned, throwing my book at her playfully.

"You'll have a good time," she added, patting me on the knee. "Zeke seems friendly… pretty cute too."

Cute? Puppies are cute.

And Zeke's voice -

If southern sweet tea could talk, that is how it would sound.

Trying not to give away exactly how *cute* I found Zeke to be, I shrugged my shoulders in an attempt at indifference. "Yep, he's pretty cute alright."

"Well, it seems he thinks that about you too," she casually dropped as she got up off the bed.

"What?" I wasn't sure I had heard her correctly.

He told Sara that you're the prettiest girl he's seen in a long time." She emphasized the word long and with a wink of her own, Mom strolled out the door.

Chapter Three
Sparks

I couldn't stop the incessant humming that droned in my ear. Even after a few swats in that direction , it wouldn't go away; must be a fly that came visiting from a nearby farm– yet another perk of the green acres life. Maybe if I opened my eyes I would have better aim.

I lifted one eyelid and gazed around the room.

There was no annoying fly to be seen, yet the buzzing continued.

Wait a minute…my phone!

I rolled over and grabbed it off the nightstand.

"Hello?" I sounded as disoriented as I felt. Apparently, lack of sleep had caught up with me on this Friday afternoon and I had conked out for several hours. Because of my physically draining and emotionally charged week, I had found it hard to settle down to sleep for the last several nights; I would stay awake until the middle of the night developing theories for the strange encounter at the cemetery.

And I couldn't get Zeke Marlow out of my head. Whenever I closed my own eyes, his twinkling ones and sly grin appeared. With each vision I found myself growing more and more excited about spending time with him tonight.

"Hey, Sallie," a familiar voice greeted, "it's Will."

Now I was awake. It was about time I heard from him. I had waited patiently all week. Well…somewhat patiently - there had been a few anxious and even aggravated moments. I had texted Kaye during one of those moments demanding an explanation as to why I had not heard from her brother.

I don't know. She had replied. I haven't heard from him again either.

I assumed that my worst fear had come true. Will had met someone else while at soccer camp - probably some tall, golden-haired soccer goddess, and it had taken him all of two seconds to forget about me. It serves me right for not being less old-fashioned and calling him myself.

"Before you even say a word," Will continued, "please let me explain to you why you haven't heard from me."

No explanation needed, I thought to myself. Let's get this over with - dump me for the soccer goddess.

Moonshine Serenade

"I know this sounds lame, but I let my phone die and I had forgotten to pack my charger – I didn't have your number anyway. I should have gotten that from Kaye when I called her."

Will was right. It did sound lame. Couldn't he have borrowed a phone and made a one minute phone call? Okay, two minutes - one to call Kaye, then one to call me. Even a short text message to let me know he was thinking of me would have been enough.

"I'm home from camp now, and the first thing I did was to grab Kaye's phone and call you. So how are you doing?"

That was it?

I should have felt relief. There was no mention of a soccer goddess, and it didn't sound as if Will was dumping me; although we weren't technically in a relationship, so he couldn't technically dump me.

But instead of relief - I felt…well…irritated.

Was it because he had woken me up and I was feeling grumpy in general; or had I expected a better excuse for not hearing from him – for instance, maybe he had been lying in a coma for most of the week?

"Sallie? Are you still there?"

"Yeah, I'm still here. I was…um…making sure that you were finished with your explanation."

"Yeah, that was it," Will's voice sounded curious as to why I would think there would be a need for further clarification.

"Okay, then. Well, I'm fine. We've been really busy here with unpacking and organizing and stuff."

I didn't mention that *stuff* included finding a diary that talked about a murder, seeing a strange man wandering around a cemetery - a man who my sister could not see, and meeting Zeke - possibly the most appealing and annoying guy ever.

"How was soccer camp?" I was interested and not because I kept expecting him to tell me that he had met someone else.

"Oh, it was great! I got to lead a whole group this year, which will look awesome on my college applications."

The rest of the conversation continued in much this same vein. Will chatted a little bit more about camp and his plans for the upcoming week. I kept my tone pretty neutral; trying not to let the aggravation that I felt come through my voice.

He sighed. "Well, I guess I better go. Kaye will gripe at me for keeping her phone too long."

"I better go too. I need to get ready for a cook-out with

some family friends." I still hadn't mentioned Zeke. I didn't really see the point in it. Will hadn't told me about any of the girls I was sure he'd met at camp.

"I'll miss my running buddy this week." The words were said thoughtfully.

I felt my heart melt a little with those words. It made me feel guilty about being aggravated with him. What I wanted to say was: *It hurts me that you didn't try harder to contact me. Has anything changed in the last week?*

But of course, I didn't. Instead, I told him that I would miss him too. Will seemed pleased with that. I asked him to say hello to Kaye for me, and that was the end of the conversation.

As I sat on my bed still holding the phone in my hand, I realized it bothered me that I hadn't mentioned anything to Will about the man in the cemetery. Was it because I was afraid he would think I'm crazy? Or, did I not tell him because I wasn't comfortable sharing something that was that kind of crazy personal with him? In Will's defense, I had not mentioned the incident to anyone in fear of either the relentless ribbing that I would endure for the rest of my life or my parent's insistence that this move had affected my brain after all as they carted me off to the nearest psychiatrist.

I laid the phone down and noticed the time. It was past five o'clock and we were due at the Marlow's around six. I hopped up and grabbed my things for a shower. Samantha and I share a bathroom that is a few steps away from my room. My parents have their own in the master suite.

The shower seemed to ease away some of the tension I had felt during and after my conversation with Will. I was probably making a bigger deal out of everything than was necessary. Leave it to me to over think every word and action someone says or does.

It didn't take long to fix my hair; it has some wave to it which is both a blessing and a curse – the blessing being that it doesn't need much styling; the curse being that with a little humidity my hair begins to resemble that of a French poodle. I applied a little powder, blush, black mascara and dabbed my lips with some pink gloss.

I padded down the hall to my room and opened the armoire hoping for some clothing inspiration; I had lived in shorts and tees all week and decided to wear something different tonight. Although not a fashionista, I enjoy clothes and prefer to dress myself in outfits that are stylish - yet a little quirky. I especially love vintage and will often raid Mom's closet for any old stuff she's held onto. Not that my mom is old, both of my parents are only in their mid-forties, in great shape and what my friends have always referred to as "totally cool."

When U2, the greatest rock band in the world (as Dad calls them), came on tour to Charlottesville, my dad bought a ticket for me to attend with him and Mom. That show is one of the highlights of my life. Our seats were near the stage and Bono - the lead singer, noting that I was there with my parents - leaned close to me and with his lilting Irish brogue advised, "You have fantastic parents, you know that?"

After a few moments of hemming and hawing, I grabbed a blue jean mini-skirt and the t-shirt I had bought at that concert; which ended up not being too significant a departure from my daily summer wear. Both were form-fitting, but not in a suggestive way. Dad wouldn't let me out of the house dressed that way. With some sandals and a final inspection in the mirror, I was ready to go. It was a good thing, too, because Mom was calling me from downstairs.

Zeke had been telling the truth when he said they lived just down the road. It took us less than five minutes to reach his driveway, another few minutes to drive down it. It was as if we were riding into a scenic postcard. The road was gravel, and meandered away from the main route through a field that smelled freshly mowed. At one point we crossed over a small wooden bridge which spanned the creek that also flowed past our house; there was a clickety-clack sound which reminded me of horse hooves as we drove across. It would be a great private place to jog, I made a mental note to ask the Marlow's if they would mind if I began to use their driveway as part of my running route.

From the zany path my thought process had cut through my brain, it suddenly occurred to me that I had not heard anyone mention if Zeke had any siblings.

"Hey, Mom," I called out from the back seat of our sedan.

This was my mom's car; also known as the family car, and the one I was relegated to drive since I had received my license last summer. It's a nice car - but not mine. My parents have said they are willing to help me get one, but I have to put forth some monetary effort myself, so a job is definitely in my future. I will be a seventeen-year-old junior in a few weeks, and seriously do not want to be riding a bus to school.

"Yes, Honey," my mom replied from her position in the

passenger's seat.

"Does Zeke have a brother or sister?"

"No. He's an only child. Sara tried for years to have another baby, but it never happened."

"How sad," Samantha exclaimed in the seat next to me echoing my own thoughts.

"Yes, it is," Mom continued.

I sat there quietly, feeling sorry for Zeke and his family. My sister could sometimes be annoying, but I certainly couldn't imagine my life without her.

It wasn't much longer before we were pulling up to their home. Sara Marlow was standing outside to greet us. It was a modest but sweet bungalow-style house with a long covered porch where two lush ferns dangled and a wicker swing sat invitingly to the right of the front door; a dormer window overlooked the roof of the porch. Someone who lived here must be blessed with a green thumb because a profusion of colorful flower gardens decorated the front yard; among them I recognized lilies and roses. Though we had parked at the house, I noticed that the gravel driveway continued over a small knoll.

Sara grabbed each of us up in a hug before guiding us around the house to a stone patio where Mr. Marlow was standing at the grill.

"James, they're here," she called excitedly.

"Kevin, Beth, girls - it's been a long time. Welcome to the neighborhood!" He was enthusiastic as he turned to welcome us with one hand outstretched and his grilling tongs in the other. "Come on over and sit a spell."

James Marlow stands as tall as Zeke, but his hair and eyes are darker. He sports a mustache and goatee and wears his hair short and spiky, much trendier than I would have imagined of a minister - certainly different from Pastor Bob, the grey-haired gentleman who led the large congregation we had attended back in Springfield.

Feeling something furry brush up against my leg, I lowered my gaze to a yellow lab that was offering up a friendly greeting of its own. Samantha dropped down on her knees to pet him. She had been begging for a dog for years, my parents had said they would consider it since we had moved to a more dog-appropriate area.

As I reached down to pat the dog on the head, I heard someone strumming a guitar. I tilted my head toward the sound of the music and found Zeke sitting casually on a wrought iron lounge chair head bent down and instrument in hand. My heart fluttered at the sight of him sitting there with his shaggy hair and bare feet, his fingers moving tenderly over the strings of the guitar.

With a quick perusal of my surroundings, I found my parents engrossed in conversation with the Marlow's, and Samantha seemed occupied by the happy dog. Feeling brave, I walked over to where Zeke sat.

I gave a slight wave. "Hey there," I said offhandedly. "I see you chose not to dig up our naked pictures after all."

He glanced up at me with a breathtaking smile and chuckled. The sound of it was smooth and warm, like his voice.

"So, you've decided to forgive me?" Zeke motioned for me to sit next to him.

"Let's call it more of a truce," I offered.

"Deal," he accepted, reaching out his hand.

"Deal." When I took his hand to shake it, a spark shot through my fingers and up my arm; it made me think of what happens when I plug my hair dryer into an outlet during the dry winter weather.

Embarrassed, I dropped his hand and averted my gaze downward. A tattoo on the inside of Zeke's left forearm caught my attention. It appeared to be a cross. Not wanting to stare I dared to peek back at him. His green-gold-gray eyes were gazing at me thoughtfully. I assumed it was sympathy; he probably had girls reacting crazily to him all the time.

"Love your shirt," Zeke said abruptly.

"Really?" I stuttered like I had just started speaking the English language yesterday. "Thanks."

"Which show?"

"Charlottesville. With Mom and Dad. It was awesome!" My voice was possibly too exuberant – I love talking about music. "We were close to the stage and the lead singer spoke to me." I relayed the story of my encounter at the concert. I realized I was hoping it would impress him.

"Wow! That's a much better story than mine. I had to drive all the way to Raleigh to see them and sat in the nosebleed section. But it was still… as you said, awesome."

We continued to chat. Our main topic of conversation was music - apparently we share some favorite bands. My taste in music is varied; there's really no rhyme or reason to what I enjoy - it's whatever strikes me. Kaye has often commented on my ability to listen to an alternative rock song one minute, and shuffle to a country tune in the next. It kind of drives her bonkers. She absolutely does not get the country music thing, but I was raised on it – singing *He Stopped Loving Her Today* along with George Jones as I bounced around in Grandpa Jesse's beat-up blue Dodge pickup.

During our talk Zeke mentioned he owned over a thousand albums. I thought he was joking and insisted that he prove it, so our parents gave the go ahead for me to visit his bedroom to see his collection.

We walked into the house through the kitchen. To the left was a small dining corner surrounded by windows and furnished with a simple table adorned with a vase of fresh flowers cut from the ones I had seen in the yard.

We continued through to the living room, passing a brick fireplace. Family photos lined its mantel. One of Zeke as a youngster holding a vivid red guitar caught my eye. He had bright blonde hair and a wide snaggled-toothed smile. We reached a stairwell near the front door; I followed Zeke as he made his way upstairs. Though I tried hard not to bore a hole into it, I couldn't deny the fact that my view of the backside of his Levi's was impressive.

Zeke's bedroom encompassed what must have been the original attic of the house. The room was in the shape of a large square, the ceiling slanted on each side with a window in the middle – the one I had noticed above the front porch. A stereo sat in a corner and beside it an electric guitar on a stand. A bed and dresser were pushed up against one wall with an overflowing cabinet of books serving as a makeshift nightstand. True to his word, another wall was lined with row after row of Zeke's compact discs.

I walked over and ran my fingers across the titles listed in his collection. The variety of musical styles was amazing: rock, country, folk, blues, alternative, Christian, jazz, classical; I thought my own tastes ran the gamut. It was nice to finally find a kindred spirit.

He must have caught my surprise at his selection, because Zeke walked up beside me and chuckled. "What did you expect, all bluegrass?"

I turned, rolled my eyes at him and shook my head no.

"Well, there *is* some of that too." He grinned playfully.

Despite his good-nature, I felt the need to explain my reaction. "If I appeared surprised, it was only because I've found few people with such wide musical interests as mine. It's the one area where my best friend and I have some difficulty connecting. She's more hip to the hip hop."

Zeke nodded his head in understanding.

I glanced back at the rows of his music collection. "Don't you download?" I was mystified that he had amassed such a collection in this age of modern technology.

"Yeah, some," Zeke replied, "but I'm still a bit old-school in some ways. I enjoy the physicality of the album; holding the case in my hand and reading the liner notes. You don't get that downloading songs."

I hadn't thought of it in that way, I wondered if his being a musician influenced his need to own the music in a physical sense – akin to a librarian preferring to hold a novel in her hand rather than reading it on a screen.

I pointed to the electric guitar in the corner. "How long have you been playing?"

He shrugged his shoulders. "I guess I started when I was about four."

"Wow, are you a musical prodigy or something?"

"No, Ma'am." Zeke ran his hand through his hair before he continued. "Music comes naturally to me; it's something I instinctively knew I was meant to do. I can't really explain it."

I couldn't seem to tear my eyes away from his as Zeke spoke to me. It was as if they were speaking their own words, but I couldn't quite make out what they were saying.

"But at the risk of sounding like I'm bragging, I do play several instruments." Zeke finished up quickly.

"Brag away!" I tried to sound encouraging because I found myself wanting to know as much about Zeke as possible. Maybe if I kept throwing the ball in his court, he'd keep talking.

The scary thing is…I'm a terrible ball player.

Zeke shoved his hands in his pockets – as if suddenly shy. It occurred to me that he might be worried that I *would* think he was showing off.

Batter up!

"Go ahead," I prodded.

"Well," Zeke drawled with that honey dripping voice, "the guitar – which you already know, and the banjo, fiddle, violin, mandolin, and bass guitar. I dabble a bit with the piano, but I'm not very good."

My eyes must have grown large as saucers as the list rolled off his tongue. I could barely play the piano, having made a poor attempt at lessons while in elementary school; and, although I can hold a tune, I'm not self-confident enough to sing for anyone. I envied his natural ability; I couldn't think of anything that had ever felt intuitively right to me.

"Impressive," I admitted. "And I *love* the banjo and mandolin."

It was Zeke's turn to be surprised. "Well, now I'm impressed."

"It's something about the sound they make - the twang. I'm not sure – it's almost as if I can hear a voice there…" I let my sentence trail off, kind of embarrassed that I had said so much. Zeke probably thought I was wicked weird talking about hearing voices in instruments. "Or maybe it's because my mother says *Mandolin Wind* used to calm me as a baby."

It was time to hit the ball back over to Zeke.

"Do you know that song?" I said quickly.

"Yeah – I can play it." Zeke answered softly. Maybe it was my imagination, but he seemed to understand the whole crazy thing I was rambling about before.

My volley.

"So, how often do you play?"

"As often as I can. I'm not much of a TV watcher; video games have never interested me, so," Zeke added with a wave of his hand around the room, "listening to and playing music is mostly how I spend my free time." Then he added with a shrug. "And I read a bit too."

Zeke hit the ball back to me. "So, do you play anything?"

"No. I'm definitely not gifted in that way."

"Well then, let me show you a few chords." He pulled his hands out of his pockets.

I shook my head from side-to-side. "Really, it's okay."

Zeke grabbed the acoustic guitar from where he had dropped it on the bed. "Aw, come on." He pulled me down so that I was sitting on the bed next to him and laid the guitar in my hands. "I usually get paid to do this, you know." His voice was teasing.

Wrapping his arms around mine, Zeke placed my fingers against the strings along the neck of the guitar. I could feel the hairs rising on the back of my own neck as he leaned in closer.

"Okay, so if you hold your fingers this way, that's a G."

With Zeke so close, my fingers felt too tingly to hold onto the strings and my hand dropped squarely into Zeke's groin. "Sorry," I remarked, surely red-faced and self-conscious at my own ineptness and bad aim.

As if he had noticed nothing, Zeke picked my hand up and

placed my fingers back along the fret. "That's alright, I'll help you," and he pressed my fingers in place as we tried again.

"So, there's the G." Zeke slid my hand and repositioned my fingers. "And here's a C," he moved my fingers again, "and there's the D."

He was breathing directly into my ear – making it extremely difficult to concentrate on anything he was attempting to teach me.

"This is harder than I expected." I admitted...harder for more than one reason. "My fingers hurt."

"Yeah, it takes a little practice, over time you develop calluses like these." Zeke held up his hands for me to inspect. "So, let's do this one more time. I'll move your fingers and you concentrate on strumming the guitar."

And I did as Zeke instructed. With him positioning my hand correctly for the chords and me focusing on strumming, we actually made a pleasant sound together.

"See. You're playing. Good job."

"Thanks, but I believe I need a few more lessons."

"I can arrange that," Zeke hummed into my ear.

His mom shouted that dinner was ready before I had the chance to take him up on the offer, even though I could really care less about learning to play an instrument and would rather sit there with his arms around me and his breath in my ear.

I awkwardly laid the guitar back on the bed and followed Zeke unsteadily down the stairs to join everyone outside. The food was laid out across an over-sized picnic table that fit all of us comfortably. I sat across from Zeke and suddenly felt self-conscious chowing down on my barbequed chicken and potato salad.

Conversation buzzed around the table. Sara joked that she had been afraid that Zeke and I had started off on the wrong foot but seemed to be getting along famously now. He gave me a wink and a grin. I forgot to breathe for a second, almost choking on my food. That would have been lovely. I could see it now – my face turning purple and red as Dad performed the Heimlich maneuver to dislodge the errant glob of chicken from my throat which flies out of my mouth and smacks Zeke directly in the middle of his forehead.

Something James said pulled me out of my embarrassing daydream. "Zeke plays at the nursing home on Tuesday afternoons, which is why he must have been in a hurry."

So, that's where he had been headed earlier this week; to

play for people in a nursing home.

I found myself intrigued.

Who is this guy?

It was my turn to return the smile, but Zeke was noticeably uncomfortable about the secret his dad had given away.

As we finished the banana pudding Mom had brought for dessert, the sun was dropping lower in the sky and the air seemed cooler. Samantha left the table to play catch with the dog whose name I had learned during dinner is George; and Mom and Sara went inside the house to clean up and start some coffee. Dad and James were debating North Carolina versus Kansas City barbeque sauces. I wasn't even aware that there are different types because I'm certain that ours comes from a bottle Mom buys at the grocery store.

Sitting dangerously close to the discussion, Zeke and I cast furtive glances at each other as we mashed soggy vanilla wafers with our forks.

Zeke stood up. "Hey, let's go for a walk."

He didn't need to ask me twice. I was up and ready to go in a flash...a little too eager, almost banging my knee on the underside of the table.

"Can you wait here for a second while I run in and put on some shoes?"

I nodded my head. Zeke was in and out of the house in a couple of minutes.

We strolled side-by-side toward the driveway and began to follow it up the small hill that I had noticed when we arrived at the Marlow's home. Our feet made crunching noises as we walked across the gravel, but neither of us had made a move yet to talk. When we reached the crest, I could see a flat valley below; it was sprinkled with daisies like decorations atop a green-frosted cupcake. To the left was a field where row after row of red earth had been plowed for a garden, to the right was a faded barn where the gravel drive dead-ended. Though it wasn't an uncomfortable one, I decided to break the silence.

"If I ask you a question, will you answer it honestly?"

"I'll try my best," Zeke smiled.

"Do you like living in Franklin County?"

It didn't even take Zeke half of a second to answer. "Yes, I honestly do."

Zeke paused for a minute to ponder; then started walking again. "Have you ever noticed how it's almost impossible to be in a bad mood on a bright summer day? There's an ease about it

–kind of like pouring honey from a jar. The sun is shining, the sky is blue, birds and bees are flitting around, and everything seems to glow around the edges."

Sincerity was apparent in his face as he looked my way. "That's what I love about living here – the easiness of it all. I can see myself in about fifty years being one of those old men hanging out at the local mom-and-pop store in my bib overalls, the unofficial town council with no serious agenda - just gossiping about people and complaining about the weather."

Zeke bent over to pick up a rock and tossed it to the side. "Anyway, it's really all I've ever known. Born and bred, basically. Sometimes I think about taking off to Austin or Nashville to try my hand at music professionally – my dream is to play the Ryman Auditorium. But I don't believe there's any place that I would rather live permanently than right here. It gets in your blood…in your bones." He shot me a glance. "I guess you think I'm pretty boring, huh? Your life in Northern Virginia must have been much more exciting."

"I don't think you're boring at all," I replied earnestly. "And to be truthful myself, I've visited my grandparents enough to kind of understand where you're coming from. Though, I'm not sure if I could imagine myself living here for the rest of my life."

"Really?" Zeke didn't seem surprised, but a bit disappointed. "Where could you see yourself living in five or ten years?"

"Oh, I don't know - different places. New York might be fun for a while, or a cool southern city, Savannah or Charleston, maybe. I've even thought about living abroad - maybe London or somewhere in Ireland." I nudged a piece of gravel with my toes. "I guess I have more of a gypsy spirit than even I realized."

"What if you found something here that you made you want to stay?"

I jerked my head up. "I'm not sure. I've never considered *that* possibility. Anyway," I glanced over at him with a smile, not wanting him to think I hated this place, "this will work out for now. Don't think I'm some big city girl come here to make fun of the locals."

Zeke chuckled. "Oh, we wouldn't allow that. If you tried poking fun at us we'd take you out snipe hunting."

"No thanks, I'm not a fan of guns."

Zeke stopped abruptly and bent forward - his entire body

shaking with laughter.

Was it that hysterical that I have no interest in guns?

Anyway, it's not as if he appears to be much of a huntsman to me…not that I know all that much about hunting. The only hunters I have ever known were Grandpa Jesse's two brothers, Frank and Clem, who would show up before dawn on Thanksgiving Day to drag him with them out into the woods to watch for deer. Of course, they always seemed to straggle in empty handed about the time Grandma Ellen laid a twenty pound turkey and steaming bowls of mashed potatoes, gravy and green beans out on the table. Having filled up there, Uncles Frank and Clem would head out to eat another Thanksgiving feast cooked by their own wives in their own homes.

After the snickering stopped, Zeke apologized and made a comment about my being "too funny" before he explained. "Snipes aren't real, Sallie. It's a silly trick to be played on unsuspecting city folks. I really thought you'd probably already heard of that one."

"No. I can't say that I have." I pointed a finger at him. "Cow tipping, now that one I know. My cousin, Wallace, tried that one on me a couple summers ago – even talked me into sneaking out of my grandparents' house in the middle of the night to do it. I felt like an idiot when I found out it was a joke at my expense."

"Well, that wasn't a very cousinly thing to do."

"I guess he's more of a second cousin."

"We are living in the South – so kin's kin - even the crazy ones."

It was a comforting thought - in a bizarre sort of way, to know that my family would still consider me one of their own should they ever learn about my hallucinations.

Zeke gestured with his hand toward the garden. "Speaking of family, that's my mom's baby over there. She cans vegetables for us to eat on during the winter and sometimes sells produce at the farmers market in Rocky Mount."

Mystery solved – Sara Marlow sports the green thumb. I wondered if Zeke shared her talent. "Do you help out?"

"Yeah, I do some of the plowing and also help with the harvesting." Zeke chuckled. "I don't help with the canning."

"Oh, so you think that's women's work?" I kidded with him.

"No," he said with a smile. "My mama would shoo me out of the kitchen if I tried to help. She'd say I was in her way."

My mind wandered to the summer afternoons I had spent sitting cross-legged on my grandparents' front porch with Grandma Ellen and Mom, a bowl of green beans fresh-picked from the garden sitting in my lap. I'd snap off the ends and throw them into a big bucket before they'd be hauled off to the kitchen for cooking and canning. I enjoyed those times listening to family stories – especially the scary kind. My grandma loved to tell a good ghost story. I was all ears when she did. As a child, I had believed them, the way Samantha does; but as I got older the enchantment of those tales faded away.

Now, here I was facing my own supernatural story; afraid to share it with anyone.

"You'll be a junior this year, right?" I realized Zeke was saying to me.

Yeah, my seventeenth birthday is next month."

"Really, when?"

"The fourth. When I was younger, I used to think the fireworks were a national celebration of my birthday."

Zeke laughed. "Well, I have to celebrate mine with ghosts and goblins. I'm a Halloween baby."

He tried saying this with a campy vampire voice, and waving spooky fingers. It cracked me up; his voice was so lovely with its southern cadence that I couldn't imagine it ever sounding menacing.

"You don't seem scary to me."

Zeke's face unexpectedly turned wistful. "It's a more appropriate birthday than you know."

I couldn't imagine what he meant by that, but I suddenly felt an awkwardness and decided to change the subject.

"So, you'll be a junior too…"

"No," his good mood had returned. "I'll be a senior – I turn eighteen on my birthday."

That meant Zeke was older than Will, who wouldn't turn eighteen until January; which for some reason reminded me of a conversation I'd had with Will in my kitchen after spring break.

"Hey, what's the big deal with moonshine around here? You know - Moonshine Capital and all."

Zeke shrugged his shoulders. "I guess that's what Franklin County is *really* known for – the iconic corn liquor in a glass jar. I don't know… there's a rich tradition of it. There was a time when men could make some serious money from bootlegging. I don't think it's so much that way now."

"Do people still make it?"

"Oh, yeah. It's not as prolific or dramatic like it used to be – car chases and stills getting busted up. Have you ever heard the story about the guys back in the seventies who hid their still under some sod with cinderblock headstones to disguise it as a cemetery?" I replied with a shake of my head that meant, no, I had not. "Pretty crafty; I think it ran for a couple of years before the revenuers found it."

I had an idea what it might be, but wasn't sure I knew what Zeke was referring to, so I decided to ask. "And a still is?"

"Sorry, another assumption I shouldn't have made." He nibbled on his lower lip while searching for an easy explanation that I would understand. "I guess you could say it's the kettle the liquor's cooked in…short for distiller. It can be a big or small operation." Zeke let out a long breath. "In a way it's kind of sad; making moonshine the way old timers did is probably a dying art."

"Like quilting." The words kind of jumped out before I had even given much thought to what I was about to say.

Zeke shot me a puzzled expression.

"My Grandma Ellen says the same thing about quilting; it's not being passed down through the generations any more, women aren't making their own stuff the way used to do – it's easier to buy it at Wal-Mart."

"Wal-Mart. Now, if you're need of some entertainment that's a place to hang out on a Friday night." Zeke's tone was sarcastic, and for that I was grateful. I was imagining the next couple of years as rather dismal if the most exciting thing to do on the weekend was hang out at the local Wally World.

"Do you mind if I show you something in the barn?" Zeke asked. I had been so engrossed in our conversation that I didn't even realize we were standing in front of the old red building I had seen from the top of the hill. Honeysuckle rambled up its walls and hung heavy like clusters of grapes on a weathered split-rail fence that stood nearby, its sweet fragrance perfumed the air.

"I don't mind at all. Do you have animals?"

"No, well, except for George – but he's not a barn animal. Every now and then my mom will decide she wants to raise chickens, but we don't have any of those at the moment either. We mostly keep our equipment in there."

Zeke pushed the barn door open and walked in. I followed close behind. My nostrils were overcome with the smell of hay, aged wood and dirt. It was a warm, earthy scent – musky and very pleasant. This country thing must be growing on me or maybe it was the company.

It was dim inside the barn, what little sunlight that was left filtered through the windows and cracks in the boards. Zeke grabbed a flashlight that must have been hanging beside the door. We didn't need it quite yet, so I guessed that was in case it did become a necessity.

"Are you afraid of heights?" Zeke questioned.

"It depends on how high you're talking about," I admitted. "Some heights do make me a little nervous."

He pointed up with the flashlight. "How about the hayloft?"

"Oh, that I can handle."

"The only way up is with this ladder. You go ahead of me." I started up the ladder using both my hands and feet to work my way up, instantly regretting my decision to wear a short skirt; relieved when I realized his head was closer to my waist and he would miss the peep show. About half-way up the ladder, I felt Zeke support the small of my back with his hand. That same spark of electricity coursed through my body. I had read about that sensation in books and would roll my eyes at the overused simile. It's not something I had ever experienced before, not even with Will. I used a second to compose. It must be this place, I assured myself. How many times had a hayloft been used for a romantic setting in a book or a movie? But, that line of thinking didn't offer me any comfort. What if that was *exactly* what Zeke had in mind – a romantic encounter? At once my knees felt weak, and my legs turned to jelly. I stumbled over the next rung and Zeke caught me with his hand.

"Are you okay?" Concern was in his voice. "We can go back down if this bothers you."

"I'm fine," I lied. "It's a little dark and I missed one of the rungs."

Zeke turned on the flashlight. I was able to climb the rest of the way with a few butterflies in my stomach, thankful when I made it to the top and stood up in the loft.

It was stuffy up there and much darker until Zeke walked over and shoved open the doors to a large window. Faint light illuminated the room.

"Come over here," he called with a wave. "This is what I wanted to show you."

I walked over and stood next to Zeke careful not to get too close to the window ledge which was a straight drop down to ground much further below.

The view through the window was breathtaking. The sun was beginning to set and the cerulean sky was streaked with shades of red, orange and pink; the sun itself was a glowing red-orange ball. Lines of white stretched across the sky; looking like tread marks left by a cloud race from earlier in the day. From our perch, I felt close enough to the horizon to almost reach out and touch it.

I whispered, "It's beautiful."

"If you think this is amazing," Zeke murmured, "you should be here during a full moon."

We stood there in the tranquil splendor of the moment; admiring the sunset and lost in our own thoughts. I wonder what he's thinking about; I deliberated as I glanced up at him. His profile was stunning: a perfectly straight nose which rounded slightly at the end; thick, long lashes that I could make out even in the dim light; a strong square jaw line; and his lips - the bottom one slightly fuller than the top.

Zeke turned toward me. My first instinct was to turn away. I was embarrassed that he had caught me gawking at him, but something in his eyes kept me there – returning his gaze. He reached out his with his left hand, tucked it under my chin tilting it up, and it was very clear to me exactly what he was thinking as he leaned his face closer to mine.

Just before our lips met, a movement in the corner behind Zeke caught my attention, alerting me to the fact that we were not alone. I hoped it wasn't a bat; I sort of have a phobia about what I consider to be creepy flying mice.

I jerked my head away from his to get a better glimpse of what it might be; it was too big to be an animal.

Was it…a man?

All of a sudden I felt uncomfortable - not threatened, unnerved. How long he had been watching us?

Zeke misunderstood the reason I had abruptly wrenched myself away from him and began to apologize profusely.

"Oh, Sallie, I am *so* sorry," he stammered, "I should have never have tried to kiss you without asking your permission."

"No, Zeke, that's not it. I didn't mind that… it's…do you know that man standing in the corner?"

He rotated his body so that he was facing in the same direction as me. I heard his sharp intake of breath as the flashlight he had been holding in his right hand fell to the floor with a loud thump.

Zeke grabbed my wrist as he spun back around; his eyes

had switched on like a lamp. I could feel his body trembling, ever so slightly. His voice was distorted as he began to speak.

"That man…in the corner…you can see him?"

"Yes, Zeke. I can see him."

"Are you sure?" His voice was still uneasy.

"Of course I'm sure," I practically shouted pulling my hand away, "didn't *I* tell *you* that he was there."

A huge grin spread across his face as Zeke grabbed me into a bear hug and lifted me off the floor. "Sallie," Zeke's voice was excited as he sat me back down, "no one else has ever been able to see that man but me. I think he might be a ghost."

And with those words, my weak legs finally gave out. I collapsed into a heap on the floor.

Chapter Four
Guilty

Zeke knelt down in front of me, rubbing my arms with his hands, his eyes fraught with concern. "Are you alright, Sallie? I promise you he's not dangerous. He won't hurt you."

But I was already aware of that. The same sort of sixth-sense I had felt with the other man at the cemetery had signaled me that this one was different. There were no creepy-crawlies – instead, something more along the lines of familiarity.

I peeped over Zeke's shoulder to see if this man was still in the corner and, if he was, to get a better view of him. He hadn't moved, but continued to watch us, offering no other form of communication. This man appeared to be young. He couldn't have been much older than Zeke when he died. His hair was a cap of dark curls, and he wore clothes that were seen more often in a different era: a button-down shirt and dark blue pants with suspenders. He wasn't transparent and hovering above the floor as you would imagine a spirit to be. Instead, he was whole – like a real, live person standing before me. As I examined his appearance, I felt a glimmer of recognition. My mind sprinted in reverse attempting to unlock the memory of how this man could be familiar to me. The recollection unfurled as if I was turning a page in a picture book...Letitia's diary *and* my dream.

Now, I had seen both of the men in her diary.

Ghosts. I finally felt comfortable admitting to myself. It couldn't be a coincidence. I had never before in my life set eyes on a ghost. Why now? Was the diary the connection? But then, how could Zeke see him too?

Zeke! I was so intent on my observation of this specter that I had almost forgotten he was holding on to me. I guess he was under the impression that I was about to topple over, faint, or perform some other such act of the panic stricken.

"I know he won't harm us. I can sense it." I whispered, aware that I was not only directing those words to Zeke but to the corner as well. For some reason, I felt compelled to let them both know that I was not afraid; and especially wanted it...him...the ghost...whatever...to understand that I knew intuitively that he posed no threat of malice.

I diverted my attention back to Zeke. "How long have you been able to see him?" My lower lip trembled as I posed this question - not because I was upset or scared, but due to the fact that I was overcome with relief to find out that I was not the only one seeing ghosts…and maybe – possibly – that I was not crazy…and if I was, then so was he, and we could be insane together.

Zeke's eyes were somber as he loosened his grip. "For as long as I can remember." He spoke this softly but matter-of-factly with not a hint of sadness or dejection. I found that my heart ached for him. I had been dealing with the uncertainty of what I had seen for a mere matter of days. Zeke had been faced with this his entire life. I wondered how he had coped or if there was anyone else who knew.

"Have you ever told anyone?"

He let go of my arms and dropped down beside me, crossing his legs out in front of him. "Of course I have," Zeke smiled tentatively, "but as a child it was passed off as my imaginary friend."

Zeke waved his hand toward the corner, as if in a formal gesture of introduction, "Sallie, let me present to you my imaginary friend."

My eyes followed the movement of his hand. The man continued to stand motionless, watching us. His body had not shifted – not even one inch as far as I could tell. I could hardly believe I was sitting here so casually having a conversation in the presence of a non-living entity. It must have been Zeke's calm demeanor that kept my own emotions under check. He'd had many more years of living with the paranormal than me, so I guess it felt normal to him.

Feeling chilled despite the heat in the loft, I pulled my legs up and wrapped my arms around my knees as Zeke continued his story.

"As I got older, the excuse of an imaginary friend obviously no longer applied. A ten-year-old still discussing one quickly moves from cute to quack, so I quit mentioning him. I've never felt afraid of him. I guess when I first began to see him I was so young that I didn't realize that most people would be afraid."

I interrupted to ask, "Has he ever spoken to you?"

"No…not really. Sometimes he makes a sound, he could be calling out to someone, but I've never been able to hear it clearly."

As Zeke answered, a memory from last night's dream popped into my head - the man had been calling out then as well. I recalled that it sounded vaguely my name or at least the beginning of it.

I turned to Zeke, realizing that what I was about to ask him would require me to admit my own strange link to this ghost, and probably also to the frightening one I saw earlier in the week. This would be a big step for me; I could keep my mouth shut, let Zeke finish telling me his story, and share with him only the knowledge that both of us could see this particular spirit. Clearly, that alone would be a huge relief for him - a sort of validation.

But, I felt a need for my own liberation with a confidante who would not only believe me but who could understand.

So many times this week I had considered telling Kaye – even practiced the conversation in my mind. There had been so little that I had not confided in her throughout our friendship; when I hadn't, it wasn't out of fear but usually because I had been sworn to secrecy by another person or considered the matter so irrelevant that it wasn't even worth mentioning.

But the incident at the cemetery had bewildered me to the core, so much so that I couldn't even find the courage to discuss it with my best friend – even though she was someone who would totally get into the whole supernatural thing. I quickly made the decision that confessing to Zeke could only help me sort this thing out, not make me feel worse.

Summoning as much nerve as I could rally, I turned to Zeke and asked, "When you hear him calling, does it sound like he's saying "Sa…Sa..?""

Zeke's eyes widened in surprise, he shifted forward leaning closer to me. "Yes…but how did you know that?"

I sighed, an effort to calm my nerves before divulging the rest. "Because I had a dream about this man and another one I saw earlier this week in the graveyard near our house."

He raised his eyebrows and cocked his head; curiosity and kinship were both brimming in Zeke's expression.

"Samantha was with me. She couldn't see him. I had to pretend it was all a joke to try to scare her. That's where we were returning from when we met you in our driveway. It's been making me crazy all week; I've been second-guessing my vision - but mostly my sanity."

I attempted a faint smile, but Zeke must have sensed my uneasiness. He grinned and reached over to touch my hand. "So, it wasn't just me causing you aggravation that day?"

"I guess not," I admitted, recalling his sense of humor.

"You'll find this amusing…the man in the cemetery was wearing a straw hat, and when I saw you standing in our driveway wearing one, I was ready to check myself into the nearest looney bin. Fortunately, Samantha *was* able to see you."

At the description of the presence I had encountered in the cemetery, there was movement from the one in the corner. Fury spread across the face of the man who had otherwise remained aloof and motionless this entire time. He held his hand up, I thought he was about to wave hello but didn't. Instead he reached toward me, his face softened. Concern replaced the anger; then a deeper concern mixed with affection… as if cared….about *me*. On impulse I stood and reached for him, as I stepped in his direction, he dropped his hand. A breeze swirled around my body as he vanished.

I felt Zeke's arm around my waist. "What was that about?"

"I don't know." As I muttered this reply, my thoughts turned to the diary again. Was it a connection between the two? It could be. Both of the apparitions I'd seen fit the description of the men Letitia had written about, and one of them was violently attacked by the other – possibly murdered.

Before I could decide whether or not to mention this to Zeke, he laid his hands on my shoulders and gently twisted my body to face him. "How are you dealing with everything that's happened tonight?"

I nodded my head. "I feel better now than I did before tonight."

Zeke smiled down at me in understanding. "I do too." He twisted his lips into a frown. "That's why I hate to have to do this, but I really need to get you back before the search party comes looking for us."

Our families - I had forgotten all about them. I'm sure they would be wondering where we were. It was getting dark outside.

"Yeah. I guess if they found us in this hayloft, they might get entirely the wrong idea."

"I'd definitely need to do some explaining to your daddy," Zeke teased. "Come on, let's get out of here. We can talk more about this later."

I followed Zeke closely down the ladder; he was one step in front of me, and because of his height our heads were almost touching. He kept his hand on the same rung I was grasping at the time and aimed the flashlight at my feet. When his feet touched the barn floor, Zeke circled his arm around my waist and lifted me off the ladder placing me gently on the ground.

"Thanks," I gasped.

"My pleasure," he drawled.

Zeke pushed one of the doors open and we stepped out into the night. I had completely lost track of time while we were in the barn and had no idea how long we had been there. Outside, the fireflies were already flickering and the crickets were chirping in conversation. Zeke reached over and clasped my hand; we followed the beam of the flashlight which bounced up and down erratically as he juggled it in his other hand.

The walk back seemed to take less time than our earlier one. Maybe it was because I was enjoying holding Zeke's hand so much.

I felt guilty as soon as that thought crossed my mind; I realized that Will deserved better than my so easily succumbing to the charms of Zeke. Kaye, *my* best friend and Will's sister, deserved better than this. I had known Zeke mere days - Kaye and Will for years.

But I couldn't ignore the fact that it wasn't just Zeke's charming personality that had made me forget Will with ease. The evening's events had connected us with a common thread that was intricate and complicated; we had quickly established an intimacy that it takes most people a great deal more time to develop.

At this moment, I felt closer to him than anyone else.

Just before we crested the hill that would lead us down to the house and our families, Zeke stopped and brushed his thumb lightly across my cheek, "She walks in beauty like the night," he whispered and then smiled. "When can I see you again?"

My heart starting pounding in my chest from both Zeke's touch and his poetic appeal to spend more time with me; but in the rhythm I was sure I could hear the words "guilty, guilty, guilty" like a judge slamming his gavel down to announce a verdict.

"Um…" I was speechless. I wanted to see Zeke again; more than that, I *needed* to see him again. He was sort of my sanity at the moment. I stood there, choosing sides in my head…Will, Zeke, Will, Zeke…when I realized that I didn't have to do so. I could maintain a platonic relationship with Zeke while I tried to iron out my uncertain relationship with Will.

It could work - maybe.

Well?" Zeke murmured as he squeezed my hand.

Sigh. It would be really hard if he kept touching me this

way.

I let go of Zeke but smiled back at him; after all, I didn't want to give him the impression that I am totally uninterested.

Sallie, you are a horrible person, I scolded myself. But the self-berating wasn't going to work. I had to see him again. At least for right now, I didn't care one single bit about any judges or juries.

"Well, how about tomorrow?" I spit the words out like an atomic fireball that had grown too hot to keep in my mouth for one second longer.

"Tomorrow evening?" Zeke sounded hopeful. "I have to work during the day."

Work? He had a job too? Between his job, helping out around the farm, and entertaining the elderly, when did he have time for this free time he had referred to in his room?

"Oh, that's too bad. I can't do tomorrow evening; we're having dinner with my grandparents."

"Sunday won't be easy either," Zeke said in a defeated tone. "Church and band practice."

A band? Zeke was in a band? Seriously, what free time?

It seemed to be getting darker by the minute, and we weren't easily resolving the issue of when to see each other again. We were running out of time; I needed to come up with something quick.

"Why don't you call me or send me a text tomorrow to see what we can work out? If we don't get back soon, it may not matter. Our parents might not let us see each other again."

Zeke leaned over and kissed me on the forehead. "Deal. I do not want to get on your dad's bad side already."

Okay. So this platonic thing was going to be a real challenge, especially since I wasn't letting him in on the agreement I had made with myself.

He didn't try to grab my hand back as we started down the hill toward his house. I guess Zeke wasn't ready for my dad to see that either. It was a good thing; if he had, it would have been really hard for me to let go this time.

Torches were burning brightly around the patio. As we got closer I could see that our parents were gathered casually around the picnic table chatting. Samantha was deeply engrossed in conversation with them. It had never bothered her to be left alone with the adults; she was able to fit in anywhere. Who knows what she was saying to them. She could be quite the vivid storyteller.

"Well, there you are!" Sara called in a friendly manner as we approached. "Where have you two been?"

All eyes were turned on us. Suddenly I felt nervous like I had been up to something which they wouldn't approve of. It didn't help that Samantha hopped up to add her two cents worth.

"Yeah, what were you doing?"

Zeke glanced over at Samantha and gave her his drop-dead gorgeous smile that could make a female of any age swoon.

"Well, Little Red, your sister and I were watching the sunset which, by the way, reminds me of the beautiful color of your hair."

I didn't think that Samantha would easily fall for his charm; but she didn't have anything else to offer, so she plopped back down on the picnic bench. I could hear my parents chuckling at her lack of a comeback... not something that happened often with Samantha.

"*You* must be tired," Dad placated her as he wrapped an arm around her shoulders giving her a squeeze, "and we need to be going anyway."

I felt exhausted too, despite the nap I had taken that afternoon; it was less physical and more of an emotional fatigue. Although I would have relished more time with Zeke, I was ready to head home where I could escape to my room and sort out what had occurred tonight - not just the encounter with the presence that had interrupted our almost kiss, but also the fog of the confusion I was fighting regarding my feelings for the two guys who were pulling at my heart strings.

Plus, I was eager to pull the diary out again, hoping that it would provide more clues to the strange events happening to me.

Zeke and his parents walked us to our car. Before we left, I borrowed a pen from Mom and wrote down my phone number on the back of a silver gum wrapper and handed it to Zeke.

"Good Lord willing and the creek don't rise," He gave me an assured grin before folding the paper carefully, sticking it into his jeans pocket, "and I'll be seeing you soon."

Samantha yawned a few times on the ride home. My mom asked if I had enjoyed hanging out with Zeke. I responded yes; detailing his musical talent and music collection. When she asked about our walk, I kept it brief, leaving out the fact that we were in the hayloft and happened to experience a ghostly encounter.

"He seems to be a good kid," Mom commented, "and he can certainly handle you, Samantha."

"Whatever." She grumbled from the back seat.

"You sure you two weren't hiding out sippin' on some 'shine?" Dad teased as he glanced back at me through the rear view mirror.

"Whatever." I responded, mimicking Samantha.

"Just checking," Dad said with a laugh, "most of the PK's I knew growing up were wild."

"What's a PK?" I asked.

"Preacher's Kid. You've never heard that before?"

"Nope."

That was a new one for me. The only minister's children I'd ever known were from our church back home. His kids were several years older than me, so I'd never spent any time with them as friends.

"Speaking of moonshine..." I guess the conversation I'd had with Will upon our return from spring break was still hanging out in the back of my mind and since Dad had taken it upon himself to be facetious, I decided that I would be, too, "Will Landry said his dad gets some from a friend who visits here on a regular basis. Do you know who that might be because I was under the impression that's illegal?"

Mom giggled. My dad paused to slide his glasses back up his nose, but he didn't provide an answer as we conveniently pulled into our drive at that moment.

I bid everyone good night as we entered our house and headed upstairs to get ready for bed. I grabbed the cotton shorts and tank top that I wore as pajamas from my bedroom; then hit the bathroom to scrub my face and teeth. I brushed my hair and pulled it up into a sloppy twist against the nape of my neck before heading back to my room. I dropped onto the bed and sat cross-legged, opened my bedside table drawer and pulled out Letitia's diary. Before reading the next entry, I read the first two over again, wanting to be sure of the description that she had given of the two men.

One of the men had his back to me, but I could see that he had dark, curly hair and wore blue pants with suspenders.

That certainly fit the man I had seen tonight, but it was still rather generic. Her diary was written in the 1930's, so I tried to think about how people dressed at that time. I could easily come up with something for the 1950's – poodle skirts and bobby socks... maybe I had seen one too many movies.

Movies - wait a minute. Dad loves movies. I often pile up on the sofa and watch them with him. What is that baseball movie that he's watched over and over again? Wasn't it set in the 1930's? I guess I could see where the ghost from tonight was dressed in a similar fashion to the clothes that were worn in that film. So, possibly he and the young man mentioned in the diary could be one and the same.

The other man was dressed as if he'd been farming. He wore a wide-brimmed straw hat that was pulled down so low it hid his face.

No mistaking this one - definitely cemetery and dream man.

Why would his spirit be hanging around? For that matter, why would the young man's spirit still be here? I didn't know much about the spirit world, it's not really something that you study in school, but I remember watching a television program recently about a team of people who investigate haunted places. One of the members had explained that some spirits remain earth-bound due to unfinished business.

Maybe Letitia's next entry could provide me with more clues.

June 1, 1939

There's a new grave in the cemetery. I saw it today, piled high with fresh red dirt. Whenever someone is buried there, Daddy teases that we have a new neighbor. So tonight at supper I asked him if he knew who our new neighbor was. He looked up at me with a serious expression on his face and then looked over at Mama. Without answering my question he told me that he did not want me going into the woods alone anymore and to not tell anyone else what I saw the other day because it really wasn't any of our business. Then he smiled and reached over to touch my hand. Besides," he said, "you probably jumped to conclusions." It hurt my feelings when he said that. I know what I saw, and either he doesn't believe me or is hiding something from me. Either way, I hope that the man in the straw hat is long gone from here.

That was all she had written on that day. I felt no more knowledgeable than I had before I had started reading it.

I was about to turn to the next page when I heard the sound of chimes – the notification I had set for a text message. I snatched up my phone debating who it could be…Will or Kaye.

Don't make plans for Monday. I have a

surprise for you. Wear a bathing suit. Pick you up at 11 a.m. Z

Z – that one letter could only represent one person.

My heart did a somersault. I allowed the elation for three seconds before I threw my head back against the pillow and groaned.

Sallie, what in the heck do you think you're doing?

I should not be getting this wound up over another guy. I haven't even given Will a real chance. Plus, what would Kaye think if she knew I was already flirting with someone I had just met? Of course, if Will were not in the picture, she would have no criticism of my situation after spending a few minutes with Zeke. After all, Zeke is so yummy that you can practically sop him up with a biscuit.

But Will is in the picture and so is Kaye and I care about them both. The last thing I would ever want would be to hurt either of them.

I stole a quick glance at the photo sitting on my nightstand. The guilty gavel in my heart banged so loud that I was surprised my parents couldn't hear it from downstairs.

Zeke had been dead wrong.

My life in Springfield had never been this exciting.

Chapter Five
Falling

There was no kicking the buzz I was feeling in anticipation of spending Monday with Zeke, despite my guilty conscience over Will and Kaye. And lucky for me, I would have Sunday morning to help keep that buzz humming along. We were planning to attend James Marlow's church and I was hoping to find a few minutes to chat with Zeke and confirm the plans for our outing.

The first thing Saturday morning, I asked for my parents' permission to spend Monday with Zeke; but Zeke had already beaten me to the punch asking them himself at some point when I wasn't paying attention - though I couldn't recall a single moment spent at the Marlow's when the entire span of my attention had not been focused on Zeke.

Not only did they give me their consent, but Mom seemed overly pleased with the idea. I imagine that she and Sara had been scheming behind our backs - maybe before we even had actually moved here. I couldn't understand why Zeke's mom would feel the need to conspire to set him up with anyone. Even though I had not yet been privy to any sort of display, I was sure that most girls practically dropped at his feet, unless they were afraid to approach him because they were intimidated. He was certainly on a different plane in both appearance and personality than any other guy I had met his age.

But Will has a lot of great qualities too, I reminded myself and decided immediately to march right up to the computer and send him a message.

I was grateful that the area of Boones Mill where we lived used a cable service which provided us with internet as well; I couldn't imagine having to use dial-up again - that would be reminiscent of the dark ages. Thanks to the speedy service I was quickly up on my social network page. Both Kaye and Will had posted messages last night.

Miss my running buddy.

That was all that Will had written. His handsome profile face was smiling at me.

How's my BFF? XXOO

That was Kaye's simple post. She had changed her picture to a funny sketch. Only Kaye could still be beautiful in caricature form.

A wave of sadness washed over me as I read the messages they had left me. Without Zeke around to cloud my focus, I realized how much I missed the two of them. We had moved here one week ago today, but it already felt akin to a lifetime with the bizarre happenings that had occurred and the undeniable connection I had formed with Zeke - not to mention the undeniable attraction that I was also feeling for him.

I thought about what I might be doing this morning had we not moved from Springfield. Zeke would not even be in the realm of my consciousness. Perhaps Will and I would have gone out on a date last night instead of having the brief, almost uncomfortable phone conversation that had taken place yesterday afternoon. Would I have spent the night at Kaye and Will's home? I pondered if overnight visits with Kaye would have become weird if Will and I were dating.

Hmm – if I had not moved, would we actually be dating at this point? Or, without the catalyst of the move would Will have even expressed any feelings for me? That was the first time that thought had crossed my mind. If it were not for this transition, Will and I may have maintained status quo for who knows how long.

I decided to send Kaye a private message rather than a wall post; there are some things you don't want everyone to be able to read.

Hey Girl. Things are going good here. Finally heard from your brother yesterday and then had dinner last night with some old family friends.

I paused right there watching the little icon flicker on the screen. It was tremendously difficult for me not to mention Zeke. Typically, I would be gushing about a guy with his first-rate qualities to Kaye. And, of course, there was the whole supernatural adventure that I didn't feel quite comfortable talking about either.

Looks like it will be dinner tonight with the grandparents and church in the morning. Not sure what else I'll be doing today. What's up with you? Miss you. Call me. Visit soon!

I wrote that last part without even thinking about the potential complication. Of course I wanted her to visit, the sooner the better; but that also meant a probable introduction to

Zeke. I don't know how she'd get here anyway, so I wasn't going to stress about it.

Next up was a reply to Will. I decided to send him a private message as well.

Hey Will!

I suddenly had writer's block.

"What to say? What to say?" I said the words out loud in rhythm with my fingers tapping on the edge of the keyboard - as if the perfect light, but personal words would spring from my tips onto the screen.

Sorry I'm not there to share the pain with you anymore. I've laid a route here already; it's different – no sidewalks, but the view is nice. Miss you too. Can't believe it's been a week already.

After rereading it a couple of times I felt pretty at ease with that message so I hit the send button. I was anxious for his reply. Hopefully, I'd get something today.

"Hey, Sallie," Samantha chirped behind me.

"I'm almost done. You can have it next." I said without turning around. I assumed that she wanted to get on the computer to play one of her virtual pet games.

"Thanks, but no thanks. I came up to tell you that Mom wants to know if you want to go to the mall today."

Shopping! That would be a fabulous way to pass the time.

I spun around in the chair. Samantha was tapping her foot while waiting for my reply. "Sure! That sounds great."

"Well, we're leaving in about fifteen minutes."

I'd already had my shower earlier in the morning, so it only took a few minutes for me to slide on some flip-flops and grab my handbag. I checked inside my wallet - not much there. Maybe Mom would be feeling generous today. All of a sudden, I felt the urge to buy a new swimsuit.

The nearest mall is about twenty minutes away in Roanoke, and seems teeny-tiny compared to the mega ones we shopped at in northern Virginia. There is a larger shopping center not too further away that has more stores, but Mom feels some nostalgia for this one - something about hanging out there on the weekends as a teenager. I enjoy the mall but I hope there will be more to do around here than that.

On the ride over, I had mentioned to my mother that I

needed a new bathing suit, so she immediately steered me into one of the larger department stores. With Mom and Samantha's help I had quickly found several bikini-style suits to try on. I was on the fourth, and this one was decent enough for me to step out and model. The three of us were weighing the pros and cons of this particular swimsuit when we heard a gasp.

"Beth Reilly, is that you?"

Collectively the three of us turned to face two stunning statuesque blondes.

"Carla?" Mom said in surprise as she reached over and gave the beautiful woman a hug, "it's been a long time. Actually, it's Beth Songer now. These are my daughters, Sallie and Samantha. Girls this is Carla; we went to high school together. I'm sorry, but I don't know your married name either."

"Brock. This is my daughter, Adrienne."

I nodded a hello to both, uncomfortably aware that I was standing in a bathing suit next to two women who could have been models for Victoria's Secret.

Carla and Adrienne both appeared to be close to six feet tall with flowing blonde tresses and blue eyes almost as spectacular as Will's. They were dressed to the nines just to come to the mall – mini-skirts, high heels and silky tank tops which left nothing to the imagination regarding their obvious endowments, particularly Carla's.

Never before had I felt so inferior in my appearance. It wasn't that I was conceited or considered myself a raving beauty (I had grown up next to the lovely Kaye after all), but I had always felt that I kind of held my own in the looks department.

Not so with these two around. I felt skinny, gawky and flat chested. I could sense Adrienne looking down on me both literally and figuratively.

I shifted from foot-to-foot. "Ah, do you mind if I…" I pointed my thumb at the changing room.

"Go right ahead," Carla answered with a sickening sweet voice. "By the way, that is darling on you. Bless your heart, such a cute little figure."

I may have recently moved here on a permanent basis, but one thing I know for certain is that *bless your heart* is definitely not a compliment and is primarily reserved for use in the South as a thinly veiled insult.

"Thanks." I added some saccharine to my own tone.

Just as I made my swift exit, I saw Carla turn her stenciledon cat eyes – drawn that way with the judicious use of blue eyeliner – back to Mom. From the stall I could overhear the conversation.

"Are you visiting your folks?" Carla probed.

"Actually, we moved to Boones Mill a week ago."

"Really? How nice. Where are you living?"

I couldn't tell if her interest was genuine or fake. I was betting fake…like her bosom.

"We bought a house near James and Sara Marlow. I don't know if you're familiar with…"

Carla interrupted before Mom could finish, "Yes, I know them. Adrienne and Zeke have been friends for a long time."

The way she phrased the words made me think she was trying to imply that they had been more than friends. I felt an unexpected surge of jealousy course through my body and was glad for the safety of the changing stall to conceal my reaction. I could easily imagine Zeke and Adrienne together – the rock star and the super model.

And I thought I couldn't feel any *more* inadequate around her.

"So, Adrienne, will you be a senior next year?" I heard Mom inquire.

"No, a junior." Adrienne's voice was so breathless that she could have passed for a B-movie bombshell. It fit her style which was very much like that of her mother's.

"Sallie will be a junior, too. Maybe you'll have some classes together."

"Maybe," Ms. Breathless replied without enthusiasm.

Fine with me. I wasn't that enthralled with the thought of seeing her again either.

Mom and Carla chatted a bit more, then the mother and daughter Barbie's departed with a promise to "do lunch."

Samantha cracked me up when she asked innocently, "Do you think her boobs are real?"

Mom burst out laughing, "They weren't that big in high school."

"I guess that means it's safe to come back out?" I called over the wall.

"Yes," Mom answered with another chuckle.

I displayed a few more suits for them, and much to my chagrin we all conceded that Carla had indeed been correct about the bikini I had been wearing when they showed up. It did flatter me the most - a pink and brown paisley print which had a bit of a vintage vibe. The top was designed like a tank which made me feel more comfortable in terms of coverage.

My dad would be pleased with that too. Poor guy. He was stuck at home trying to figure out how he was going to maintain a lawn that was considerably larger than the one we had moved from. I had heard some talk about a riding mower and maybe even some bush hogging (though I have no clue what that means). In all honesty, mowing the lawn was probably more preferable to him than shopping with the three of us.

We strolled around the mall a little longer. Both Mom and Samantha picked up a couple of items each and we were fortunate not to run into the beautiful Brocks again.

When we got home, Dad was unloading a green tractor from the trailer hitched to his truck. Evidently, he had also done some shopping today and was thrilled with his new purchase.

"Men and their toys," Mom commented, shaking her head.

"Isn't it pretty," Dad replied with admiration as he ran his hand over the hood.

"Lovely…for a tractor." Mom retorted with a smile.

We all were treated to a jaunt around the yard on Dad's new toy. I could have been riding back in time to one of the sunny days I had spent plowing up Franklin County red clay while perched on Grandpa Jesse's tractor. He would sit me on his lap and let me turn the steering wheel while he kept his hands below mine out of my sight, allowing me to think I was the one really doing the driving.

Once, when I was about eight years old, I had begged him over and over again to let me try some of his chewing tobacco; and, after hearing it repeatedly throughout the course of the day, he finally gave in and gave me a tiny pinch from the crumpled Red Man pouch he pulled from his back pocket. I stuck that stuff in my mouth thinking that I was really something; not a minute later, I was spitting it out and retching. It took most of the day and a whole lot of tropical punch flavored Kool-Aid for me to get that foul, burning taste out of my mouth. Mom wasn't happy when she heard that story, but I never asked for chewing tobacco ever again. I think he gave it up not long after that too. "It's a nasty habit," Grandpa Jesse would say, "and a darn waste of money."

I was looking forward to seeing him this evening and partaking of Grandma Ellen's scrumptious cooking. I had asked specifically for chicken and dumplings, one of her specialties. It is a personal favorite of mine and a recipe that my mom has never been able to duplicate probably because she insists on using canned biscuits for dumplings as a short cut instead of rolling out and cutting the dough from scratch as Grandma has always done. All-in-all I can't complain, though, since my mom is a pretty decent cook – she had a great teacher after all.

The joy riding was swiftly ended so that we wouldn't be late for supper, and the four of us piled into the car to head to my grandparents. Samantha immediately stuck her nose into a book, and my parents were lost in conversation regarding lawn maintenance; so I stared out the window.

Once leaving Route 220, the main road through Franklin County which will take you straight to North Carolina, the drive to my grandparents' home in the Callaway community turns into something you'd see in a folk art painting. The landscape is laid out like a patchwork quilt of fields and farms. We passed several dairy operations which make their presence known by their smell before we can even see their tall grain silos. The stinging odor of manure is always thick in the air during the warmer months but isn't entirely unpleasant – to me, anyway. My sense of smell has always been rather sharp at evoking memories, one whiff of the cologne my dad wore when I was younger will bring back a flood of them – him holding me in his arms as we danced around the kitchen, saying prayers as he tucked me into bed, his hands tight over mine as we grasped the handlebars of my bike when I learned to ride without training wheels. So the pungent smell of the dairy farms has served as an almost friendly welcome, greeting me on many visits to this area. It means we are getting closer to the home of my grandma and grandpa.

Theirs is a small farmstead which, as my grandparents have aged, has become less and less of a working farm. It has never been the core of their financial existence; they have always been part-time farmers. Like my parents, Grandma Ellen and Grandpa Jesse met in college and married soon after graduating. Because my grandmother had inherited the farm, my grandfather set up his small veterinary practice nearby; and my grandmother worked as an elementary school librarian. Both are now retired and keep a few chickens for the egg supply and one very friendly goat as a pet. They continue to plant a garden each summer to live off of the rest of the year.

My family has been the lucky recipient of a boatload of canned goods that we pick up from them during our late summer visits. Many times Samantha and I have had to ride back home with our feet propped up on our suitcases because the trunk has been loaded down with glass jars filled with green beans, tomatoes, corn, and pickles.

As we parked in the driveway, Grandpa Jesse was coming up the stairs that lead from the cellar of their traditional white farmhouse and was carrying a couple of glass jars in his hands. A big grin spanned his face as he recognized our vehicle. He was wearing his usual attire: short-sleeved button-down shirt, khaki work pants, and a baseball cap that usually advertises a farm supply company and covers his mop of gray hair that sticks out every-which-way beneath the brim. When it is hot enough, he exchanges the button-down and work pants for a t-shirt and shorts; though for some reason, he wears dark socks pulled up to his calves along with stark white tennis shoes, which never makes much fashion sense to me. I don't know what keeps me from telling him how wrong that looks.

We had barely come to a stop when Samantha jumped out of the car and with a quick wave to Grandpa Jesse, headed off in the direction of Daisy, the goat. I went straight for the kitchen, delighted to see that Grandma Ellen had a pot of chicken and dumplings bubbling on the stove.

"It's not anyone you know," my grandma said, startling me as she walked up behind me. I turned and gave her a hug - her body was soft and cushy like a down pillow - and chuckled inwardly at the story behind her comment. A couple of years ago, we had been treated to a meal at which the main course consisted of a chicken for which Samantha (unbeknownst to anyone else) had developed a fondness. Upon discovery of our dinner's identity, Samantha was horrified and vowed to never eat chicken again. That only lasted a couple of months until her love for fried chicken exceeded her desire for animal rights.

The table was not yet set, so I offered to help, opening the cabinet doors and pulling out the worn yellow and white sixties-style plates and matching glasses that my grandparents had used since they were new. Grandma has always said that she was a product of her grandparents who had lived through the Great Depression; she was a packrat who rarely threw anything old away, unless it was in such bad shape that she had no choice. As I busied myself at the table, she worked around the stove emptying into a large pot the jars of green beans that Grandpa Jesse had delivered from the cellar, and checked on the cornbread she was baking. Its warm aroma perfumed the kitchen as she opened the oven door.

"How was dinner with the Marlow's?" She asked after she laid her oven mitt on the counter, stuck her hands in the pockets of her apron and faced me. If she had been wearing a red dress with a white fur collar, she couldn't have been more similar in appearance to the typical Mrs. Claus you see in Christmas displays. Her snow-white hair is a ring of fluff about her head; she is short and plump, sometimes wears silver reading glasses perched on the end of her nose and has a smile so welcoming it takes up almost half of her face.

"It was nice," I answered, not elaborating any further. Apparently my grandma was having none of that. She went straight for the punch.

"What do you think of Zeke?"

Bam – there it was. Did Mom and Sara Marlow get to her already too?

"He's nice too," I said slyly. I wasn't sure if I was going to give in and play this game.

"If I were your age, I'd be thinking he's a little more than nice," she smirked. "That boy is one tall, cool drink of water."

"Grandma!" I shouted with surprise. Although I shouldn't have been shocked; she is as honest as the day is long.

"Well, I would," she remarked while stirring one of the bubbling pots on the stove.

Suddenly I felt the urge to confide in her about my dilemma with Will and Zeke. Grandma Ellen has always been so easy for me to talk with. I called her before I told my own mother the first time my heart was broken by a boy with dimples in the sixth grade. Although she may be a bit prejudiced since she knows Zeke personally, she has met Will more than a handful of times when they've visited us in Springfield; so I feel pretty sure she could be an impartial jury to my crime.

"Okay – you're right. I do think he's more than just nice." I tried to sound casual about it as I laid out the silverware.

She cleared her throat a little - kind of an "ahem" - but otherwise didn't respond, so I started to blather.

"When I first saw him earlier this week I was a little irked with him, but last night I found him pretty irresistible. He seems more mature than most guys his age and a bit intense, but so down to earth, too. Does that make any sense? Anyway, do you know that he's a talented musician?"

"Yes, I do. I've heard him play many times at church since we started worshiping there last fall." She replied, stirring the pot some more.

Moonshine Serenade

"He seems a bit interested in me too, but there's another situation I need to deal with."

"Do tell," she faced me again.

I had finished setting the table at this point, so I pulled out a chair and sat down.

"Do you remember Kaye's brother, Will?"

"I think so. If I recall correctly, the last time we were up there that he had grown quite handsome, as well."

"Yes, he is. He's a great guy too – he's a soccer coach for a little league team." I was hoping this tidbit would impress her, I'm sure that she was already aware of Zeke's volunteer work at the nursing home. "Well, I've had a crush on him since last fall, and out-of-the blue, when we announced that we were moving, he started showing me some attention – different than just being his sister's best friend. Then the night before we moved, he kissed me."

She raised her eyebrows at that confession, but her face suggested it was more of a *you go girl* and not a *does your mama know* expression - which reminded me….

"I've not told *any* of this to Mom."

Not that I couldn't talk to my mom, I had not been in the mood to go into the amount of detail that would be required to have this conversation with her.

"I promise not to say a word," she vowed, laying her finger across her lips in a "shhh" gesture.

"The added complication to all of this is Kaye." I continued to pour out my predicament. "She's excited about Will and me being together. I can't stand the thought of hurting either one of them if it doesn't work out."

"Well, that sounds like a right fix you got yourself into." Grandma nodded her head in understanding. "So what are you planning to do about it, Sallie Beth?"

Sallie Beth is my full name, and what my family called me until about the fifth grade when I insisted with a stomp of my foot that I was too grown up to be called by two names. It took them a little while, but my parents eventually got in the habit of using only my first name (unless I am in trouble). My grandparents, however, had never gotten out of the routine of calling me by both names. I haven't bothered trying to belabor the point with them, so I was stuck with letting them call me whatever they wanted. Frankly, it really was the least of my concerns at this point.

"I'm not sure, but I'm thinking that I'll keep things on the down low with Zeke while I try to figure out what's going on with Will."

"Well, you're young. It's good to keep your options open," she advised. "Though, it will be tough to maintain a long-distance relationship."

Was she already showing her bias?

"But ultimately, you should go with your heart."

Something about the way she said that made me think of my great-grandmother.

"Grandma, what do you know about your father?"

"Not much. He died while my mother was pregnant with me. She would never talk much about him, or tell me who he was, but she made it very clear that it was not because he was a bad person. He was a very good man who went out of his way to help other people." She said this as if remembering the very words her mother had spoken to her as a child. "As I got older, I realized that she had been protecting me by not revealing his identity, but I don't know from what. It's too bad that she died so young. Had she lived to old age, she may not have felt the need to protect me any longer."

By the time she reached the end, I had walked over to my grandmother and squeezed her ample waist; it obviously still bothered her, and not knowing the identity of her father was a missing link in our family. I wished that I could find out who he was and join all the pieces together completing our family picture. My mom had tried before without any success. It was assumed that my great-grandmother had gone to her grave with this secret. If she had told anyone else, that person had never divulged it.

Grandma sighed, patted me on the shoulder as if she was comforting me and then smiled. "Go tell everyone that supper is ready."

We assumed our places around the table; grace was said, bowls were passed and stomachs were filled. It wasn't long before my dad scooted his chair back, patted his belly and praised Grandma's cooking. "You've outdone yourself this time, Ellen."

When the dessert plates were empty, the women cleared the table and cleaned the kitchen, while the men escaped to the living room undoubtedly to check out a baseball game score. Samantha hand washed the dishes while I dried and put them away. My grandmother had never owned a dishwasher, claiming it would be a waste of money and energy.

Moonshine Serenade

But our chores didn't feel like work as the four of us chatted about trivial matters and laughed over family stories. Grandma Ellen stayed true to her word, not revealing one thing about what we had discussed, though Zeke's name did come up as she good-naturedly teased Samantha about him getting the best of her.

When we arrived back at our house, I decided to go for a run. Despite the lateness of the hour, it was still light outside. I jogged down the stairs and poked my head into the living room to let my parents know that I was going out. Mom and Samantha had already claimed their spots on either end of the couch where the lamps were located so they could read. Dad was reclined in his favorite chair, his eyes focused on another one of his recent proud purchases - a flat screen TV that Mom had reluctantly agreed to hang above the fireplace. Dad was pushing his luck; she was already unhappy with the fact that the shabby recliner had made the move with us.

"Don't you think it's a bit late for that?" Mom's eyes were apprehensive.

"Nah. I'm going for a short one. It won't take me long."

"Well, be careful," she replied before returning her attention to the June edition of *Country Living* magazine.

I left for the route I had used for most of the week, deciding that tonight I would include the Marlow's driveway, or at least part of it. I didn't want it to appear that I was running straight to their front door, especially since I had forgotten to ask permission last night, though I didn't think they would care.

It wasn't long after I turned down their road that I noticed it seemed to be getting dark fast. It quickly covered the trees and the ground like a mother drawing a heavy blanket up over a sleeping child.

Even as the moon continued to rise and glow it wasn't enough to light my path. I was only able to see a few feet ahead of me. Because stupid me had left my phone at home, I wasn't in the position to call someone to rush right over and pick me up. I was getting nervous, but determined to finish my run. I decided that the bridge we had crossed on our visit to the Marlow's would be as far as I would attempt to journey down their driveway. The sound of my running shoes hitting its wooden boards would serve as an easy landmark, and fortunately, I didn't have to run much further before I could vaguely make out the railings. It was a blessedly short bridge; I made it to the end and turned around within a minute, the soft thud of my sneakers rose to a clatter as I quickened my pace in an effort to get home fast.

I was rounding a bend in the road when the bright glare of lights hit me square in the face, rendering me as blind as the proverbial deer in headlights.

I threw my hand up to shield my eyes and jumped to the right to get out of the way of the oncoming vehicle; but the ground there was uneven and I found myself tumbling backward into the darkness. I felt a sharp pain in my right ankle as I tried to regain my footing. With my body twisted in an awkward angle, I fell with palms forward -sliding my arms, stomach and legs along the floor of the ditch.

I lay there catching my breath when I heard a car door slam shut.

"Sallie! Sallie!" It was Zeke's voice.

Great.

Just.

Great.

Dear Lord in Heaven, why must you humiliate me this way?

"Sallie!" Zeke had a flashlight and was shining it down on me. "Are you okay?"

"Yes, I think so," I called back as I rolled over and tried stand up. An intense pain shot from my ankle straight up my leg.

I dropped back to the ground. "Ow! Ow! Ow!"

In a second Zeke was at my side, his hands caressing my arms. "You are obviously *not* okay. Where does it hurt?"

I pointed to my ankle. He shined his flashlight in that direction.

"I think it's already starting to swell. What were you doing out here in the dark anyway?"

Fabulous. Now Zeke will think that I'm stalking him.

"I was running. I run almost every day, and I mistakenly thought your driveway would be safe because it's off the main road."

"But it's dark as molasses. We don't have streetlights and sidewalks like you're used to at your old place." Zeke admonished, but with concern in his voice.

I interrupted him angrily, "Don't you think I realize that? It got dark quicker than I expected." Maybe it was due to the embarrassment or the pain, but his last comment seriously ticked me off.

I tried to push myself up again, but Zeke's arms were

around my back and under my legs before I made it very far.

"No you don't," he said as he lifted me up without even the hint of a groan at my hundred and twelve pounds. "Hold this," Zeke directed, handing me the flashlight. I did as I was told and grabbed the flashlight aiming it in front of us.

Zeke carried me easily up the small embankment to his Jeep, pausing only to ask if I was able to open the passenger side door. Once I had accomplished that task, he sat me gently inside and fastened my seatbelt.

"Thank you," I said with downcast eyes, shamed by my earlier irked retort.

"No problem," Zeke replied, brushing a stray lock of hair out of my eyes.

I could only imagine how bad my appearance was…sweaty, red-faced, hair sticking out every which way and probably covered from head to toe in dirt - maybe even stinky. Hopefully, my deodorant was working overtime today.

While Zeke walked past the front of the Jeep to the driver's side, I covertly sneaked a sniff under each armpit. Thankfully, they both still smelled like baby powder.

Zeke opened his door, and the thought suddenly occurred to me that he might take me to his home; it was mortifying enough that Zeke should see me like this – but his parents as well? "Where are you planning to take me?"

His face scrunched up in a way that made me think he was concerned that I had hit my head instead of twisting my ankle. "We're going to your house, of course."

I sighed in relief as he jumped in, efficiently executed a turn-around and accelerated back down his driveway. Occasionally we would hit a bump and my ankle would throb; only once, on a particularly large one, did I cry out loud causing Zeke to apologize profusely. I made every effort to console him; it wasn't his fault that this particular stretch of road was filled with potholes.

At my house, Zeke was adamant about helping me to the front door and escorting me in. For the first time tonight, I noticed that he smelled faintly of perfume. I didn't have time to contemplate its origins because Mom had hurried to the foyer when she heard the door shut. I could tell she had been worriedly awaiting my return. The sight of Zeke's holding me up while I hopped on one foot only added to the anxiety in her eyes.

She rushed over to me, "What happened?"

"I fell and twisted my ankle."

"It's really all my fault, Mrs. Songer. I blinded Sallie with my headlights, and to get out of the way of my Jeep, she fell into a ditch and twisted her ankle."

Leave it to Zeke to take all the blame for something that was due to my stupidity, or, if truth be told, stubbornness. I had my mind set on running, nightfall or not. Maybe I had been subconsciously hoping to run right into Zeke...be careful what you wish for.

Assessing that I was not seriously injured, Mom was quick to place the blame where it really lay. "Zeke, this is not your fault. I told Sallie it was too late for her to be out running, but she can be a bit obsessive about it. "

Hello! Does anyone here care that I'm hurt *and* humiliated?

"Mom, I think I need to get upstairs and prop this ankle up on a pillow."

"Oh, honey, I'm sorry. You're right." She turned back to Zeke, "Thanks so much for your help."

"I'll get her up the stairs for you before I leave," he offered.

"No thank you. I can do it myself," I started to say but was interrupted by Zeke scooping me up in his arms again.

"Show off," I whispered so that only he could hear.

Mom sprinted up the stairs ahead of us, "Follow me. I'll show you to her room."

Holding me closer to his chest than necessary, he started up the stairs.

"Wrap your arms around my neck," Zeke said with a devilish grin. "That will make it easier for me to carry you."

I knew he was right, so I complied. I actually felt quite contented draped around Zeke, but I couldn't let him get by with it that easily.

"You shouldn't take advantage of a girl when she's down." I scolded with a smile.

Zeke beamed.

Mom motioned with her hand toward my door. Zeke carried me into the room and carefully laid me down on my bed. Using one of my extra pillows, Mom carefully propped up my ankle and examined it.

"It's swollen alright, but not broken."

She would know. My mom has a nursing degree and had worked for years on the orthopedic floor of the same hospital as Dr. Landry. She enjoys nursing, but her dream has always been to open an antiques store of her own. She plans to do that here in Franklin County. She has been saving money to do so, which leads me to think my parents have been orchestrating this move for much longer than they had admitted.

"Zeke, do you mind sitting with her while I run down and get an ice pack and some ibuprofen?"

"My pleasure," Zeke drawled as he sat softly on the edge of my bed. He perused our surroundings. "Nice room. I bet you have a great view of the mountains."

"Thanks, I do actually."

"Who are they?" Zeke pointed towards the picture on my nightstand.

"That's my best friend, Kaye, and her brother, Will. We lived in the same neighborhood. Kaye and I have been best friends since kindergarten."

He stroked my hand. "Moving has been really hard on you, hasn't it?"

Zeke could read me well considering he had known me for such a short time – not counting our encounter as toddlers. I felt traitor tears stinging my eyes, but I fought them back. I hate crying in front of people.

I peered up at Zeke through damp eyelashes. "Yes, it has," I acknowledged quietly, "in a lot of ways."

"Well," he said as he leaned in closer, "I'm hoping that I can help make it all better."

At that exact moment Mom came barreling back into the room with Dad right behind her.

She held up the ice pack and bottle of pills. "Here you go!"

Zeke jerked away from me, my parents had not noticed our close proximity, although I was sure the pink flush of my cheeks would give it away.

"Thanks so much for bringing her home." Dad patted Zeke on the shoulder as he handed me a glass of water.

"It was no problem, really. It was kind of my fault too that this whole thing happened." Zeke glanced over at me and smiled. "I guess I should be heading out."

I didn't want him to leave, even though I knew he had to. I was anxious for him to explain in exquisite detail exactly how he planned to make it all better, but regardless of how pro-Zeke Mom seemed to be, it certainly wasn't enough to let him sit at my bedside all night.

This time I reached over to grab his hand giving it a squeeze as I gave him a sincere smile. "Thanks for everything. I mean it."

Zeke squeezed my hand back, then stood up and walked to the door. "Take care of that ankle. We're still on for Monday, gimpy or not."

Zeke waved to my parents and was gone. He had barely left the room before I began to miss him. Despite my supreme embarrassment regarding the entire falling flat on my face situation, I couldn't deny that I had enjoyed him doting on me tonight. Though both excited and confused by it, I had fully realized my fondness for Zeke Marlow. He was the best part of my new life here.

Mistaking the pain in my eyes to be from the discomfort of my injury, Mom started the helicopter hover around me. I was anxious to be alone and expressed my need for assistance in getting ready for bed. She helped me to get cleaned up and into my pajamas, positioning me on the bed so that I could keep my ankle raised while sleeping.

For many reasons, I wasn't expecting it to be my most comfortable night of sleep. I was hoping the pain meds would kick in soon and help me to rest. I could sort through the emotions that were racing through my body in the morning, so I settled into my bed as comfortably as I could and closed my eyes.

Before long, I was standing in a circle of trees, a cool breeze stirring their leaves into a soft whisper, urging me forward into the dark night. I was here to meet someone; the earth crinkled beneath my bare feet as they propelled me to that promised rendezvous.

"Zeke," I eagerly called out. There was no reply.

I spun on my heels hoping to find him arriving from the other direction; instead I was greeted by a stabbing pain in my right foot. Glancing down, I could see a trickle of blood slowly ooze from beneath my toes, spreading out in a pool and darkening the earth beneath them. I crouched to the ground, searching for the culprit. I shoved leaves and pine needles aside with my fingers, discovering something hard and sharp. I held it up toward the light of the moon – a large, jagged-edged piece of thick glass. I studied the specimen, turning it around in my hand. It appeared to be the bottom half of a broken jar, its cavity blackened as if it had been burnt by the rot of age and forest sediment.

A rustling in the leaves turned my attention away from the container. I blinked my eyes to focus in the dim light: emerging from beyond the long branches of an evergreen, a young man with suspenders stepped softly forward, his voice clear this time as he spoke.

"Sallie, I've been waiting for you."

Chapter Six
Univited

Mom came in to check on me before she went to bed and without meaning to do so, woke me before I could utter one word to the young man in my dream.

This isn't the first time that I've experienced recurring dreams, or at least ones with the same setting and cast of characters. For several months when I was about ten years old, I had vivid nightmares about spaceships with colorful blinking lights descending from the sky, landing on the front lawns of the homes in my neighborhood, and loading us all zombie eyed onto their ships via staircases that opened like the steps to an airplane. Mom said Dad was to blame for that one. He had let me watch a science fiction flick with him, which at the time didn't scare me, but it must have left a subconscious impression.

The other dream I've had on a continuing basis is also the most horrifying: I'm strolling down the halls of my old high school, waving and chatting with my friends as usual when I notice that they are all gawking at me with puzzled expressions; bystanders are breaking into laughter. Then I glance down and observe with abject mortification that I have been prancing around the school wearing nothing but a matching red and white polka-dotted bra and underpants.

After a few nights of providing everyone in my high school with a free peep show, I told Kaye about my embarrassing nightmare. She grabbed a hardback on dream interpretation that she keeps on her bedside table. Using her pink-polished fingernail, she scrolled the index for *Being Naked in Public* and a found a plausible explanation.

"This makes sense," she said as we sat cross-legged on her purple satin bedspread. "It says here that when you dream about being naked (or practically naked) in public, it means that you feel exposed in some part of your life - awkward or vulnerable. Or it could mean that you have a subconscious desire to be less secretive."

"I'd go with the secretive reason," she concluded with a wink. "So if I understand this correctly, to make the dreams go away you'll need to jump on Will. Or we could use one of my love spells to get him to jump on you."

Kaye reached for another self-help guide on her nightstand,

Camilla Cabot's Complete Guide to Love Spells and Potions.

"No and No!" I replied with emphasis then added sarcastically, "Besides, can't you use your cards to read my future? Then we'd know the answer to all of this right now."

"Oh, very funny. You know I haven't practiced enough to be accurate with that."

I really, really miss Kaye.

I'm sure today's weather was only contributing to the mood.

From my perch on the bed, I can see streams of water rolling down my window and hear the pounding of raindrops that sound as if someone is pelting rocks onto the old tin roof.

I'm a prisoner in my room, my mother had strongly suggested that I stay put and keep my ankle raised in an effort to encourage the healing. This meant that while my family is privileged to enjoy Zeke's gorgeous face and guitar playing during church service this morning, I'm stuck here alone, but with Dad's iPad for company – giving me some sort of connection to the outside world.

I checked my social page first. I had received several messages from a few friends, but nothing from Kaye or Will.

That was odd.

They must be staying busy even without me.

But of course they are, Sallie. I hadn't been their entire world before I moved, and I certainly wasn't now.

I decided to write them both a short note on their profiles, relaying my running injury to Will (carefully leaving out the specifics as to who had escorted me home and carried me to my bedroom) and asking Kaye if she had grown more adept at casting spells and reading fortunes.

Not that either of us truly believed in that mystical stuff.

Okay - maybe Kaye a little. She did have a lot of fun playing around with it at least.

A couple of years ago, we went through a phase where we would lock ourselves in her room and play with her Ouija Board, a hand-me-down gift from Kaye's Aunt Cynthia – the wearer of long flowing scarves, and owner of the dance studio where Kaye had taken lessons pretty much her entire life.

We would ask Ouija the typical dumb questions. "Does my latest crush like me?" and "What age will I be when I get married?" It not only told us at what age we would marry (24 for Kaye, 23 for me) but also that I would marry the front man of one of my favorite bands and that she would marry the latest here today, gone tomorrow, hot throb movie star gracing the pages of every tabloid magazine.

Yeah. Obviously *that* couldn't be trusted.

Ouija frightened us once. After that experience, we hid it in the very back of Kaye's closet and never played it again.

Earlier I had explained to Kaye that some people consider the board to be evil and that wicked spirits can use it as a guise to make contact with humans. I had received this information after casually mentioning to my mother that Kaye had a board and that we had been interrogating it on all matters of special relevance to a fourteen-year-old.

Mom chuckled at some of the examples I had given her and shared some of the crazy questions she had asked the Ouija when she played with her best friend as a teenager. According to one of her consultations, she should be married to the lead singer of a popular 1980's band and that I, her first born, should be named Ursula. She then went on to say that her mother had not been particularly happy to find out that she had been using the Ouija Board since she had been raised to believe it to be a channel for the unholy.

Like my mom before me, I rejected that idea thinking it was old-fashioned. But Kaye and I both totally embraced the idea that ghostly entities in general were the driving force behind the planchette. We decided to test this theory on a blustery Saturday night in January as we were holed up in Kaye's bedroom.

This night, rather than inquire about ourselves, we decided to query our spirit. We quickly ascertained that "it" was male. We asked his age, but received a ridiculous answer that was a number way to high for anyone to have lived before dying.

Frustrated, Kaye called it a liar. The words had no sooner left her mouth when the planchette began to spin erratically and roll across the board with our fingers still attached. Then, as quickly as it had started spinning, it stopped and began to slide across the board like a snake – even though we had not uttered a word to it since Kaye's angry comment.

Do not go to sleep Sallie was the first sinuously spelled message.

My eyes narrowed as I glared over at Kaye.

"Are you doing that?"

"No, I promise!" She gasped. Her cheeks puffed out as if all the breath had been knocked out of her. I knew her well, and Kaye was without a doubt as surprised as I was by this communication.

The small, triangular shaped board continued to move gracefully across the larger one.

I will kill you.

I lifted my hands from the planchette and smacked it, sending it reeling across the room where it slammed into the opposite wall. After we both spent some time in recovery, Kaye sprang from the bed and picked it up along with the larger board and shoved them both into the game box, stashing it deep into her large closet beneath a garbage bag of stuffed animals which she had intended to donate to Goodwill two years before.

Neither of us could sleep that night. Restless, we tossed and turned in Kaye's big bed, occasionally whispering about what had happened, but not sure what to make of it. Eventually we got up and crept into Will's room, sleeping under a blanket on his floor, as we were prone to do when we had been unnerved by a scary movie. We were comforted by his big brother presence. When he awoke the next morning, yawning and disheveled-haired, he wasn't surprised to find us snoozing on our makeshift bed.

It had been a long time since I had relived that memory, and that was likely the last time Kaye and I had camped out in Will's room. I guess we had eventually become too old for that - though I recall having many a daydream during the last few months where I slipped into Will's bedroom without Kaye. I would sit on the bed rousing him from his slumber as my fingers swept his hair away from his face; I would smile as his eyes opened and he recognized me. Will would wrap an arm around me and pull me close; kissing me softly and slowly – not unlike the one and only kiss we had ever actually shared.

I propped my chin in my hand, closed my eyes, and tried to concentrate on the kiss Will had given me on the front porch of my old house. Maybe if I made the effort to focus on him more, I could get back some of what my attraction for Zeke seemed to be clouding over.

I could see Will clearly in my mind's eye, leaning toward me, his stray lock of hair falling over his brow; but before we began to kiss, the face changed and sapphire-blue eyes turned to a blend of gray-gold-and-green, wavy dark hair became a tousled sandy blonde, and with the transformation complete, a sweet southern voice whispered my name.

How swiftly my thoughts returned to Zeke.

I needed a distraction.

I sat strumming my fingers lightly on the edge of the iPad, probing my brain for something to do as a diversion, when it occurred to me that I had not opened Letitia's diary in a few days. I had been so caught up in the whole Zeke-Will-Kaye situation – well, to be honest, mostly Zeke – that I had ignored Letitia, whom I considered to be the first friend I had made here.

And, seriously, what did that say about my state of mind a little more than a week ago to consider my first friend to be someone I had met by reading her old diary?

Zeke had certainly improved my outlook on this whole place. When you throw in the whole ghost thing, what would my state of mind be today if I had not met him?

I didn't even want to consider that scenario.

I sat the iPad next to me, leaned over to pull the diary from the nightstand drawer, and opened it to the page after the one I had last read. I was excited to see that this seemed to be the longest entry yet, Letitia's script graced page after page before the next date was written at the top of a sheet. She must have had a lot to say that day, and, hopefully, would divulge some helpful information in my search for answers.

June 8, 1939

I know it's been a week since I've written. I haven't had much to say until today. Mama and Daddy have forbidden me to go into the woods alone. But today they went into Rocky Mount, and I figured what they didn't know wouldn't hurt them.

Now, normally I would be chomping at the bit to go with them, but the errands they needed to run today didn't sound fun. I thought that the two of them being gone would give me the opportunity to do something that would get me into a whole heap of trouble if they found out.

From the moment I heard them mention riding into Rocky Mount; I made the decision that while they were gone I would visit the spot where I saw the murder take place. Daddy really hurt my feelings when he said that I had jumped to conclusions over what I saw, so my plan was to go back there and search for clues.

I was impressed with Letitia; she was a heck of a lot braver than I might be under the same circumstance. Although, I could relate to her irritation on being told that she had jumped to conclusions. I feel pretty sure that if I told anyone else other than Zeke about the ghosts I have been seeing, I would be given the same sort of dismissive answer that Letitia had received from her father regarding the murder she was convinced that she had witnessed.

But a ghost is an entirely different matter than a murder. Suppose the killer returned to the same spot while she was there? Among the ghost tales that I was privy to hear from my grandmother when I was younger, there always was a common statement from her at the end: "Mind you, these are all stories. I'd be much more afraid of the living than the dead." I guess this was meant to calm our fears of a supernatural encounter, but was it true - are there dangerous ghosts? The one I saw in the cemetery and my dream certainly did not appear to be friendly. I decided to clear those thoughts from my head and focus my attention on Letitia's writing. I'd frighten myself about being home alone if I continued to concentrate on those scary specters that I seem prone to come across lately.

I gave them plenty of time to get up the road before I ventured out. I would rather be out in the woods and have Mama and Daddy wonder where I was than have them catch me heading that way. They would be gone for a while, so I knew I could get back before they did.

I was walking so fast to get there that I broke out in a sweat. As soon as I crossed the woods' edge, I began to retrace my steps to the location I had sought over a week ago. Before getting too close I paused behind a large white pine to make sure that I was alone and that there were no signs or sounds of anyone else approaching. When I felt sure that I was alone, I walked cautiously, looking over my shoulder as I moved to the area where I had seen the two men.

At first glance, the spot seemed clear. There was an old tree with four large trunks that stretched up toward the sky from its base, which was open and wide so that I could probably sit in it like a chair if I tried. I was nudging the fallen leaves around the bottom of the tree with the toe of my shoe when I noticed something sticking up from beneath a pile that lay in the lap of the tree. I reached in and pulled it out. It was a glass jar filled with a clear liquid that sloshed as I turned it in my hand. There was no question in my mind what this container held – illegal whiskey.

An image from my dream last night swirled through my mind...a broken jar in the woods.

I was becoming more convinced than ever that all of this was interconnected: the diary, the ghosts, my dreams. But what is completely confusing to me is why?

And what is Zeke's part in all of this? Was there something here in the water in Franklin County that, if you drink it, allows you to see ghosts? A jest, of course, but I couldn't quite come to terms with why the two of us were the only ones seeing dead people.

Maybe, if it wouldn't totally ruin the mood, I could talk with Zeke about this tomorrow and get his thoughts and possibly some theories. It couldn't hurt to get the opinion of someone I trusted, and he had a vested interest in this himself. Maybe, if all of this is truly related and we could figure it out, then the result could help him as well. Finding out the identity of the spirit that had been appearing to Zeke for years could help it to move on, right? If that's what ghosts are supposed to do, or can do. I was treading in some very unfamiliar and unexpected water here. I would definitely be doing some research today on that subject, but first, I wanted to finish reading this entry.

I placed the jar back where I had found it and covered it with leaves and some nearby fallen pine boughs so that it was entirely hidden from view. If that container had been the cause of the argument between the two men, I was surprised to find it still there a week later. I couldn't imagine why one solitary jar of liquor would result in a murder. Although, I have seen firsthand that moonshine can be both a blessing and a curse. It has saved many a family from absolute poverty, providing a means to earn a living when no other jobs were available. By the same token, I've witnessed fathers and brothers of friends sent to prison when they were caught selling illegal liquor and the bad things that can happen when men are high off it. Fearing what might come of it, my friend, Mary, had to be sent away to an aunt's house after a drunken man had attacked her when she was walking home alone from school one afternoon. Her older brother served justice by beating the man within an inch of his life. She confided this to me before she left, and I promised never to tell this secret about her to anyone, though I'm not sure it's really a secret in our small community. It's hard to keep that kind of tragedy from spreading like wildfire. Some folks around here delight in it.

Poor Mary. I didn't need a detailed explanation to understand what had happened to her. At that time, if an unwed girl became pregnant, she would face a public scrutiny much different than today. Despite the violent nature in which it seems the pregnancy was produced, Mary and her baby certainly would have been met with whispers and sideways glances if not an outright shunning.

My own great-grandmother, Sallie, had been met with a great degree of prejudice when her pregnant belly became obvious. Although she insisted that she was married and even wore a ring on her left hand, the fact that she had neither changed her last name, nor had a husband who could be seen, led many to question the truth of what she told. Only her parents' insistence to the members of their community on the honesty of the story she conveyed kept both her and my grandmother from being truly shunned. Though they themselves were surprised at my great-grandmother's announcement, they believed in their daughter's heart and integrity.

I dug around the area a bit more searching without success for any evidence that might help to prove my account. Disappointed, I began my journey home and decided to walk past the cemetery. If my parents had returned home early and witnessed me walking from that direction, I could honestly claim a visit to the grave of my beloved grandparents with whom I had shared a home my entire life and who had died within six months of each other last year. My father was grief-stricken to lose his parents so close together, as was my mother, who thought of them as her own mother and father. It didn't help that Charles was gone either, we prayed every night for his safety. If my brother were still at home, he would certainly believe me and help me to figure this whole thing out. I decided that in my next letter I would tell him this story and ask for his thoughts on the situation.

As I came out of the woods, I turned my attention from the red-crested woodpecker that I had been watching hop from tree to tree, and saw a young woman standing by the newest grave in the cemetery. Her head was bent, and one arm lay across her mid-section as if she was trying to control the sobs that racked her body.

Not wanting to disturb her grief, I backed up and followed along the tree line until I was sure to be hidden from her view. Feeling so sad for the girl in the graveyard, I made my way back home.

"Ouch!" The complaint emerged audibly as a pain shot down my spine. Last night's awkward sleeping arrangement, plus bending over the iPad and Letitia's diary for a while, had all contributed to a literal pain in my neck. I needed to change positions, or better yet to get up and walk about the room.

I rose slowly, tenderly placed my feet on the floor, and gradually put pressure on my injured ankle. I hobbled to the window and pressed my forehead against the pane, gazing toward the mountains in the general direction of the cemetery.

Though midday, it was almost dark outside, the sun blanketed by thick gray clouds. Water tumbled down the window in rivulets, blurring the mountains and trees so that they appeared to move in a zigzag pattern. I must have been lost in a ramble of thoughts for several minutes before I realized that something was moving outside my window. I squinted to focus on the object below. As the mingled lines formed to offer some recognition, I felt uneasiness rise in the pit of my stomach.

Looking up at me was a man wearing a straw hat and bib overalls - barely discernible through the rain-distorted glass, but enough for me to make out who the unwanted visitor was.

I pressed my face against the glass, squinting to get a clearer image of what he might be doing down there. At first glance, he was standing motionless with arms at his sides. In the next second, his face flashed before me. It could have been a 3D horror movie image that filled my entire window frame - malicious eyes, a grubby beard and blackened teeth.

With one hand, I grabbed the window sill for support; the other flew over my open mouth. My scream was soundless…there was no one in the house to hear me.

I closed my eyes in an effort to steady my buckling knees; then, after taking a deep breath, dared another glance toward the angry face of the ghost.

But he was gone.

My body jerked in an uncontrollable spasm when the front door slammed. I did a quick scan around the room searching for the best place to hide.

What would it matter if I found a hole to crawl into? Couldn't he find me? This wasn't a normal person playing a little game of hide and seek, after all. And what would he do to me if he did find me beneath the bed or stuffed into the armoire? What other option did I have? I needed to prepare myself for an attack.

There was a loud thump at the bottom of the stairwell.

I poised in a kick-boxer self-defense position that I had learned from P.E. class, ready for whatever fighting I needed to do, or could do, against something that could disappear into thin air and make his face appear in my window two stories high.

Thump.

His heavy footstep seemed to reverberate throughout the house.

Thump, thump.

He was getting closer.

Thump, thump, thump.

And moving faster.

Thump, thump.

Dead silence.

A soft creaking ended the edgy stillness as my bedroom door was slowly pushed open.

I braced myself, trying to recall the self-defense instructions: knee to the groin, elbow in the ribs, a head slam to the face, bite.

But those directions were for battling a human attacker. What if you weren't exactly sure what your attacker might be? Other than something that was definitely not a human.

At least, not one who was alive and breathing.

The door moved again, a harder push this time, a louder creak.

Brace. Fight. Run.

A hand slid around the door frame.

Brace. Fight. Run.

A shadow appeared in the doorway.

Brace. Fight. Run.

And a voice called out my name.

"Sallie?" Dad's head appeared in the doorway. "We're home, honey."

Thank you, Jesus! It was my family returning from church.

I dropped my defensive pose.

"Good to see you up," then he winked, "but you better not let your mom catch you out of that bed."

I stumbled back to my bed as Dad left the room. Trembling legs hindered my ability to move about as much as my injured ankle. I had barely dropped myself down into the same position in which Mom had left me and composed my face to appear as normal as possible before she came hurriedly through the door.

"How are you feeling?" she questioned breathlessly as she sat down on the edge of the bed and rubbed my arm.

"I'm fine, Mom," I replied in my most convincing tone. I knew that even if she could see through the deceit, she would never guess the true meaning of why I really was not *fine* at the moment. There was only one other person who could understand.

I needed Zeke. I needed him to comfort me, to hear his honeyed voice assure me that I was not crazy, and to vow to me that we would figure this out together.

My mom's exploding smile brought the center of my attention back to her; it was obvious that she had some better news to share.

"I have something very exciting to tell you," she burst forth like a levee unable to hold back the torrent of water. "At the service today, I was approached by a woman who owns an antiques store in downtown Rocky Mount. She wants to sell and had heard that I was interested in opening a shop of my own. She offered to let me take over her lease and to sell me the entire contents of her store at a reasonable price, so I told her yes - right there on the spot!"

"Wow, Mom! I'm really happy for you." I truly was - all the pieces seemed to be falling into place for her since we had moved here...dream home, dream job.

"The catch is," she continued, "we have to move on it this week since her lease is expiring soon."

My heart dropped to the tips of my toes.

"Does that mean I can't hang out with Zeke tomorrow?"

"Not at all, I very much want you to spend time with him. You need to make some friends here. Besides, tomorrow I'll be taking care of all the legal stuff. But if your ankle is up for it, I will need your help for the rest of the week. I'll pay you. Consider yourself gainfully employed - if you want the job, of course."

Sweet! I could think of no better job than working with my mom in her shop. I had been worried that I would end up flipping burgers in a fast food joint or a manning the cash register at a supermarket.

"Of course I want the job!" I threw my arms around her neck. "Thanks, Mom!"

She hugged me back. "You may not be thanking me when you've dusted the same knick-knack for the hundredth time."

"What are you talking about?" I teased. "When we take over the place, people will be knocking each other down to get through the door and buy our knick-knacks."

Mom replied with a swat at my knee and attitude in her voice, "Well, your enthusiasm certainly energizes me! I'm ready to get our shop open, girl."

"Have you thought of a name yet?"

"I have a few ideas running around in my head."

I was really curious about what she had come up with. The name should be catchy, but also something that would stand the test of time.

"Well...?"

"I want to give them some more thought, and then I'll put them out there for opinions. I'm sure you'll have no problem giving me yours."

A shrill beeping sound intercepted my reply. The sound bounced off the walls and rendered me almost deaf.

"Glad to hear that the smoke detectors work," Mom shouted as she covered her ears. "Your dad must be burning our grilled cheese sandwiches."

She left the room in a hurry, and within a couple of minutes the beeping had stopped, although I could still hear it echoing in my head. My cell phone started ringing about the same time my ears stopped.

"Hello," I answered a bit loudly.

"Hey there, Gimpy! I missed you this morning."

The voice was unmistakable.

"Hi, Zeke. Hope I didn't burst your eardrum when I answered the phone; our smoke alarms have just stopped going off."

He chuckled, "Is everything under control there?"

"Oh, yeah. My dad's cooking, and unless he's grilling outside, he almost always burns something. Apparently our new detectors work very well."

"How is your ankle working today?"

"Still hurts a bit when I try to walk on it."

"Well, I guess if it's not any better tomorrow I'll need to carry you around like I did last night."

The thought of spending the day in Zeke's arms was almost enough to make me fake not being better tomorrow, even if I was.

"It's certainly tempting, but I'm sure I'll be back on my feet by then."

"Okay then, but my offer still stands - please pardon the pun."

"Very funny, Zeke."

"Well, I guess I better let you get back to your scorched lunch."

The beating of my heart stopped for a full second. I wasn't ready to let him go yet; I really needed to tell him what had happened this morning.

"Umm, Zeke."

"What's wrong?" He sounded disappointed. "You're not backing out on our date are you?"

"Oh, no. Not at all. It's just that…"

I wasn't sure how to say it. I knew that Zeke would know that I'm not crazy, but it felt crazy to even think about saying out loud: *Oh, by the way, I happened to see a ghost this morning.*

"What is it?" Now he sounded curious.

"Do you remember me telling you about the man I saw at the graveyard…the one that Samantha couldn't see?"

"The other ghost? Yeah. Why?"

I could tell that my voice was going to be shaky before I even said the words, "I saw him again this morning. He was standing outside my bedroom window."

"What? Are you alright? Do you want me to come over? I'll skip band practice if you need me."

"No. I mean, yes, I'm fine, but don't skip your band practice. I needed to tell someone, and well, you're the only person I can tell without it sounding as if I've taken way too much pain medication." I successfully calmed my voice down so he wouldn't feel the need to rush right over, although that's exactly what I really wanted, but it wasn't fair for him to miss his practice time. "We can talk about it more tomorrow…if that's okay with you."

"Yeah, yeah, of course. Are you sure you don't need me now?"

"Yes. I'm sure." I was becoming quite the liar today, first with Mom, and now with Zeke.

"Tomorrow, then. But you call me if you need me."

"Thanks, Zeke. I'll do my best to stay ghost-free until then."

He laughed. It was like warm sugar. "Bye, Sallie."

Not long after my conversation with Zeke, Samantha came bouncing into my room balancing a bowl of vegetable soup and a plate laden with a grilled cheese sandwich and grapes on a wooden tray with legs. We have used this tray every Mother's and Father's Day as long as I can remember to bring our parents breakfast in bed. They've always been gracious about eating it - even when we were younger and it couldn't have looked appetizing, much less tasted it.

"Mom asked me to bring this up to you."

"Thanks, Samantha! How was church today?"

She sat down on the other side of my bed cross-legged facing me. "It was fun. I met a couple of girls who invited me to the youth group meeting tonight."

I sipped from my soup spoon as I listened to her talk a little more about the people she had met this morning. I was hoping to find the right time to inconspicuously ask some questions that would lead her to eventually bring up my favorite guitar player.

".....and a bunch of them go to the middle school here in Franklin County, so I'll already know a few kids when school starts. But I'm thinking what you really want to know about is Zeke."

The little bit of soup that was in my mouth spewed out, fortunately right back into the spoon. I underestimate the perceptiveness of my sister.

"So, here's the scoop. Yes, he's an awesome guitar player, and he's a great singer too; he's, like, the praise band leader or something. Yes, the girls were all over him – especially that Adrienne girl we met yesterday at the mall. And no, he didn't seem to pay that much attention to them other than to be nice."

Samantha was good - I would definitely give her that. She knew exactly the important information to relay.

"Samantha, get down here, honey - your food's getting cold!"

My little sister jumped up off the bed at the sound of Mom's voice.

"See ya later!" Samantha called as she skipped out the door.

I finished up my lunch and settled in for what was sure to be a long afternoon.

Chapter Seven
Son Of A Preacher Man

The birds are singing my song.

A happy little ditty, something you might hear in a Disney movie just before the heroine dons a frilly dress and rides off on a white horse toward a castle in the sunset with her handsome Prince Charming.

However for me, instead of the setting sun there is a brilliant blue and cloudless sky with the temperature already hovering around 80 degrees despite the mid-morning hour. And my potential prince would be whisking me away in a black Jeep to an unknown location that requires a bathing suit.

But handsome...handsome I got.

Anxious for the day to begin, I hopped out of bed forgetting about my injury, reminded as my feet hit the floor. The pain was fleeting, and as I moved around, the discomfort faded so that I only slightly hobbled. No need for Zeke to carry me around today.

That's sort of a bummer.

Mom was coming in from her morning run as I came down the stairs to fix a bowl of cereal. I gripped the wood rail tightly for support but otherwise was able to make it down without much trouble.

"You're certainly much improved," she commented while watching my descent. "Aren't you glad you took it easy yesterday?"

"Yes, you were right." I admitted, glad that she had insisted I stay in bed and rest my ankle. I would much rather be able to spend all day with Zeke today, than watch him from a distance for an hour or so yesterday.

"What time is Zeke picking you up, anyway?"

"He said to be ready at eleven o'clock."

I was worried that the anticipation would make the next hour-and-a-half move slowly, but the exact opposite happened, it was almost as if I didn't have enough time to prepare myself.

I'm not one of those girls who takes a couple of hours to get ready; but by the time I had finished breakfast, taken a shower, dried my hair, brushed on some waterproof mascara and dabbed some gloss on my lips, it was already close to time for Zeke to arrive.

I cut the tags off my new bathing suit and pulled it on. With hands on hips, I evaluated my appearance in the mirror, turning front-to-back and front-to-back all over again.

All-in-all not bad, but what girl is ever totally pleased with her body?

I wasn't comfortable parading about in my bathing suit, so I put on a gauzy tiered skirt to cover-up the lower-half. Because the top was designed like a tank, I could get by with wearing it alone. Next came the go-to flip-flops and then I filled a straw bag with sunscreen, lip gloss, a rubber band for pulling up my hair, and a change of clothes. I grabbed my sunglasses and cell phone off the dresser and headed out my bedroom door.

I was leaning up against the island in our kitchen chatting with Mom and Samantha when the ringing of the doorbell made me jump; I wasn't consciously aware of how jittery I had been while waiting for Zeke to get here. I walked as fast as my ankle would let me, allowing a deep breath before opening our front door. There he stood…in cargo shorts and a white tee that showed off his tanned and muscular arms. Today, the top of his hair was covered in a red bandana tied in a knot at the back of his head.

A broad smile crossed his face as he moved his right arm from behind his back and presented me with a glass vase full of flowers. "I guess I have some competition," Zeke said matter-of-factly.

I was totally confused. "What?"

"These roses. A delivery man was dropping them off as I arrived, and I volunteered to bring them in. Your name is on the envelope. I have to admit I considered ripping it off and pretending they are from me."

I bit my lip as I took the flowers from Zeke and motioned for him to enter.

"Well, even though they're not from you, I guess you can still come in." I said in jest. I thought with his sense of humor that he would find the remark funny, but I only got half a smile from Zeke as he stepped into the foyer. "Roses aren't my favorite anyway. I prefer daisies."

I sat the vase down on the credenza and pulled the card from the plastic pitchfork-like object holding it. My finger was shaking a bit as I slid it under the flap of the envelope to open it, it didn't help that Zeke was standing there propped up against the banister, arms crossed against his chest watching me. The card easily slid out of its confines, its message twisted my heart.

I haven't forgotten you. Will

Well, he had some good timing.

"May I ask who they're from?" Zeke questioned politely.

I glanced up at him through my lashes. "Yes, you may ask."

Zeke cocked his head, but didn't alter one inch from his position. "Does that mean you're going to allow me to ask but not tell me the answer?"

I was thinking about doing just that but I didn't want to play games with Zeke.

I sighed. "They're from Will."

Zeke nodded his head and pursed his lips. "Will, as in your best friend's brother?"

"Yep."

He opened his mouth to say something else when Mom and Samantha strolled out of the kitchen. In two seconds flat my mom noticed the flowers sitting on the table in the foyer.

She bent over to smell them, "Zeke, how sweet of you to bring Sallie such pretty roses."

Zeke shook his head. "They're not from me."

"Oh." A crease furrowed my mom's brow. "Who would send me flowers?"

I was about to reply when Zeke answered for me. "No, they're for Sallie, alright."

I gave him the evil eye, in return received his trademark smirk. Zeke wasn't upset about the flowers at all; he was calling me on the carpet – making me 'fess up about Will.

Mom inclined her head in my direction.

I shrugged my shoulders attempting to act as if it was no big deal; for both her and Zeke's benefit. "They're from Will."

"*Will Landry?*"

I nodded my head yes, deliberately not elaborating more, then watched as the dawn of realization rose across my mother's face. I could imagine what she was thinking: *Sallie and Will, and I never noticed,* and then, w*hy hasn't she told me?*

"Really, Mom," Samantha rolled her eyes and added her own two-cents-worth. "Don't tell me you didn't see them running together every day for weeks before we moved."

And having done her good deed for the day, she turned on her bare heels and headed back toward the kitchen.

It was a slightly awkward walk out to the Jeep with Zeke; I couldn't get a feel for what he was thinking regarding the whole Will situation. As we reached his vehicle, Zeke paused for a

Moonshine Serenade

moment on the passenger's side, leaning me up against the door so that we were face to face –sort of – if I tilted my head back. I could feel my pulse begin to race as he placed his hands on either side of my head and stared down at me.

Zeke's expression was serious. "Are you dating Will?"

"No. We are technically not dating." It was true; we had not been out on a single *actual* date.

"So the vase of roses, does that imply that he's interested in you?"

"That is affirmative."

Zeke gave me another half-smile. "And you are…interested in him?"

"I was…well…still am. It's complicated."

He moved his face even closer, our noses were almost touching. "Am I a part of that complication?"

Despite the difficulty I was having concentrating enough to put two words together, I was able to answer rather boldly. "That is affirmative as well."

Zeke's mouth exploded in a bright smile before he kissed the tip of my nose. "Well, that's all I needed to know." Then Zeke opened the door and helped me get inside.

With the sunshine pouring through the windows, I noticed things about the Jeep that I had not the other night. It was well used with a faded dashboard, the gray vinyl seat torn in some places but otherwise tidy. It smelled like Zeke – musky with a hint of what reminded me of Ivory soap – clean and crisp.

Zeke hopped into the driver's side, donned his aviator-style sunglasses, started up the engine and shifted it into gear. The radio was playing softly as we pulled out of the driveway. I recognized the song; it was an older tune – something from before my parents were even teenagers.

Zeke reached over and turned the sound up; he had a huge grin on his face.

I smiled back at him. "What are you smirking about?"

"Don't you hear the song on the radio?"

"Yes."

Zeke kept his eyes focused on the road. "Well, I'm the son of a preacher man."

"I'm fully aware of that fact."

His grinned widened. "Do you think I'll ever be able to teach you anything?"

If I could see through his shades, I'm positive there would have been a wicked glint in Zeke's eyes.

I slid my sunglasses up to shield my own expression. "I guess that depends on what you're teaching and if I'm in the mood for learning."

Zeke shook his head and chuckled.

For a couple of minutes we were the only car on the road; a world of difference from Northern Virginia where by now we would have passed at least ten Volvo station wagons, Toyota mini-vans or Honda sedans. It wasn't too much longer though before an old red truck passed us going in the other direction. Zeke raised a hand from the steering wheel and waved. The old man driving the truck did the same.

"You know him?" I asked.

"Nope."

"Then why did you wave?"

Zeke shrugged his shoulders, "Just being friendly."

We turned onto the main highway and headed south. I still had no idea where we were going; Zeke had given me no clues whatsoever. I gazed out the open window watching the scenery as it flowed by. Kudzu grew thick on the hillsides, morphing the banks and the trees it covered into dinosaurs, swamp creatures and other sorts of green-leafed monsters reaching out for us with vine draped arms.

Zeke was enjoying another song that was playing on the radio, his fingers drumming against the wheel in time with the beat.

Wander as it does, my mind drifted to Will and the roses. It shocked me when I realized I hadn't even thanked him yet – normally I would have been punching his number as soon as I read his name on the card.

"Zeke, I realize this is a bit awkward, but would you mind if I sent Will a quick text? It's rude of me not to say thank you for those flowers."

"You're right – it is rude." Zeke replied in a fake admonishing tone. "Go right ahead, I don't mind at all. In fact, tell him hello from me."

Tempted to stick out my tongue at him, I grabbed the phone out of my bag instead. I pressed the keys slowly, literally all thumbs - I am not talented at texting. Kaye's fingers can fly across the keys.

Thanx 4 the flowers. Call u later. Sallie

The guilty feelings I had been attempting to suppress started to rise up in my chest again; I suffered an actual pain there. I had never experienced this situation before because not once in my almost seventeen years had two guys been vying for my attention at the same time. Well, I take that back – two that I would actually consider. There was Randy Crane, the science whiz and my biology lab partner, who had tried to earn my favor all through ninth grade; but no matter how sweet he was or how hard I tried; I couldn't find a way to click with him. I chose instead, Julian Blake – a tall, strong-jawed basketball star who could chat up a storm in a group but was so shy when we were alone that he could barely speak or even look directly at me for that matter.

But this time the two guys were Zeke Marlow and Will Landry.

Will reminds me of my favorite pair of pajamas - easy to throw on, hard to throw away.

On the other hand, Zeke brings to mind a Christmas morning when I had received a gift I wasn't expecting, realizing it was something I had wanted all along.

And of course, there is our kooky common denominator: we see dead people.

We turned off the main road, riding a couple more miles when Zeke pulled behind a church building with an empty parking lot. He shut off the engine, slipped off his sunglasses and turned toward me with a mischievous grin. "We're far enough away from the parents now - time to take the top off."

My heart submerged deep into the pit of my stomach.

I was hurt at first.

And then I was straight up angry.

What a waste of my time spending the last couple days thinking almost exclusively about Zeke and allowing myself to be drawn to him regardless of the feelings I had for Will - who I knew would never make such a flippant request of me.

And now after going on and on in my head about how exceptional Zeke is (I had compared him to Christmas morning!) he had transformed into some generic teenage boy seeking a quick thrill.

This was not the Zeke I thought I had come to know.

And I'm not the type of girl who rolls over and complies.

Crossing my arms over my chest, I lit right into him. "I am not taking my top off, and you can take me back home."

Zeke looked at me as if I had transformed into a creature from another planet and then burst into laughter. "Not *your* top, silly – the *Jeep* top."

"Oh," was all I could manage to force from my suddenly

strained vocal chords.

Previously, I would have summed up my most embarrassing moment as the other night when I laid splayed out flat-faced in the ditch, but that was nothing compared to this conversation which a recording of could probably win first prize on America's Funniest Videos.

Still shaking his head, Zeke climbed out of the Jeep and walked around it, peeling off the cover as easy as if it was the lid of a soup can. I had never been for a ride in a convertible before, and I might actually enjoy it if I could recover from my total humiliation.

Zeke jumped back into the vehicle wearing an expression more serious than the one he had left in...wounded but not physically. He jerked the bandana off, stuffed it in his back pocket and then ran his hands through his hair.

"Zeke..." I began to sputter my attempt at an apology.

Before I could say more, he interrupted by reaching over and taking both my hands in his. We sat in silence for several seconds, his thumb rubbing mine as he was taking time to consider the words he was about to convey.

I bit my lower lip nerves getting the best of me as I waited to find out what was brimming beneath his furrowed brow.

The fact that I wasn't so quick to take off my clothes was a good thing, right?

Zeke didn't keep me guessing about what he was mulling over for long. "I'm trying to decide what bothers me most - that you would think I could treat a physical relationship with you so casually or that you could conceive in general that I'm that type of guy. Have I done anything to give you this impression, because if I have..."

"Zeke," I shook my head vigorously. "You have done absolutely nothing to give me that impression. I'm a ridiculous girl who misunderstood your words and reacted without thinking clearly. I am so sorry."

Zeke's eyes narrowed as he stared directly into mine, he clasped my hands tighter, but not uncomfortably. "Sallie, there is something I want to make sure you understand. I am all kinds of crazy for you, like no girl ever before." He spoke those words slowly and clearly – a careful enunciation so that I wouldn't mistake a word or its meaning, "I knew it from the moment I saw you Tuesday afternoon. Even though we hadn't seen each other since we were what – two or three – it seemed as if you had been right by my side every single day of the last fifteen years. I know it sounds weird, but it's true; I was caught off guard by the force of that connection and was worried until I saw you again on Friday that I had made an utter and complete fool of myself by teasing you about our childhood photos."

Zeke stopped to smile at me sheepishly before continuing. "I was the one who instigated the dinner party, asking my mom to call and invite your family. I was anxious to see you again even before Friday. I almost pulled up your driveway several times as I passed by. I needed to know if the bond I felt was real," Zeke laid his forehead against mine, "and after Friday night there is no doubt in my mind that it is." He pulled away and gazed directly into my eyes, "At least for me anyway. You see, Sallie, the way I feel about you isn't a choice for me. It's a calling."

Zeke halted, almost as if he were waiting for an answer from me to a question he didn't specifically ask; but I could only stare at him, because the words he said could have gone from my brain to Zeke's lips, and I had either been too preoccupied with my loyalty to Will to recognize the fact or plain too dumb to admit to myself that I am also all kinds of crazy…for Zeke.

I opened my mouth to say something. Anything. Though I wasn't sure what it would be, I was positive that whatever it was would not be as eloquent or coherent as what had emerged from Zeke's lips.

But Zeke burst forth with more of his speech before I could get my words out. "Regardless of what you may think because I tried to kiss you that night in the barn, I am not usually so forward with girls. And there's something else - something about us," He waved his hand back and forth between us, "whenever we're together it's like striking a match to gasoline." As if trying to explain by example, Zeke leaned forward and lightly brushed his thumb across my cheek. "Can you feel it?"

Could I feel it?

Every time there was a touch, a stroke, a caress – even close proximity with Zeke, I could only relate it to being jacked up by a jolt of electricity.

And I could make that claim based on experience. It had happened to me once at church camp when I grabbed a live microphone on the cement stage in my bare, wet feet - a shock of electricity had coursed through my body scaring the holy heck out of me. I was shaken only for a moment and quickly realized that I was fine and there was no lasting damage.

But like that swift zap of electricity, was all this that was happening with Zeke going to be over quickly too?

As of this moment it didn't seem that way.

The emergence of my feelings for Zeke was fast and furious and wholly different than what had occurred with Will. Those emotions had crept up slowly and built over time to affection; it only seemed as if it had happened overnight.

I now realize that's not how it had gone down.

Those romantic notions were the result of the many years I had been close to his family and the fact that Will happened to be one awesome guy. Before Zeke, I had not met any guy who could compare to Will.

And with Zeke, I had tried to deny the connection giving every bit of effort to remain focused and loyal to Will; but Zeke's admission today made it blatantly apparent to me that I was fighting a losing battle. These emotions were deep and natural.

Even so, it felt like I was winning and losing at the same time. I couldn't help but be a little scared.

I knew Will would never hurt me intentionally; Kaye would kick his butt.

I didn't believe Zeke would ever hurt me intentionally either, but I was laying my heart on the line here and potentially stomping all over Will's. I felt the sincerity in Zeke's sweet talk... had faith in it. And that would make it all the easier to end up shattered – albeit accidental.

As much as I wanted to do so, I did have a hard time believing that I was the only one who had inspired such intense feelings in Zeke. I didn't think he would lie about that sort of thing. Maybe it had been a while, and he had forgotten the powerful feelings he had once felt for some other girl.

Honestly, a guy like Zeke could not have made it this far in life without some romantic encounters with a female. Just the other night he had smelled of perfume.

As soon as the memory surfaced in my brain of Zeke helping me to the door Saturday night scented by something that was definitely not Ivory soap, I felt queasy - kind of like the little hint of jealousy that had occurred when Mrs. Brock had mentioned Adrienne and Zeke together. But it was stronger this time – more along the lines of a bad school lunch kind of sick.

I swallowed hard. This was an over the top and stupid reaction. Only stupid girls behaved this way. *I* am not one of those stupid girls.

I inhaled, the sound caught Zeke's attention.

"What's wrong?"

I did not want to tell him how silly I was…didn't want him to see the jealousy simmering in my appropriately green eyes. I wasn't sure where this relationship with Zeke was heading, but I knew for sure that I did not want him to take me for an immature teenage girl right here at the beginning.

I shrugged my shoulders. "Oh, it's nothing." It was a lie that women had been using for centuries. I'm not sure why because no man ever seems to fall for it.

Zeke was no exception. "It's obvious that it's something. Come on, you can tell me."

Maybe it was his voice: smooth, sweet, languid; or maybe it was his eyes staring directly into mine; or maybe it was his general proximity that made me so easily give into him.

"Oh, you're right. It is *something*." The words came out as if they were almost too painful to say.

Zeke leaned closer laying his arm on the back of my seat. "Go ahead, I'm all ears."

By this time I had passed the point of no return. I had to give him some sort of an answer, particularly after that speech he had made. I went through a quick thought process. The way that my brain was performing it could have been a scanner running a bright red laser over a list of decent possibilities that didn't make me sound like I was overreacting (which I was) or that I was absurd (which I also was). Despite the fact that Zeke had acknowledged the way he feels about me, I still had no reason to behave like a jealous girlfriend; and besides that, he had not responded in a covetous rage when he presented me with Will's flowers this morning.

So my brain scanner settled on a reply, hopeful that it was the right choice.

"If this feeling you have for me is so strong – you said nothing ever before, right?" Zeke nodded his head in affirmation. "Then why did you *reek* of perfume the other night when you almost ran me over?"

Zeke paused for a minute. His teeth grazed his bottom lip; I realized that this is a tendency of his whenever he was thinking something over. Whatever or whomever had been the cause of his Saturday night scent was not immediately obvious to Zeke.

I wasn't sure if that was a good thing or a bad thing. Did he have so many girls draping themselves all over him that he couldn't quite remember them all?

Or was it honestly no big deal?

I was hoping for the latter.

"Oh!" He exclaimed. "You were bothered by that?"

Zeke reached over and held my hand in his again. "That was nothing, Sallie. I stopped by a party on my way home from work and helped escort a girl who had way too much to drink to the vehicle of a buddy of mine who was very happy to be driving her home." He raised one of my hands to his lips and swiped a kiss across my knuckles. "So are we good now?"

"Yeah. It really wasn't a big deal," I lied. "Just curious."

Zeke laid my hand back in my lap and placed one of his on the steering wheel, using the other to turn the key in the ignition. As the engine revved to life, he hesitated as if a sudden inspiration had entered his brain. I could almost see the light bulb burning brightly above his head.

Zeke, his eyes gleaming, turned to face me. "Wait a minute. Were you jealous?"

Glaring up at him through my eyelashes, I said nothing; but, my wordless response screamed multitudes.

"Woo hoo!" Zeke shouted and then choreographed the Jeep in an exuberant reverse spin like a driver who has won a much coveted race. I grasped the roll bar for support.

Zeke braked and shifted the Jeep into first gear, glancing over at me with a huge smile. "You made my day." He winked. "But of course, the day has just begun."

Ten minutes later my seat had turned into a trampoline. I was bouncing up and down (off-roading Zeke called it) as we made our way down a rocky drive; my hair was no longer whipping around my head from the wind because it was stuck to my lips.

Reminder to self: lip gloss and convertibles do not mix.

Despite the sticky situation, I loved riding with the top off of the Jeep – several times turning toward Zeke with a Cheshire grin spread across my face.

We rounded a bend. I could see water ahead of us spread out in what appeared to be a quiet, private cove. To my right sat a small cottage.

Zeke pulled the Jeep up next to the house and parked. Excited to have finally reached our secret destination, I opened my door and hopped out – wincing when my feet hit the ground.

Zeke came up behind me and grabbed my hand. "What do you think?"

"It is absolutely lovely," I gushed.

The cottage could have been lifted straight from a lakeside New England town. It was covered in white clapboard siding, a cobblestone path led from our parking spot to a red front door that was sheltered by a pergola decorated with tiny climbing pink and white roses. As we walked past the front of the house, I could see a grassy lawn that stretched to the shoreline and was dotted with full grown trees; a faded wooden dock extended into the water. A glance backward revealed a screened-in porch that encompassed the rear of the home and a patio that was laid out with the same stone as the front path.

"I'm glad you approve," Zeke smiled as he squeezed my hand. "This is where we ran naked as toddlers."

Chapter Eight
Summer Rain

Zeke dropped my hand and raced back to the Jeep, retrieving a picnic basket and cooler in one hand, grabbing a rolled up quilt and his well-used black guitar case in the other.

"Do you need some help with that?" I offered.

"Nope, I can handle it." He motioned with a tilt of his head. "Follow me."

I walked behind Zeke at a slow gait for a short distance across the yard. He dropped the quilt on the ground beneath a large oak; its long branches piled thick with green leaves provided the perfect canopy for shade. It had become one heck of a hot day, and due to the humidity leftover from yesterday's rainstorm, I could feel each hair on my head swell and curl – there goes my good hair day - soon it will appear as if I have been the recipient of one bad perm.

Zeke placed the other items gently on the ground, then opened the quilt by flapping it in the air, and spread it underneath the tree.

"Have a seat," he sat on his knees and opened the basket. "I hope you're hungry. I called your mom to find out what you like - and don't like," Zeke added as he pulled out items wrapped in tin foil, "so I promise these sandwiches do not have mayonnaise."

I thanked Zeke as I sat down on the quilt, pulling my legs up beside me. We both removed our sunglasses; beneath this tree, we didn't need them.

"Turkey and provolone on whole wheat," Zeke offered me one of the wrapped packages. He continued to dig in the basket. "Let's see what else is in here. Salt and vinegar potato chips…"

Another one of my favorites…this guy is good.

"Strawberries," Zeke continued to pull items out of the basket, "and white chocolate chunk macadamia nut cookies that I baked myself."

"Really? You bake?"

Zeke sat back on his heels with an impish grin on his face. "I guess saying that I baked them is a little deceiving. I pulled them out of the package pre-cut and placed them on the baking sheet and stuck them in the oven for eight to ten minutes."

I couldn't help but smile at his honesty. "Well, I do bake, so next time I'll put a dessert together."

That wasn't an attempt to impress him with my Betty Crocker talents; I really do enjoy baking. I picked it up because my mom is not a big fan of all the precise measuring that's involved. Most of her cooking is performed by memory – a pinch of this and dash of that. Fortunately, she had found a non-baked banana pudding recipe which has become her typical go-to dessert for company and potluck dinners. But the teaspoons, tablespoons, and half-cup measurements don't bother me, so I've been awarded the title of resident baker of the house.

Zeke remained perched on his heels with an expression on his face that I couldn't quite make out. Was it disbelief that I could bake?

"What?" I asked. "Are you surprised?"

"No. I'm happy that you are already planning a next time."

"Thanks for all this," I was impressed with the spread Zeke had laid out, "it's great."

Zeke sat down on the blanket, grabbed a couple bottles of root beer out of the cooler and pulled off the caps with the bottle opener on his key chain. "You're welcome, darling." But he dropped the *g* so that it sounded closer to darlin'.

"So tell me about this place," I remarked as he handed me a root beer almost too cold to hold, icy droplets were running down the side. I took my napkin and wrapped it around the neck of the bottle. "The last time I was here, I was what - one or two years old? Unfortunately, I have absolutely no memory of that, or should I say fortunately since apparently I was naked the whole time."

A fountain of root beer spewed from Zeke's mouth. "Thanks for that," he chuckled as he grabbed a napkin to wipe his mouth. "My mom's parents bought this land before she had even had started elementary school. The lake was new at that point, and the real estate wasn't as expensive as it is now. My grandpa wanted a good place to escape for fishing anytime he wanted. He had no idea what this property would be worth forty years down the road."

I sipped from my own drink as Zeke handed me a plate loaded down with a sandwich, chips, and strawberries. I had been to a few places around Smith Mountain Lake during summer visits with my grandparents. There was a restaurant my grandpa loved called Moosies that served his favorite Reuben sandwich; we were usually treated to a lunch there and a game of putt-putt nearby while we were in town, but I really had no idea about the history of the lake and was surprised when Zeke said it was new when our parents were children. I had assumed that it had always been around.

"When was the lake built?"

"I think sometime in the middle to late nineteen-sixties. It was built for generating electricity; local folklore has it that homes and barns – minus the people and animals of course - still sat intact as water from two rivers flooded them to create the lake," explained Zeke.

"My mom mentioned that we camped here with your family when we were kids, so I guess that means the house was not here at that time?"

Zeke had popped a strawberry into his mouth; I watched his teeth sink into its delicate skin. He chewed and swallowed before answering my question.

"It was under construction. For years my grandparents kept a camper down here, but when my parents got married and I came along, grandma decided that we needed something bigger than that little camper, so my dad and grandpa decided to build this cottage themselves. It took them about a year, but they did it. As you can see, it's not very big, but it works for us. I'll take you inside and give you the grand tour before we leave."

"Do your grandparents come here often?" I asked hesitantly, hoping that if they did something would keep them away today.

As if he grasped the true meaning behind my question, Zeke replied with a wink and a smile, "They've been given strict orders to stay away today."

We sat munching on our food for a moment before Zeke broke the silence. "So tell me about this other ghost you've been seeing?"

These words sounded funny to me emerging so easily from Zeke's mouth, almost like we were two best friends and he should have been saying instead "tell me about this other guy you've been seeing." But Zeke and I weren't experiencing the typical romantic relationship, so given the context, it was entirely appropriate, albeit comical. I guess the questions about Will would come later.

I gave him a more detailed account of the morning at the cemetery with Samantha when I had first spotted the spirit with the straw hat, as well as my encounter yesterday morning. Zeke listened attentively, stopping me only to ask a couple of questions.

"And then there are the dreams too," I continued, pausing to make sure Zeke was still following me and that I hadn't lost him with the word dream. Some people have no interest in interpretation, but Kaye finds it so intriguing that she makes me more attuned to my own dreams. Zeke didn't seem to be comatose yet, so I kept going. "Like I told you the other night in the barn that was how I knew your ghost sometimes calls out 'Sa… Sa… Sa.' But in the last dream I had, he actually said my name. In fact he said, 'Sallie, I've been waiting for you.' And here's the really interesting part to this whole complicated mess."

Zeke raised his eyebrows when I made this remark as if to say *could this particular conversation could be any more out of the ordinary?*

"The day after we moved, I found a girl's diary from nineteen-thirty-nine in a closet in one of the upstairs rooms. In the first entry, she claims to have witnessed one man kill another in the woods near my house."

That grabbed Zeke's attention. "You're right. That is interesting."

"I haven't told you the best part. The two men she describes in her diary match that of our two ghosts. The murderer wears a straw hat, and the man who was murdered has dark curly hair and is wearing pants with suspenders."

Zeke's eyes widened. "Well, it certainly seems like it all could be more than a coincidence, but what could be keeping the spirits here, and why can no one else around us see them?"

"I'm sorry to say that I don't know the answer to any of those questions. But while I was laid up yesterday, I did some research on earthbound spirits which turned up quite a bit of information." I leaned in closer to him excited to be relaying my newly discovered information. "According to several sites that I came across the spirits of those who have died may remain on earth for a variety of reasons - confusion if the death was sudden or unexpected…or sometimes the spirit stays because it realizes it's dead but chooses not to go into the light, so to speak."

Zeke chuckled.

I smiled back at him knowingly. "The movie, *Poltergeist*, right?"

He nodded his head. "I'm impressed. You're into scary movies?"

"Dad is – science fiction especially, but he'll watch horror too. I can't tell you how many seventies and eighties era films I've watched with him."

Zeke nodded his head in agreement. "I've endured a few of those with my parents as well. So what were you saying about those reasons?"

"Oh, yeah. Some stay behind to take care of unfinished business - that one I already knew - or because a loved one here is having a hard time letting go. Darn, I can't remember the last one."

I bit into my sandwich, staring off in the distance as I thought for a minute. Zeke patiently waited, polishing off his sandwich and grabbing a cookie.

I snapped my fingers. "Now I remember – guilt."

Sounds like you did your homework, girl," he praised and offered me a cookie as if it were my prize for a job well done.

I shrugged my shoulders. "Well, I didn't have much else to do, and besides…" I let my voice trail off. I had said way more than I intended.

"And besides what?" Zeke's curious eyes focused on mine.

I bit my lip, frustrated that my mouth had jumped ahead of my brain. "It's important for me to figure this all out for you. You deserve to know why you've been seeing this guy your entire life."

Zeke took my hand and kissed the palm. "Thank you."

His lips were soft, warm, and sent a ripple down my spine. At some point, I'd have to 'fess up to him that I feel sparks too.

Zeke sighed as he placed my hand back in my lap. "You deserve to know why you're seeing ghosts as well. This can be a team effort."

"I'd like that very much."

He broke into his trademark wicked grin. "Then it's a deal, but before we delve too far into our ghostbusting…"

I grinned at the reference to another eighties era movie.

Zeke smiled back. He knew I got it. "We need to have some fun. What's your pleasure – fishin' or floatin'?"

I laid a hand across my belly. "I'm too full to go swimming right now."

"Fishing it is then," Zeke declared as he jumped up.

I peeked up at him with a fretful face. "I have to warn you. It's been a LONG time since I've been fishing. I don't think I even remember how to cast a line."

Zeke grabbed my hands and pulled me onto my feet. "Don't worry. I'll help remind you, but the fact that you used the term 'cast a line' gives me some hope. Do you want to wait here while I run up to the house and grab a couple of poles?"

I nodded my head yes. Zeke dashed up to the cottage and entered through a back door. I starting clearing up the picnic area, grabbing one last bite of my dessert. I guess I wasn't too full after all – or the more probable explanation would be that I have absolutely no willpower when it comes to sweets. I had just finished putting the soda bottles back into the cooler when Zeke returned carrying two fishing poles and a tackle box.

He motioned with his head, and I walked beside him. Zeke whistled a tune as we strolled along; it was pleasant, but didn't sound familiar. When we reached the water's edge, he handed me one of the poles and knelt down to open the box full of lures.

Zeke feigned a sigh. "Looks like I forgot to stop and get some fresh worms on the way down."

"Oh, you're funny." I wrinkled my nose in disgust. "That's quite alright; I think I would prefer a fake one anyway."

"I figured you would." Zeke picked out a squiggly greenish-black rubber worm that closely resembled one of those gummy candies and dangled it teasingly close to my face before attaching it to the end of my line. He stood beside me and gave me instructions on how to cast out. I practiced a couple of times and by the third time had caught on rather well; it was like riding a bike. My line lay bobbing in the water when Zeke stepped away from me to pull off his shirt. I caught a glimpse out of the corner of my eye and had to check myself to make sure my mouth hadn't hit the ground beneath me.

Zeke's body was tanned a light bronze that showed off his muscles to perfection, and his abdomen was ribbed like the old-fashioned washboard my grandmother has sitting on her front porch as a decoration.

"You better watch your line," Zeke directed with a smile. His naked torso had distracted me to the point that I didn't notice my fishing wire had gone completely slack in the water. I turned the reel slowly, bringing some tension back.

Zeke picked up his pole, cast it effortlessly, observed it for a few minutes, and then laid it down on the ground. I continued to stand quietly on the shoreline holding the fishing pole as advised by Zeke and watching the line for any sign of a tug from a fish who had found its way to my lure. The water lapped gently against the rock embankment. In the distance I could hear the hum of motorboats and jet skis zooming along the main channel away from the purview of our exclusive cove. Zeke moved behind me, gazing over my shoulder with one hand resting casually against my back. The brilliant yellow sun was directly overhead in the cloudless sky and the back of my neck was sweltering. Wishing I had thought to pull my hair up before walking all the way down here; I reached back with my hand and pulled the length of it over my right shoulder futilely fanning my bare neck with my fingers.

"Are you hot?" Zeke was quick to ask.

"Just a little."

He lightly laughed as if amused by his own private joke.

A minute or two passed with no signal from a hungry fish when I felt Zeke's finger trace a line from the base of my skull to the top of my back. I paused, holding my breath wondering if that had been my imagination.

It was most definitely not because Zeke lowered his mouth to my ear and whispered, "This time I'm gonna ask your permission. May I kiss you?"

My legs turned as jiggly as the worm dangling from my hook when Zeke cupped my face in his hands and touched his lips to mine. The kiss was soft at first, quickly becoming more insistent. I dropped the fishing pole, wrapped my arms around his waist and stood on my tiptoes in response – pressing myself closer into him. We stood there melded together for what could have been hours and seconds at the same time when I felt a dull throb start in my ankle, then shoot up my leg.

"Ow," I muttered in frustration as I shifted my position.

Realizing the problem, Zeke lifted me up in his arms and carried me to where our picnic blanket lay beneath the shade tree. He positioned me gently, propped his head on his hand and stared down at me, unspoken words passed between us before Zeke leaned forward and kissed me again. I ran my hands through his hair and down his back when Zeke pressed his lips across my cheek, down my neck, and then to my collar bone; the scruff on his face felt pleasantly scratchy. I held my breath when I felt his hand slide down my tank top. Zeke raised the hem and ran his thumb across my belly; my heart pounded so loudly I could feel it in my ears.

I had so little experience with this kind of thing - what should happen next? Should I make Zeke stop? I probably should stop it, but I didn't want to because it felt really, really good.

I didn't have to make the decision because Zeke abruptly pulled away from me with blazing eyes and flushed skin.

"Sallie, I'm sorry. I should never have let it go that far," he whispered in a husky voice that was different from his normal sweet tea tone.

I sputtered a reply, "It's not completely your fault...I wasn't trying to stop you."

"That doesn't make it right though." Zeke rolled onto his back, laying his right arm behind his head like a pillow and fixed his vision intently on the sky. "It's like everything moves in fast forward with you."

I sat up, pulled my knees to my chest and faced Zeke. His left arm lay stretched out in front of me. I ran my fingers tentatively along his tattoo, tracing the outline of the cross. Today, I could clearly see the intricacy of the artwork. The cross was a pewter color inlaid with detailed scrollwork – each of the four ends was pointed in the shape of a dagger. A gold skull with black eyes stared from the center of the cross, and from behind it several bones shot out in a circular pattern creating an X effect. Flames rose from behind the bones, which made the whole design glow. It was stunning work.

Zeke turned his head to observe my rapt fascination. "Do you like it?" he asked as if he thought my answer would be no.

"Yes, I do," I replied...almost as if I was still trying to make up my mind. "I wasn't sure about the skull at first, but it's growing on me. Is there a story behind it?"

Zeke shifted his position, sitting up so that he faced me. I stretched my own legs out and cradled his left arm in my lap.

"Do you know much about my namesake, the prophet Ezekiel?"

"A little bit. The one lesson I vaguely remember from Sunday school had something to do with bones, there was a little song we used to sing about him...*them bones, them bones, them dry bones*...or something similar to that."

"Yeah, that's right." Zeke nodded head. "I hated my name as a kid for that song alone. Anyway, as you probably remember, the story goes that the Spirit of the Lord carried Ezekiel to a valley covered with bones and commanded him to speak to the bones and tell them that God would breathe life into them again. So Ezekiel did as God asked, and the bones of each body lying there came together. He watched as the skeletons became covered with flesh, but they still weren't alive because they weren't breathing. Then God tells Ezekiel to order the four winds to breathe into the bodies so that they might live again. Ol' Zeke did as he was told, and those bodies came right to life. Well, the rest of the story talks about how God explains to Ezekiel that the bones represented the people of Israel who had no hope, but when God breathed life into them, hope was reborn…life was renewed."

Zeke chewed his lower lip, clearly in his thinking mode, while he stared at the forearm lying in my lap. "Enough of the sermon, now for the story you really wanted to hear – my tattoo…" His voice trailed off as he glanced over at me.

I could see in his eyes that this story had turned personal. "Go on." I hoped the prodding would offer him some encouragement.

"I got it last summer. I'd been going through a rough time – personally, spiritually – I had made some decisions I regretted, was ashamed of even. I guess it was pretty normal teenage stuff, but kind of out of character for me. On top of it all, I was starting to question God… my faith… all the stuff I had been taught from birth. I'm not sure if that was a result of the poor choices I had made or if it was the reason. Either way, they kind of go hand-in-hand, you know?"

I nodded my head in agreement, but it was really my turn to feel ashamed. Though I had been a good girl in conventional teenage terms, it was mostly because I hadn't had that many opportunities to be bad and not because of any close spiritual relationship I had developed with God. My parents were not to blame for my lack of connection. I was born and bred in church, had memorized the Beatitudes in my fourth grade Sunday school class, and was baptized at twelve. I guess I hadn't put much effort into it beyond Sunday mornings.

Zeke kept going with his story. "One night I was sitting in my room strumming my guitar – frustrated because I wasn't feeling inspired when I noticed my Bible laying covered in dust on the bookshelf. I grabbed it, laid it down on the bed, and flipped through the pages rougher than I normally would. Looking back now I think I was mad at God and challenging him to respond in some way. When I had finished my little tirade, I noticed that the pages had fallen open to Ezekiel Thirty-Seven. I'd read the passage before and knew it well, but felt compelled to read it again. This time, as I looked over the verses, it became a different story for me. I realized that I had become like those dry bones. For whatever reason – shame or indifference - I had allowed myself to die inside…to give up because I didn't care anymore. I realized then and there that the only thing that would truly change my life- make me a different person- was to allow God to breathe new life into me, to open myself to His renewal." Zeke shrugged his shoulders as he continued, "I had wanted a tattoo for a while, so I decided to get this one as my reminder not to allow myself to become that way again. I designed it myself and had it placed where I would see it every day, sort of my own version of the Jewish tefillin."

Confused, I shook my head. "A Jewish what?" My knowledge regarding Jewish customs was rather lacking.

"A tefillin. It's a small leather box strapped on the left arm and forehead by some Orthodox Jews as a symbol of readiness to do what God's word tells them to do; the left arm is chosen because it's closest to the heart."

"Like a wedding band."

"Yeah, like a wedding band." Zeke nudged me on the arm with his elbow. "See, I told you I'd teach you something today." His voice was teasing, but his eyes seemed to be in a far-off place. "I've never told that story to anyone else. Not my own parents. Not even my best buddy. I think they all assume I got inked on some wild whim."

"Thanks, Zeke," I reached out and touched his hand, "for sharing that with me. It's a privilege to be the only person besides you to know the real story behind your tattoo."

Zeke locked his gaze with mine. "I can't imagine you not knowing."

I dropped my eyes, running my fingers across the design once more. "Did it hurt when you got it?" It was a silly question but one I had to ask.

Zeke laughed. "Yes. It burned like hell!"

I couldn't help but laugh too and then laughed harder when I imagined the expression on his parent's faces when he asked if he could get a tattoo. I imagined what my own parents would say. Probably something along the lines of when pigs fly, when you no longer live in this house or how about this one… NEVER. "How did you talk your parents into letting you get it?"

Zeke's mouth spread into a mischievous grin. "Oh, I didn't. That's another long story. Let's say it involves a trip to North Carolina and a tattoo parlor that didn't ask for an ID. Mom and Dad weren't thrilled, but I guess it made it a little easier for them because it was a cross and not a hula dancer."

"Or a girl's name," I chimed in.

Zeke's eyes danced. "Hey, I'd be okay with that."

"You're crazy." I remarked before kissing him square on the lips. Surprised by my own boldness, I jumped back before he had a chance to reciprocate.

Zeke let out a long sigh; then chuckled as he stood up. "I need to cool off. Let's jump in." He nodded toward the lake as he pulled me up.

I shimmied out of my white skirt; Zeke let out a low appreciative whistle.

"You do not disappoint, girl."

I rolled my eyes and muttered *thanks*. What I really wanted to say was *neither do you*, but instead I grabbed Zeke's hand.

A sinful smirk crossed his face. "You can swim, right?"

"Yes!" I replied emphatically. I am in fact quite a good swimmer – having spent many summer hours in our neighborhood pool back in Springfield.

In one swift movement, Zeke threw me over his shoulder and started running across the lawn towards the lake. I barely had a chance to register what he was planning to do before Zeke sprinted down the dock and jumped high into the air, plunging both of us into the cool water with a loud splash. The sound of my voice screaming *"Zeke!"* trailed behind us.

Zeke's arms tightened around me as we sank into the water, then he let go, keeping a tight hold of my hand as my body floated away from his. He pulled me up with him as we kicked our legs in unison and resurfaced together, shaking our heads and smiling.

My hair could have been an octopus wrapped around my neck. I leaned back in the water and it fanned out behind me; this time, as I drew my dripping head from the lake, my hair fell straight down my back.

With an arm around my waist, Zeke drew me close to him. His eyes were luminous, his lips sweet as they caressed mine. The water was freedom. Zeke smiled as we parted; giving me one, two, three more quick kisses. It suddenly occurred to me that I had never kissed anyone as much as I had him today, and out of the few kisses I had given or received, none of them were with this much carefree abandonment. I was happy. I couldn't help but wildly grin back at him as we bobbed up and down.

"Follow me." Zeke tugged on my hand and pulled me toward the dock. "Not that I mind being that close to you at all," Zeke emphasized as he glanced back at me, "but eventually our legs will get tired."

"Speak for yourself," I teased. "My legs are in great shape."

Zeke's eyes glinted with amusement. "Oh, pardon me, Miss Marathon."

As we reached the dock, I could see that roped to one of its posts were two large black inner-tubes. Zeke let go of my hand as he swam over and began to untie one of them.

"It'll be easier to get on if you stand on the ladder," he instructed.

I climbed a couple of rungs up the dock ladder and waited as Zeke brought my float to me. He held it steady as I plopped down – as gracefully as I could, and managed to settle my rear end into the center hole with my arms lying casually on each side.

Zeke untied the other one and climbed aboard. His long tanned legs were stretched out, his feet dangled in the water. He paddled over next to me and reached out to hold my hand. We floated there side-by-side with hands clasped across the water – heads laid back on our tubes, soaking up the sun. The warmth that was penetrating the outside of my body was not unlike what I was feeling on the inside – a glow emanating from my heart, coursing through my veins.

Time seemed to melt like crayons in the sun as we lay there adrift. My eyes squinted as the colors merged – leafy green trees melded into a cobalt sky, grey waters reflected a rippling yellow sun.

All was calm and quiet. Occasionally Zeke would hum that same tune he had been whistling earlier. Combined with the gentle lapping of the water against the dock, it became a lullaby; so I rested my eyes. We felt no need to speak, yet the silence wasn't deafening. It was easy to *be* with him – relaxed, normal. It was so normal in fact that after a while the darn call of nature was beginning to make itself abundantly clear.

I turned to Zeke. With his tousled half-dried hair, taut bronze chest, head tilted back and eyes closed, he could have been a male model. One of those you'd see getting all the girls in a country music video. I wish I hadn't kept my eyes closed for so long; I would rather have stared at him.

Too bad my bladder had other plans.

"Ahem," I cleared my throat attempting to get his attention.

Zeke peered at me from the corner of his eye. "Yes," he replied in his slow southern style.

How could I put this delicately? "I think you're going to need to give me that tour of the house now."

He sat up, resting his elbows against the tube, "Gotcha."

Zeke slid off his tube and disappeared. I pushed up with my hands and searching for any sign of him beneath the calm murky water when out of the blue his head popped up next to mine.

Startled – I sputtered, "Geesh, Zeke. Are you trying to scare it out of me?"

He smiled and grabbed hold of my tube, "Just trying to get you there as fast as I can."

Zeke swam with one hand, pulling me over to the dock. While I climbed out and up the ladder, he retrieved his inner tube and then threw both of them up onto the wooden planks with a plop. He had made it up the ladder and was walking toward me when he suddenly stopped and turned his head toward the loud buzzing sound of some sort of water craft entering our cove.

"Oh, great," Zeke muttered as what turned out to be a white and yellow jet ski zoomed into our view. Water shot into the air as it skidded to a halt a short distance from the dock. The driver was wearing a bright pink life jacket and large white sunglasses, her long platinum blonde hair pulled back in a ponytail.

A wispy voice I recognized called out Zeke's name.

"Hey there, Adrienne," Zeke's reply was cordial but nothing more. Emphasizing his disinterest, he pulled me next to him and casually wrapped an arm around my waist. I naturally placed my arm around Zeke's.

I could see Adrienne's body stiffen at the sight of us standing together with so much familiarity.

Zeke gave my waist a squeeze before adding, "This is my friend, Sallie."

"We've met." Adrienne's reply was short, scornful.

Zeke tilted his head, puzzled.

"Saturday… at the mall. Our moms knew each other in school too." I said only loud enough for Zeke to hear.

He nodded. "Oh, right."

Irritated with our private tete-a-tete, Adrienne stood up on her jet ski and with what looked like a practiced strippers move, removed her life jacket – shaking it in a pretense of attempting to dry it out.

I knew what she was doing – showing off her body to Zeke. Maybe it was for my benefit as well - an attempt to make me feel as insignificant as possible. The itsy bitsy teeny weeny yellow polka dot bikini would have seemed like a granny suit compared to what Adrienne was wearing. Strings no bigger than a piece of yarn tied the front and back of the bottom part together and mere threads held together two scanty pieces of triangle shaped fabric that barely covered the top of her voluptuous body. From what I could tell, her little display had no effect on Zeke; instead, he rolled his eyes.

"Anyway," Adrienne purred as she leaned forward to lay her jacket across the handle bars, "I was hoping to find you here *alone,* Zeke." She cast what I assumed was a spiteful glance in my direction. I couldn't exactly tell with the giant shades she was sporting. "I didn't get a chance to properly thank you yesterday morning for your help Saturday night."

While I stood there trying not to imagine exactly what she meant by a proper thank you, Zeke replied indifferently. "No problem. I'm glad that Cash got you safely home." Then in an almost parental tone he added, "Maybe you shouldn't drink so much next time."

So Adrienne was the mystery girl from the other night that spurred my jealous reaction. I wasn't quite sure what to make of that, but despite her *Sports Illustrated* swimsuit model body Zeke truly appeared uninterested, the fact of which was apparent to Adrienne as she dejectedly dropped back down onto the seat of her jet ski.

"I'll keep that in mind," she answered as she jerked her vest up and snapped it on.

And with a "*See ya*" she sped off - spewing a plume of water in our direction. I'm sure she was hoping it would hit us square in the face.

I don't expect that Adrienne and I will be friends in school.

Frankly, I don't really care.

Zeke turned toward me and opened his mouth as if he was about to offer an explanation, but I pointed my finger at the sky and spoke before he could say a word.

"She took off just in time. It looks like Thor's about to throw his hammer down."

Zeke tilted his back for a view of the dark clouds churning overhead - the once friendly azure sky had turned a furious gray. "I think you're right. I need to cover the Jeep."

"I'll get our picnic stuff."

Zeke ran off toward his Jeep. I hobbled as fast as I could to the tree where our picnic lay and started picking things up off the ground. By the time he had finished securing his vehicle from the rain, I was lumbering toward the house arms loaded down with picnic paraphernalia.

"You gonna make it, Gimpy?" He called out as he jogged in my direction.

I grinned, finding this nickname he had given me endearing and hoping he'd drop it when I got back to normal. Although I wasn't adverse to the attention that Zeke felt my injury warranted, I was ready to not be the damsel in distress any longer.

"Yeah. Just a little slow. Maybe I'll get there before the storm hits."

Zeke was standing in front of me before the sentence was finished. "I'll help." And he retrieved most of the items from my clutches.

He led me inside the house just as the rain began to fall. The scene before me could have been what Goldilocks saw as she strolled into the cottage of the three bears. We were standing in a kitchen with a blue and white tiled floor, white cabinets and a farm style table. Directly ahead of us was an open sitting room with a stone fireplace flanked by two oversized armchairs and faced by a sofa – all of which were covered in a simple light blue cotton. In the corner was a small spiral staircase leading to what appeared to be a loft. To my left was a short hallway with four doors, two on each side.

Zeke motioned with his hand. "The bathroom is the first door on the right."

"Oh, thanks," I replied automatically. I had forgotten that I needed to go.

The bathroom was lovely in its simplicity – beige tiled floor, a white pedestal sink with a mirrored medicine cabinet, and a small claw foot tub that included a shower head and a wrap-around shower curtain. A standing white wicker cabinet probably served as the linen closet. I paused to glance at my reflection in the mirror. My hair had dried in its natural waves, and the sun had left a slight blush on my cheeks. I ran my fingers through my hair and tossed it around a bit – that would have to do for any primping.

When I returned from my bathroom break, Zeke was kneeling next to his open guitar case. He had donned his t-shirt; I noticed that my white skirt was laid neatly along the back of the sofa. Zeke faced me as I put it on.

"I really hope you don't think you're doing that for my benefit," he smiled

"I'm not like Adrienne. I don't feel the need to flaunt my body."

Zeke's eyes narrowed. "Rest assured. You wouldn't be so appealing to me if you were like her." He glanced down for a second pretending to be studying his guitar and then looked back at me. "Not that I'm defending her in *any* way, but because you've just met Adrienne, you wouldn't know that she didn't used to be like that either."

My heart dropped with those words; they suggested a past between the two of them that I definitely didn't want to think about. It made me wonder again if she was one of the mistakes last year that led to his tattoo. I seriously needed to push that idea right out of my mind. I leaned against the couch as Zeke pulled the guitar from its case and perched himself on the edge of a chair. He ran his fingers across the strings and tuned the sound. I began considering what made me respond with such envy at the mere thought of the girls who might be in his past. I hadn't cared a bit about Will's. And then it dawned on me: the difference was that I knew Will's past – every girl and practically every not so sordid detail of his romantic life. There was virtually nothing about Will's past relationships that was left to my imagination. On the other hand, I knew very little about Zeke's – just his claims that he had never felt this way before.

A deep thunder rumbled outside shaking the very floor on which I was standing. I moved from the back of the sofa and sat down on one its cushions near to Zeke's chair. He gave me a sympathetic smile. "Are you afraid?"

Zeke had misunderstood my sudden movement. I had simply wanted to be closer to him. "Not at all; I love a good summer afternoon thunderstorm. At my grandparents' house we'll sit out on the front porch drinking iced tea and watch the downpour until the lightning gets too close, and then we'll scuttle back inside." I tucked a wayward strand of hair behind my ear. "The best part is after the sky has cleared...the smell. There's nothing I can think of to compare it to, a sort of freshness like the rain has washed everything clean."

Zeke stared at me in amazement, a warm smile spread across his face. "Summer rain is one of my favorite smells too," then he added with a laugh, "I think you're more of country girl than you're willing to admit."

"I never said I didn't enjoy the country life. It's different – you know- moving here permanently... being away from the friends I've known all of my life."

His fingers played softly across the strings as Zeke reflected on what I had said.

Without even turning away from the guitar he asked carefully, "Can you tell me about Will?"

Sure, if you'll tell me about Adrienne was the first thought that ran through my jealous brain, but, I knew that wasn't fair. I had only assumed there was a past between the two, but Zeke had not confirmed that or given me any reason to believe that they had a future. On the other hand, Will was a real and present part of my life - maybe even a real and present danger in Zeke's eyes.

"Sure. What do you want to know?"

The rain gushed, pummeling the roof in a rhythmic pattern. Zeke leaned toward me – his eyes almost the same color as the sky before it began to storm. He laughed a low chuckle and grinned. "Well, how about everything."

Thanks - way to narrow it down for me there, Zeke.

As the thunder grumbled like an angry giant, I began my synopsis: That I had known Will since becoming best friends with Kaye in kindergarten; that up until about a year ago I had thought of him only as a big brother of sorts, but then out of the blue had developed a crush that Will had begun to reciprocate a few weeks before I moved. I intentionally didn't mention the kiss and hoped that Zeke didn't ask. It felt weird now to think of myself kissing anyone other than Zeke – even kissing Will seemed bizarre to me at this point and something that had happened more like ten months ago rather than ten days.

And out of all the questions he could possibly ask, the first one out of Zeke's mouth was, "What does Kaye think about me?"

I ran through a list of possible answers in my mind - trying to come up with a response that wouldn't sound totally fabricated, but knew the best answer was the honest one even if it might hurt Zeke's feelings.

"I haven't told her about you yet," I admitted through twisted lips.

I watched his face for a response, but with my admission, he had simply stopped playing and stared at me…not in surprise or in anger – an intent gaze that I couldn't quite read because of my rather meager experience in this whole arena of love triangles – still I felt that I needed to say more to him.

"Zeke, please realize that *yet* is the operative word there." I laid my hand on his. "It's not that I don't want to tell her - *we* happened so fast, and this whole thing is all mixed up with her brother being the other guy and all. And honestly, I probably should tell Will first even though Kaye is my best friend. I'm trying to figure out the best way to handle all this without hurting anyone."

Zeke raised my hand and intertwined my fingers with his own. "It's fine. I understand." His voice was calm.

I must have unconsciously scrunched my eyes in disbelief – a motion not lost on Zeke.

"*Really,* I do," he added for emphasis. "I can see this is a difficult situation for you, and I admire the fact that their feelings mean so much to you."

He dropped my hand and moved his fingers nimbly across the guitar strings; it seemed to be Zeke's way of ending that conversation. I recognized the tune as the one he had been humming all day.

"What's that song?"

He raised a shoulder. "A little something I'm working on."

"It's really good," I was being honest.

"Thanks." Zeke smiled widely. "I haven't finished writing the lyrics yet, so hopefully it will get even better."

By the time the thunder had stopped rolling and the rain was no longer pounding the roof, Zeke had told me about the band he had formed at fourteen with his best friend and a couple of other guys.

What he deemed an intentional folksy version of the Oasis song, *Wonderwall,* was the first song they had ever played for a crowd. They performed it on the back of a flatbed truck at a local festival.

"We were a mess," Zeke laughed, "but we kept practicing and now we're not too shabby. We play bars occasionally, but since all of us are under twenty-one, we need someone who is legal to chaperone us, so we mostly play parties at this place Cash's dad owns. We make a little money, but most of it we put right back into the band."

"What kind of stuff do you play?" I asked him, intrigued by the thought of Zeke being in a band that actually got paid to play.

Zeke rolled off a list of artists and songs – mostly rock, folk and country with a little bluegrass thrown in; not wanting to self-proclaim their genre as anything in particular he explained with a shrug, "We mostly play whatever we're into, while trying to stay true to our roots. We change it up - gauge the mood of the audience. Occasionally we'll play something unexpected like an old punk song. You've got to hear a Ramones tune done with a banjo."

Late afternoon came earlier than I expected, so we packed up the Jeep and headed back to my house stopping once so that Zeke could rescue a slow moving turtle trying to cross the road. We walked to the front door arm-in-arm, pausing beneath the portico for the day's last kiss.

"Will I get to see you tomorrow?" I asked as the kiss ended.

Zeke shuffled his feet. I knew that wasn't a good sign. "Unfortunately, no."

I scrunched my eyebrows in irritation – partially at him and partially at me. I was irritated with Zeke for saying no and irritated with myself for this growing dependency on him for affection *and* protection from ghosts.

Sensing my frustration, Zeke rubbed the back of my neck "It's not that I don't *want* to see you," he said with assurance. "I won't be in town. I'm leaving with my parents as soon as I get home to head to West Virginia for a service project we do together every year. We'll be back home Friday evening."

I did the math in my head, from tonight that would be four full days without him – around ninety-six hours depending on what time he returned Friday.

That sucked big time.

"Will you have time to call?"

"I will do my best. We'll be in the mountains, and the cell phone reception is really poor at our campsite. But hopefully I can get off that mountain at some point."

Zeke let out a sort of half-laugh.

"What?"

He smiled broadly. "It's that, I've not had to worry about my cell phone reception before because there's never been anyone that I needed to talk to. It's a great feeling, you know. This time there's someone back home waiting for me."

"Assuming I'm still here when you get back…"

Zeke raised his eyebrows in a *what do you mean by that* expression.

"What if those ghost guys come back around while you're gone?"

"Hey, I'm sorry you have to deal with that alone for a few days, but you already know that my guy won't hurt you. As for the other one, stay away from the cemetery and keep around other people as much as possible."

I bit my lip, thinking. "That shouldn't be hard. I'll be helping Mom get the store ready this week."

Something behind my head caught Zeke's attention and he chuckled. "Oh, and make sure Little Red keeps you company while I'm gone." His voice was a few decibels higher than normal.

I rotated half way to check out what was going on behind me and was positive I saw the living room curtain flutter.

As I turned back around, Zeke was pulling something out of his back pocket. "Keep this with you to remember me by." He laid a folded piece of red cloth into the palm of my hand. It was the bandana he had been wearing earlier today.

"Thanks." I resisted the urge to hold it up to my nose and inhale his warm scent. "I don't have anything to give you."

"No worries." He tapped the side of his head with his finger. "I'll have my memories of today." Zeke pulled me close and took a deep breath. "Hmm…lavender."

"What?" I had no idea what he was talking about.

"Lavender. *You* smell like lavender."

I stepped backward and angled my head, confused that he would recognize such a scent. "Lavender. Really?"

Zeke smiled. "There's a patch that grows wild beneath my bedroom window. Mom thinks one of the previous owners planted it. The scent blows into my bedroom window sometimes. It's nice."

He planted a kiss on my forehead. "And I'll enjoy it even more now." Zeke sighed, his expression changing. "Well, Gimpy, I better get going."

I wasn't sure how to respond – *thanks I had a good time* - didn't seem to be enough, but with lack of time to consider carefully what I should say, it's what I blurted out anyway. "I'm really going to miss you – even if it is for only a few days."

He planted a kiss on my ear and whispered. "I'll miss *you* like crazy."

Zeke walked away, I felt my heart strings pull. His body was a homing beacon that urged me to follow. I watched as he opened the Jeep door and climbed inside, but before he sat down, his tousled head popped back up over the door.

"Oh, by the way," Zeke called out, "I'm in love with you."

Before I could lift my jaw up off the ground to respond, he was behind the wheel and pulling away. I wondered that if I were standing on the sidelines watching this happen – a sort of out of body experience – would I consider myself out of my mind for not scrambling after him and declaring *my* love right here and now.

That night, rain poured steadily outside my window as I lay snuggled beneath the blankets with Zeke's bandana wrapped around my hand. I propped it on the pillow next to my head, holding it close to my nose. It smelled of him – musky and earthy, very much like the scent of a summer storm that we both love so much.

And as for my dreams...

Sweet.

Chapter Nine
Ring Of Fire

Downtown Rocky Mount is a meandering little stretch of roadway flanked by one and two story buildings, some old, some new. The difference is easy to spot by the bricks that have faded to a soft shade of red, a reminder of the times when mega stores didn't exist, and people supported their community by shopping in the mom and pop stores located on the sidewalks of the downtown streets.

Though larger than the creek side Boones Mill town center, Rocky Mount's has that same small town atmosphere - the good kind of small town charm where you know where your stuff comes from and the people who sell it to you. With an amazing café (the chef of which has catered to actual rock stars!), the county library, and Zeke's music store all within walking distance, I was feeling pretty good about my new place of employment.

The new kids on the block, we had been welcomed with open arms. The news of our takeover had spread quickly. Mom had already joined the Chamber of Commerce, agreed to a store opening ribbon cutting, and been interviewed by a reporter from The *Franklin News Post,* the thrice-weekly local newspaper.

I was parked on the street outside of our antiques store, bent over with my rear end sticking out of the trunk of the family sedan when a voice from behind me asked, "Are you Sallie?"

Surprised someone would know my name since Mom had done the majority of the meeting and greeting, I raised my head too fast, knocking my noggin on the roof of the trunk. With what I am sure was a grimace on my face, I turned to see a tall, wiry guy who appeared to be in his late teens, but could have stepped straight out of the Woodstock concert that was held back in the 1960's. He sported a short beard and shoulder-length brown hair pulled back into a ponytail. A tie-dyed shirt, cut-off blue jean shorts, leather sandals, and small metal glasses perched on his skinny nose completed the retro ensemble. He must have heard that we would be selling vintage clothing and was here to check out the store.

"Yes, but I'm sorry. We're not open yet." I answered, rubbing the knot already forming on the back of my head.

"Oh, I'm not here to shop. I'm Cash. My dad owns the music studio around the corner." His words were drawn out in an easy going manner that matched his laid-back style.

"Where Zeke works. It's nice to meet you."

"It's nice to meet you, too," he replied with a wide welcoming grin. "Zeke and I have known each other a long time. We took guitar lessons together for years until he got better than me."

I had finally met someone who could give me an honest assessment of Zeke's abilities, since Zeke himself was too humble brag about himself. "Zeke's pretty modest about his talent. How good is he really?"

"Good enough for a record deal my dad says...Zeke's an awesome teacher too. Since he's been offering lessons, we've had more girls than I've ever seen clamoring to learn to play the guitar. It's like the guy already has groupies." Realizing how I might construe that last comment, he added without missing a beat, "But he's totally professional about it. Anyway," he said with a clap of his hands, "Zeke asked me to check in on *you* while he's away, so that's what I'm here to do." Cash bowed formally with a sweep of his long, skinny arm. "Where may I be of assistance, Milady?"

I couldn't help but laugh at the disparity between his hippie garb and the extravagant gesture. "Actually," I reached back into the trunk for the item I had been attempting to retrieve when Cash came along, "this box isn't heavy, but you could get the door for me."

"No problem," he skipped ahead of me and grabbed the door. "Zeke said you moved into a house near him," Cash commented as he followed me inside.

"Yeah, we did. It's down the road from his home. It's the old brick house with all the apple trees."

"I thought that might be the one since there was a for sale sign in the yard until recently. Well," he said the word with two syllables – so that it sounded more like we-ell, "I hope this doesn't freak you out or anything, but that place has always given me the creeps."

Thank goodness the box I was carrying was not marked as fragile because it dropped out of my hands with a huge thud and came darn close to landing right on Cash's Birkenstock clad feet.

"I mean it's a beautiful place and all," Cash continued as if nothing had happened as he bent over to pick up the box. "It's this feeling I get whenever I pass by on my way to Zeke's house. It's not like I've seen ghosts floating around the place or anything. I'm sure you're quite safe there."

Cash didn't realize how right on his intuition was; I wasn't about to tell him. At any rate, our new house had been rather harmless the last few days – maybe because I had hardly been there to find out otherwise.

Mom had spent most of Tuesday still working out all the legal stuff pertaining to taking over the store, so Samantha and I had spent the day with our grandparents. Grandma Ellen had tried to fatten us up by fixing country fried steak, mashed potatoes and pinto beans for supper with homemade ice cream as our dessert. She still uses an old-fashioned ice cream maker, and Samantha had cranked on that thing until she whined that both her arms hurt.

After that meal, I had no choice but to finish the day with a run and a shower before quickly checking the computer for a message from Kaye or Will. But still no word – how weird was that?

I called and left Kaye a voice mail, surprised that Will had not responded to the one I had left him the night before. Even though my head was still swimming from my day at the lake, it had been important to me to call Will and thank him properly for my beautiful flowers.

Wednesday and Thursday had now passed without hearing from him or Kaye. I was beginning to wonder if I had done something to make them angry with me. I racked my brain over and over but couldn't imagine what it could be. I was certain there was no way they could know about Zeke – even though I knew that, at some point, I was going to have to tell both of them about him.

And if she was upset, it would be unlike Kaye not to let me know exactly what she was feeling as soon as she felt it; it's impossible for her to hold back any sort of emotion. It's a personality trait of Kaye's that is both admirable and aggravating at the same time.

Zeke, on the other hand, had managed to make it off the mountain and call Wednesday night. They had made it to West Virginia without any problems, set up camp late, and had already spent a couple of days helping to build a community playground at a church ministered by one of his dad's old college roommates.

His voice huskier than normal, Zeke sounded exhausted,

but relieved to hear that I had no ghostly sightings to report - unless you count Zeke himself who seemed to be haunting my every thought. Lucky for me, he still planned to be back late Friday afternoon, which meant I had less than forty-eight hours to kill before I would see him again.

Fortunately, killing that time would not be a difficult task. Mom had kept me busy working at our newly named shop most of the week. Though not open yet, a sign made out of punched tin and bearing the title of *Blackwater Antiques* hangs above the front entrance of our store. The inspiration had come from a river that flows through Franklin County and one of Mom's favorite Doobey Brothers songs.

One of my jobs has been to sort through her collection of old concert tees. Mom's been buying them for years, coming across them mostly at flea markets, yard sales, and thrift stores. She has amassed quite a few and occasionally lets me swipe one that I am particularly fond of. My favorite is an Elvis shirt from his Vegas years that someone had donated to the Goodwill. It is kind of flashy with some glittery stuff on it, but the kind of quirky thing that I have fun wearing.

Also on my agenda, and this is what has taken up most of my time, is painting the inside of the store a soothing shade of sage green with paint purchased at the nearby hardware store. The guys there had been super helpful, even lugging the buckets back to the shop for me.

I know it sounds weird, but I love to paint. I guess maybe I'm a frustrated artist. I can't draw or paint on a canvas worth a darn, but give me a paint brush and a wall and get out of my way. There's also that instant gratification part - one day and a gallon of paint can totally change a room for the better; or maybe not, if the color on the wall turns out to be completely different than it appeared on the paint chip.

Case in point: Samantha had chosen the color Princess Pink for her old bedroom in Northern Virginia, but once it was on the walls more closely resembled Puked Pepto Bismal.

Another reason I enjoy painting is that it gives me time to think. Usually, no one bothers me because they're afraid I'll ask for help, so I can let my mind wander without any interruptions. This week, as my mind drifted away in the hypnotic flow of my hand and paint roller against the wall, I had come to the conclusion that the two old adages of absence making the heart grow fonder or forget are both true.

It depends entirely on the circumstances.

Zeke's absence this week had certainly made my heart grow fonder, while the time I had spent away from Will, although I wouldn't say made me forget, had certainly changed my perspective.

Now granted, if Zeke was not in the picture, *maybe* things with Will would be different. But Zeke is sitting front center of this portrait, and I had to quit beating myself up over that. Call it what you want – fate, destiny, God – whatever it is; Zeke and I are bound together in some way that I can't explain but have come to accept that it is simply meant to be.

So if I explain it to Kaye in that way, then maybe she of all the grand romantic notions about soul mates and kindred spirits would be more understanding.

Hopefully today, as I finish up the trim on this monster of a paint job, I can give more thought to exactly how I could go about pleading my case to both Kaye and Will. Again, it is not something that I would prefer to do over the phone or by email, but I have no idea how long it will be before I get to see my best friend and her brother in person, and it's pretty important that it be taken care of sooner rather than later. No use in prolonging the agony...plus, I'm ready for Zeke and me to really be together without any of my baggage dragging us down.

"Where do you want me to sit this?" Cash was standing there still gripping the box I had nearly dropped on his toes.

I motioned toward our glass enclosed check-out counter. "Over there. Thanks so much for picking that up. I guess my arms are worn out from all this painting I've done the last couple of days."

"No prob," Cash replied as he surveyed my handiwork. "Hey, are those t-shirts over there?"

"Yeah. We have some pretty cool ones. Feel free to check them out."

But Cash didn't need an invitation. He was already loping his way toward the display.

"Sallie, is that you?" Mom's voice chimed from the small room at the back of the store which would serve as her office.

She had driven Dad's truck today, filling it up with about anything in our house that wasn't nailed down; dropping him off at work after he helped her unload. I had followed later in the car which was also packed with some odds and ends for the store. Samantha had chosen to stay with my grandparents again. She's still working her way through those Nancy Drew books and claims she can't concentrate around here.

"Yeah. Come out and meet…" Before I could finish my sentence, she had already emerged from the back and was watching curiously at Cash as he rifled through shirts.

"Well, hello there," he remarked, peering back at her above his spectacles. "You have quite a collection here. I'm impressed."

Mom laughed lightly as she thanked him.

"Mom, this is Zeke's, friend Cash. He stopped by to check-in on us."

"At Zeke's request. Don't forget that part." Cash pointed at me with a wink. He wasn't shy in his attempt to score some points with my mom for Zeke.

"Ahh," I could practically see the wheels turning in her head. "That was *so* sweet of Zeke; he's always so thoughtful," She added as she glanced in my direction with a satisfied smile. No need to ask on whose sidelines she was shaking her pompoms.

Cash rummaged through the shirts and examined a couple, showing an obvious preference for a Grateful Dead tee with a skull on the front which in a vague way reminded me of Zeke's tattoo. I told him he could have it, hoping that Mom, who had made her way back to the office, wouldn't mind. Cash repeatedly thanked me as I walked with him out the door; adding that he hated to rush off but he needed to get back to the shop and prepare for a Crooked Road jam session they were hosting tonight.

"I've got a new tune I've been practicing," Cash said off-handedly as he held up the shirt to admire one more time. "This is a *seriously* sweet design."

But my mind was still stuck on his prior comment. A sign touting The Crooked Road had caught my eye before I turned off Main Street this morning and headed to our store; now with Cash's reference, my interest was renewed.

"What's The Crooked Road? Really, all of these country roads seem crooked to me."

Cash slung the shirt over his shoulder like a knapsack and turned toward me. "Oh," he cocked his head in a thoughtful pose. "Well, The Crooked Road starts right here in Franklin County – just up the street actually at the intersection of Routes Two-Twenty and Forty. It's a tourist trail that winds through Virginia and hits some historic traditional music venues." I could tell that he was trying to think of a name or a place that someone like me might recognize. "Like the Ralph Stanley

Museum and the Carter Family Fold. You know about the Carters, right?"

"As in June, wife of Johnny?"

"Yep." He grinned. "You're pretty smart for a city girl." I rolled my eyes at him. "Then you probably already know that a lot of people credit June Carter Cash's family for starting the whole country music scene."

I pretended that yes, indeed I knew all about that little piece of music history. "Isn't the Carter family place near here?"

Cash's eyes widened. Apparently my question had totally given away my little know-it-all farce.

"Heck no. That's way down in southwest Virginia. Our local spot is the Blue Ridge Institute up Forty West near Ferrum College, but we have a lot of shops and stuff around here where people get together on a regular basis to play some music."

I felt the need to redeem myself and prove to him that I do know a thing or two about music. "Like bluegrass?"

"Yeah, mostly bluegrass, old time gospel - that kind of stuff. Speaking of which," Cash nodded his head in the direction of the music store, "I better get back at it. We've been busy. Thank goodness Zeke will be getting back today though I doubt *I'll* be seeing him tonight." Cash gave me a knowing smile before he walked off.

"See ya," I called after him.

Cash gave me a backwards wave. "And thanks again for the shirt!"

After another day of painting and pondering, my brain felt deep fried and ranch dressing dippable; so around four o'clock, I called out to Mom that I was headed back to the house.

With my project complete, I was anxious to get cleaned up. Zeke was due home tonight, and I was beyond hoping that he would show up at my house as soon as possible. I had some important news to share with him. My decision had been made – well, sort of made for me because it was beyond my control. But a decision nonetheless, and the anticipation of telling Zeke that I love him too was killing me.

I had fixed my post-shower hair and makeup when a knock at the front door sent both my heart and legs racing to answer it. I threw a sundress over my head, ran down the stairs barefooted, stubbed my toe on the last step, and hopped on one foot to the front door with a grimace on my face. I managed to form a smile as I grabbed the front door and jerked it open.

"I'm so glad you're back...." The words caught in my throat as I faced Will and Kaye, both grinning from ear-to-ear. Kaye was bouncing up and down like she had a sprouted a Tigger tail.

"Surprise," they both screamed before Will grabbed me around the waist and twirled me in the air, then set me down and planted a kiss right on my mouth.

As Will moved his head away from mine, I blinked my eyes twice to make sure I wasn't experiencing hallucinations because a person who looked extraordinarily like Zeke was making his way toward us with a storm brewing in his eyes and a bouquet of wild daisies clasped in his hand.

Chapter Ten
Sweet Thing

"**W**ow! This really is a surprise! Completely unexpected!"

I said this so loud that it sounded as if I was conversing with my great Aunt Stella, who has been practically deaf since she hit her sixties, but refuses to wear a hearing aid for reasons of vanity. I'm not certain why she thinks the hearing aid would tarnish her beauty because she seems rather comfortable sporting a lacquered bouffant of jet black hair the dye from which has left a permanent dark ring around her hairline.

The point of my earsplitting greeting was not that Will and Kaye were also hard of hearing, but so that it would reach Zeke's ears as well. I didn't want him to think this was a planned visit and that I had held back any information from him.

"Yeah, that's why you haven't heard much from us for several days," explained Will, though with a puzzled look on his face. I guess my practically screaming in his face did come across as odd. "You know how Kaye cannot keep a secret." He glanced over at his sister who stuck her tongue out at him.

With my normal voice, I replied, "I'm so glad you're here." I knew it was the appropriate thing to say, and I was glad to see them, but they happened to have some really bad timing.

Kaye grabbed me around the waist and gave me a big squeeze. "Oh, me too! I've missed you so much! I can't wait to fill you in on...*hello*..." Kaye took an involuntary step backwards as she laid her eyes on Zeke.

"Hello to you," he replied with a voice that would melt every bit of ice in the southern hemisphere. "I'm Zeke, Sallie's neighbor."

And then Zeke, who had become so much more to me than just my neighbor, asked a question with such southern politeness that it made my heart hurt. "Well, Miss Sallie, aren't you going to finish the introductions?"

All three of them had turned to me as if they were expecting actual words to be able to form and emerge from my mouth. Kaye's eyes were wider and brighter than I had ever seen them. I knew *exactly* what she was thinking: Why haven't *you* told *me* about *him*. A muscle was twitching in Will's jaw; he moved closer to me.

"Um, sure. Zeke, this is Kaye and Will, my friends and *neighbors* from Springfield." I said awkwardly. "They surprised me by showing up just now. I had absolutely no idea they were coming."

"What a wonderful surprise for you," Zeke continued, although Kaye and Will wouldn't be able to tell that he had added a heaping tablespoon of lemon juice to that sweet tea voice of his. "I hope you'll be here for the weekend."

"Will you?" I asked this only half hopeful that the answer was yes.

Shame on you, Sallie!

"Yeah." Will was the first to speak up. "Dad's in Roanoke for a medical conference, so we're in town at least through Monday."

Zeke good-naturedly punched Will on the shoulder. "Great! Then you'll be able to come hear my band play tomorrow night. I stopped by to invite Sallie, but the more the merrier. Isn't that right, Gimpy?"

Kaye's shot me a look when Zeke called me by his little nickname that left me in no doubt I was going to have a lot of explaining to do later.

"Yeah, yeah that'll be awesome, Zeke." It was my turn for a squeeze of citric acid.

"We'd love to come!" Kaye interjected. "You're in a band? Like, you get paid to play and stuff? How cool is that! I've never known anyone in a real band before. Except the marching band at school, but that doesn't really count, does it? I did go out once with a guy who played on the drum line, but he constantly tapped his fingers on the table while we were waiting for our food. It was totally annoying, and I kept avoiding him every time he tried to ask me out again. Do you remember that, Sallie? I would dodge into the first available room anytime I saw him walking down the hall toward me and this one time I wasn't paying attention and walked straight into the boys bathroom…"

"So where are you playing?" I interrupted, knowing if I didn't, Kaye would go on and on and on.

"It's a barn party. We go on at nine o'clock." Zeke glanced over at Will with a smirk on his face. "Do you think your parents will let you stay out that late?"

In response, Will slid an arm around my shoulders and pulled me close. I could feel the tension between him and Zeke. It wrapped around me like a snake squeezing tighter and tighter so that I could barely breathe. "If it's a late night, I'll probably be staying here with Sallie; so whatever her curfew is..." He stared Zeke down.

I watched Zeke's eyes change from glossy marble to a gun metal slate. "I'll talk to your Mama, Gimpy. I'll tell her it's a special occasion and that you'll be with me, too. Maybe she'll let you stay out a little later than normal."

"Great! That sounds great," Kaye peeped in with a nervous laugh. The tension had not escaped her either.

"Well, I better head out then so you three can enjoy your visit."

"Zeke, I'll see you later. Right?" I said this in kind of a statement and a question combined, hoping he'd get the message that I really did want to see him later – if he was willing to see me.

"Sure. Give me a call. I'll give you directions for tomorrow night." He pulled the daisies from behind his back. "These are for you. If I remember correctly, they're your favorite."

Zeke shot Will a narrow-eyed glance before he walked away, leaving me with daisies in my hand and a gaping hole in my heart.

Sneaking out of the house was easier than I thought it would be, considering I'd never done it before.

I hopped into Mom's car, not turning on the headlights until I was out of the driveway, and then drove like Danica Patrick toward Zeke's house. I had absolutely no idea how I was going to get into said house, but I'd deal with that once I got there.

Cruising down the dark county road began to feel more like a guilt trip when I reflected on how I had left Kaye asleep in my bed. After Zeke had stormed off, I had brought Kaye and Will into the house and showed them around; the roses Will had sent earlier in the week sat drooping dramatically on the foyer table.

Will held my hand as we walked from room to room. I let him, terrified that it would lead him on. He was comfortable with his affections in Kaye's presence and had grown more handsome in the last few weeks. Will's face was tanned from the time he had spent outdoors playing soccer, and his sapphire blue eyes were glittering as if he was really, really happy to see me.

After the grand tour, Will claimed to be starving and

suggested ordering a pizza. He was stunned when I said we couldn't get one delivered. Fortunately, my family had grown accustomed to that little facet about living the country life and had stocked up on some of the almost like delivery type in the freezer. I stuck one in the oven; we hung out in the kitchen while it baked. Kaye filled me in on the latest neighborhood gossip. Mr. Cundiff and Mrs. Mason had not spoken since the Chihuahua incident, and the twins had called 911 two more times because they thought it was fun to see the ambulance and fire trucks come screaming down the street. After a personal visit from the fire chief, the neighborhood had become a quieter place.

Mom, Dad, and Samantha showed up and were surprised to see the three of us lounging around the kitchen island munching on pizza and drinking sodas. After a round of hugs, Mom exclaimed it was "almost like old times."

Grabbing a slice of pizza, Samantha stood next to me and with as much false innocence as she could muster asked, "Isn't Zeke coming home tonight?"

Kaye answered before I could. "Oh, he's already back. He stopped by a little while ago and invited us out tomorrow night. What do they feed the guys around here 'cause he sure is some sweet country boy eye candy."

"Well, we know it's not delivery pizza," Will scoffed.

"Must be something in the corn," I countered, a bit riled, shocking myself by having this feeling of protectiveness regarding my new hometown, its inhabitants and the lack of food available by delivery.

"Or something the corn is made into," was Will's returning jibe.

"Nah – I think that only affects the eye of the beholder."

"Whatever," Kaye mumbled, "I'd be happy to behold him anytime."

Spending a couple hours in my room eased the awkwardness I had felt since they arrived. Will reclined on the bean bag in the corner. Kaye lay sprawled on her stomach across the bed and complained about how bored she had been since I moved. We played a couple of hands of Rummy. It was approaching ten o'clock and my third victory when Will threw down his cards, said he was beat and ready to crash in the guest room.

Of course they would assume they'd be staying the night here.

Kaye stood up. "Let's go grab our stuff out of the car."

I led them out. Kaye went to retrieve her items from the backseat of the car. Will pulled me over to the driver's side door.

"So do you want to sneak into my room later?" Will ran his hands up my arms and squeezed my shoulders.

"Ah, no. My parents will be right next door."

"Come on, where's your sense of adventure?" He was teasing me. I reached out to swat him on the arm, but Will was quicker than me and pulled me close for a kiss. Not exactly who I thought I'd be kissing tonight. I tried to make sure it was a quick one without appearing too suspicious.

"Ahem!" Kaye pulled me away. "Get a room you two!"

Evidently having more of a clue than me, Mom had already made up the pull-out couch in the office on which Will would sleep. Kaye and I dropped him off there and barely made it back into my room before she started pounding me with questions about Zeke.

I wasn't ready yet to confess to Kaye. This wasn't exactly how I had planned it out in my head. So I faked a headache (blaming the paint fumes) and asked if we could talk about it tomorrow.

Tired from her day of travel, Kaye didn't complain when I suggested we hit the sack. We settled into bed - Kaye on the left and me on the right – just as we always had.

"Tell me one thing, why does Zeke call you Gimpy?"

I explained about my injury and his knack for assigning nicknames.

"Hmm, maybe he'll give me one before the weekend is over." She yawned.

"I'm sure he will," I mumbled into my pillow as I faked sleepiness.

"'Night, Sallie."

"Goodnight, Kaye."

I lay silent and still until I heard Kaye's deep, rhythmic breathing. By now it was approaching midnight, but I couldn't wait to see Zeke any longer.

When he had walked away, I had felt this gulf open between us that didn't exist before he had left for West Virginia, before he had told me that he loved me, before Will and Kaye had showed up on my doorstep. I had to jump across that gaping hole, and soon, not wanting to waste another minute keeping Zeke guessing about how I felt.

I slid out of the bed and slipped on my flip-flops. It was too dark to change my clothes so my cotton pajama set would have to suffice. The house was silent as I crept down the stairs and out the front door.

And Will had chided me about my sense of adventure – if he only knew.

As Zeke's house came into view, I breathed a huge sigh of relief when I saw his Jeep sitting in the driveway. It was a bonus that it was parked alone. Where could his parents be in the middle of the night? No matter - that would make it easier for me to sneak in. Pulling up beside it, I jumped out of the sedan. The clear night sky and the moon provided enough illumination to help me find my way onto the front porch. Wondering how lucky a girl could get in one night, I turned the doorknob and was pleased to find it unlocked - must be a rural thing because my grandparents rarely lock their doors either. Fortunately, it meant no tossing pebbles at windows or climbing up rose arbors for me tonight. I stepped inside, closed the door quietly and started up the stairs that led to Zeke's room.

Zeke was sound asleep, stretched out on top of his blankets clad only in a pair of cargo shorts. A bedside table lamp was still burning; an open book lay on the bed just past his hand, the tips of Zeke's fingers holding his place. The far off sound of a long, lonesome train whistle blew through the open window.

I allowed my eyes to wander over his body from head to toe for a sixty seconds.

He was beautiful.

"Zeke," I called hesitantly as I walked toward his bed, my courage draining like cold water after a long bath as I watched him sleeping so peacefully. I shouldn't have come here after all. I didn't want to disturb him any more than I already had today.

I turned to leave on tip-toes when I heard the rustling of bed sheets. I jerked around to find Zeke sitting up in bed; he rubbed his eyes and ran a hand through his hair.

"Sallie, what are you doing here?"

I drew a deep breath.

It was time for that leap.

"I'm here because I love you, too." The words came out in more of a raspy whisper than I had intended them to be.

"What?" He was still trying to shake off the sleep.

"I'm...here...because...I...love...you...too." I said it louder and slower this time, enunciating each word clearly.

Zeke leapt off the bed and took my face in his hands. "Say it again if I'm not dreaming."

"I'm here because I love you, too." The words barely made it off my lips before Zeke was kissing them.

I didn't recall leaving a window open, but the distinct chirping of a bird had awakened me from the most comfortable night of sleep I'd experienced since the move. Maybe Kaye had needed some fresh air in the middle of the night, but the twittering bird was disturbing my contented slumber. With eyes barely open, I moved in slow motion to go shut the window but didn't even make it to the edge of the bed before I was enveloped with a gentle embrace.

Muscular arms.

Bare chest.

So...that was *definitely* not Kaye.

"Good mornin'," a voice purred into my ear.

Panicked, I sat straight up in the bed and grabbed Zeke's alarm clock. "Oh, my gosh! What time is it?"

Bright red digital numbers glared back at me: 6:30.

"I am so dead." I moaned as I flopped back onto the pillow.

Zeke leaned over me, grinning. No one should be allowed to wake up that pretty; even his breath smelled great. I imagined my early morning appearance was slightly scary with my smudged mascara and hair flattened to one side of my head. And with my luck, I probably had a big, puss-filled zit perched on the end of my nose.

"Will your parents really be awake at six thirty on a Saturday morning?"

"Probably not, but I'm sure your parents noticed my car when they came home last night."

He reached down and brushed back a lock of hair that had fallen across my face. "Don't worry, my parents stayed at the lake house last night. And if they had come home in the middle of the night and seen your car parked in the driveway, do you honestly think they wouldn't have marched right up here?"

Granted, one less thing to worry about, but that still left getting home before my mother got up for a run and before Kaye could wake and find me gone. I hoped she had slipped into what I affectionately refer to as Kaye's Coma – once she's out, she is *out* and it takes a serious amount of shaking to rouse her; with my fingers-crossed, I hoped that Will would not be up and rummaging about my house this early either.

"I guess they would have – they're cool, but not that cool, right?"

"Exactly," Zeke murmured as he placed his lips along my collarbone, up my neck, resting on my earlobe. "Thank you," he whispered, "for last night, for coming to me, for loving me back."

Reluctantly, but not wanting to press our luck, Zeke let me go. Hand-in-hand we walked to the car. The morning was silent, cool and refreshing; beads of dew clung to flower petals and dripped from their leaves. Cobwebs glittered like diamonds amongst the blades of grass and the mist gliding near the ground could have been fairy smoke. It felt as if we were the only two people awake and alive in the entire world.

A lingering kiss and I was on my way. In the rear view mirror, I saw George bound to Zeke's side. Zeke rubbed his head, but his eyes never left the back of the car as I drove away. I already missed him like crazy and had been away from him for all of one minute.

The gentle mist turned into a billowy fog as I drove down Zeke's driveway. I found myself turning down the radio – as if that would help me see any better - while I navigated my way through the layers of vapor that floated around me. I slowed the car to a crawl, barely able to make out more than a couple of feet ahead. Just beyond what I could see clearly, a shape began to form – probably a deer. Zeke had warned me about them before I left; they roam in abundance around here and are most lively in early morning and at night.

I brought the car to a stop and beeped my horn rapidly. But the figure didn't move, so I inched the car forward and beeped again.

Still as a statue; that was either one stubborn or stupid deer.

I pulled the car forward again, this time in quick, jerky spurts.

Gas. Brakes.

Gas. Brakes.

As I drew closer, an outline began to form.

Not four legs, but two.

And two arms.

I slammed on the brakes.

That was definitely not a pair of antlers sitting atop the head.

The apparition stood glaring at me, inches from the hood of the car. Panicked, I hit the lock button on the door, and in the very next second realized how stupid I was – like a locked door could keep out something supernatural – yeah, right.

We stared at each other through the windshield and blurry mist, neither making a move. I inhaled and let out a couple of deep breaths trying to calm the hummingbird heartbeat hammering against my chest. Just about the time I thought I might need a paper bag in which to hyperventilate, I felt a surge of adrenaline like a fizzy mixture of soda pop and Sweet Tarts had been injected straight into my veins. I jerked the car into reverse; it was all I could do to keep myself on the road as I skidded backwards a few feet.

Satisfied with the distance, I shifted the car back into drive and floored the gas pedal. The tires spun against the gravels which held the car in place while simultaneously leaving dents in the bumper. Suddenly, the gravels released the tires and the sedan shot forward, running straight through the ghost – as if he were part of the mist itself. A chill pierced my body as the car slid through him. The cold grabbed my chest in a pain that squeezed my heart, stole my breath, and rendered me light-headed and weak, but as quickly as it had overtaken me, the sensation was gone.

I never looked back - not even when I pulled onto the main road that led to my house. I had managed to calm myself down by the time I got there by repeating Zeke's name over and over, using it like a talisman to protect me from evil spirits. I parked and turned off the engine, peering out the windows before opening the door. The fog had dissipated, and seeing plainly that there were no ghosts, good or bad, nearby, I ran to the front porch continuing my good luck chant of Zeke's name.

Except for the rhythmic tick-tock of the grandfather clock in the foyer, the house was silent as I sneaked inside. With no apparent signs of life, I tiptoed up the stairs with my back to the railing, hoping to avoid the tell-tale creaking that could alert my early morning return. Surprisingly, I had never lied to my parents before - I certainly didn't want to start now. I crept quietly and carefully into my room, where Kaye seemed to still be asleep. I crawled gingerly into the bed beside her, breathing a silent sigh of relief. It seemed as if no one was the wiser that I had spent the night with Zeke.

"Where. Have. You. Been?"

I could not roll over to face her. I was more scared of Kaye in this moment than I had been of the ghost in the fog.

"What do you mean?" I tried to sound innocent.

"I mean you weren't here at two, or four, or six. So do not even try to tell me that you're just returning from the bathroom. Have you been in Will's room this whole time?"

"No. I have not." My voice was firm.

"Well, good – I guess - because up until this moment, I didn't realize how much that might creep me out." Kaye's reply was undecided. "So if you weren't with Will, then where were you?"

The speed with which I came up with an answer surprised me. "I was out of *this* room." It was a true statement. Vague. But true.

"You snuck out of the house, didn't you?"

Kaye might not be a Rhodes Scholar, but she was no dummy.

No quick reply button to hit this time, so I toyed with the lace along the edge of the comforter and tried to ignore her.

Even though Kaye weighed all of one hundred pounds soaking wet, I could feel the load of the bed shift as she leaned over so that her face was close to my ear. "I've never known you to sneak out of the house, Sallie Songer. So for you to do something that crazy, it must be a really big deal and the only big deal I've seen around here is Zeke. I should have figured this out sooner! That's why you've been so reluctant to talk to me about him."

Kaye's voice was an excited whisper, but I couldn't tell if it was a good kind of excited or a bad kind of excited. Regardless, it was time to tell the truth – I could not and did not want to play this game all weekend.

"You're right. I was with Zeke."

"All night long? Did you…"

I knew what she was implying and was so shocked by the question that I sat straight up. "No! I went to his house to talk to him. We ended up falling asleep on his bed. But nothing else happened."

From the expression on her face, I couldn't tell if Kaye was pleased or disappointed.

"What was so important for you to say to him that you needed to sneak out of the house in the middle of the night to do it?"

The time had come to face the jury...to tell the truth, the whole truth, and nothing but the truth.

So help me, God.

"I couldn't wait any longer to tell him that I'm in love with him," I answered in a voice that rose barely above a whisper.

In a gush of words I spilled the entire story of almost everything that had happened since I had moved to this place – finding the diary, meeting Zeke, seeing ghosts, the picnic at the lake, Zeke telling me he loved me, and how -as if completely beyond my control - I had fallen in love with him as well. I made sure not to leave out how tortured I felt about it because of her and Will. It was my turn to babble on and on, barely allowing Kaye to get a word in edgewise. I watched her animated face change from surprise to shock, and disbelief to excitement – but never anger. It felt good, how I imagined it must feel to confess to a priest. The guilty gavel banging in my heart had finally quieted.

As I had hoped, the love-at-first-sight romantic in her wasn't overly upset about the Will situation. Disappointed, in Kaye's own words, that I wouldn't be her future sister-in-law, she, like me, was unsure of how we would break the news to Will. Though we both decided it would be best to wait until after tonight.

Continuing in true Kaye form, she was completely intrigued by the ghosts. She was dying to see one, whenever we were alone she would ask me to conjure one for her.

"Kaye, I've already told you," I explained for the thousandth time, "I cannot make them appear. I've only seen the nice one once and that was with Zeke, the scary one appears out of nowhere."

Due to the arrival of our surprise guests, Mom gave me the day off from the store; so the three of us met up with Mrs. Landry at a restaurant near the hotel. It was good to see the woman who had been another mother to me.

After eating, Mrs. Landry went back to the hotel, and we toured the larger mall in Roanoke. Kaye picked up a new outfit to wear to the party. Will was amazingly patient as she tried on several sets of clothes. She emerged from the dressing room over and over, never satisfied with our opinion. We eventually ended up sitting on the floor at one store after about a half-hour of Kaye modeling for us. She eventually decided on the standard khaki short-shorts with a white halter-style top and a pair of high-heeled sandals. She was a knock-out, but, of course,

Kaye would also be H-O-T dressed in a potato sack.

On the way home, Will sat in the passenger seat while Kaye stretched out snoozing in the back. She eyed me after she yawned, complaining that she didn't sleep well last night. From time-to-time, Will would fiddle with my stereo, casually lay his hand on my knee, and then go back to adjusting the volume or switching the songs.

He seemed almost nervous in his affection, which was sort of sweet. I experienced a second of remorse for not reciprocating the right sort of warmth toward Will. I would hate breaking his heart, and I was pretty sure that his heart would be broken. Before yesterday, I wasn't certain, but the more time we spent together today, the more I had come to the conclusion that absence had made his heart grow fonder.

By the time we got back to the house, it was supper time. Dad was busy grilling hamburgers and hot dogs, while Mom worked on some side dishes in the kitchen. We ate buffet-style on the patio – it was a clear, warm evening, the grill smoke fortunately kept the usual gnat invasion at bay.

The girls cleaned up the dishes while the boys sat in the living room and talked sports. After tidying the kitchen, Kaye and I excused ourselves to get ready. Samantha followed us upstairs and sat on the bed while we refreshed our makeup and styled our hair, asking us a hundred questions about where we were going and who would be there.

I loosely braided my hair into two long pigtails and donned some cut-off blue jean shorts and a cream-colored off-the-shoulder peasant-style shirt; to accessorize, I wrapped Zeke's bandana like a cuff bracelet around my wrist. Kaye laughed when I pulled on the bright turquoise cowboy boots I had found at a second-hand shop on a trip to downtown Alexandria. I had been waiting for the right occasion to wear them, this seemed to be the appropriate one – it was a barn party after all.

"Seriously, are you going to wear those?" She admonished.

"Yes. I am."

She groaned. "Some things never change."

"Don't be a hater." I teased. "Upset that I have a better fashion sense than you?"

Kaye smirked. "You wish."

Will was more appreciative as we descended the stairs to leave for the party. Whistling before he remarked. "Let me guess, a cross between Mary Ann and Daisy Duke?"

Kaye rolled her eyes. "You do realize you're about the only

person alive who watches Gilligan's Island reruns?"

"What?" Will threw his hands up in fake frustration. "They're funny!"

"I'm with you, Will. They are funny." Mom squeezed each of us in one of her giant hugs as we walked out the door. "Have a good time tonight. And be careful driving. Remember what precious cargo you are."

Zeke's directions were more challenging than any I had ever attempted to follow before. They went something like this: turn left just past the old tobacco barn, go about a mile and turn right at a white farmhouse, stay on this road (which was stretching the definition of road a bit – it was more of a red dirt rutted path) until it dead-ends.

Thank goodness I had both Will and Kaye riding with me to be on the lookout for Zeke's landmarks.

The place was already packed by the time we got there. Vehicles were lined up in the field – a lot of them were trucks with the tailgates down and large coolers in the back. People were milling around – mostly teenagers, but a few guys who probably graduated from high school about five years ago. One group had a hefty-sized plastic trash can that they were dipping plastic cups inside of and then drinking from them.

"Looks like somebody's got some home brew over there," Will chuckled. Kaye's wrinkled forehead which followed Will's statement was a clear indicator this was a side of him she hadn't seen. Will had schooled me on what he knew about illegal liquor before my move, so it was nothing new to me.

"Hey, guys," I heard a familiar voice call out.

As I rotated on my booted heel, I couldn't help the huge grin that spread across my face. Zeke was dressed much like he was that first day I spotted him in the driveway – including the straw hat that almost pushed me off the deep end. It was all I could do not to gallop straight into his arms. I wanted every girl watching Zeke cruise my way to know that this guy belonged to me. Of course, most of those girls were also checking out Will. Every come hither invitation made me feel protective of him too, but in a different way – sisterly, again.

"Wow! You look – wow!" I had found Zeke to be rarely speechless.

I felt Will place his hand against the small of my back. The intent of *his* protectiveness was crystal clear, and not at all brotherly. This was going to be a difficult charade to pull off tonight.

When I talked with Zeke on the phone earlier in the day, I told him about my confession to Kaye and warned him ahead of time about the plan not to tell Will about the two of us until after tonight. Zeke wasn't fond of the idea but understood that I was trying to make Will's trip as pleasant as possible before ripping his heart out and then stomping on it before sending him back home with his mama.

Zeke tore his eyes from me to glance over at Kaye. "And you're looking rather lovely as well." He gave her one of his giant smiles. "How'd we get so lucky to be in the company of these ladies tonight, Will?"

Will opened his mouth to respond, but before any words could come out, a shirtless guy in a baseball cap standing near the trash can yelled at Zeke.

"Hey, Zeke, want some punch?"

Zeke smiled and shook his head. "No thanks. I don't drink that stuff anymore."

The guy chugged the contents of his cup. "Aww, come on. It'll put some hair on your chest."

"If that were the case, yours would be covered in fur by now. Right, Austin?"

The group standing around Austin burst out in laughter. He rubbed his very bare torso, shrugged his shoulders, and dipped his cup into the can again.

"You can't beat a guy for trying." The gang around him cackled like chickens in a coop.

Shaking his head at Austin's remark, Zeke motioned us toward the barn. "Those guys are already wasted. Come on up so I can introduce you to the band. We're already set up and don't start playing for another half-hour."

The journey to the barn through the maze of cars, trucks and a few out of place mini-vans was filled with a chorus of party-goers calling to Zeke. He was well known, reminding me of anytime I went anywhere with Kaye back home. Strolling beside her now, I could sense her excitement in this new environment. She can enter a room with a hundred folks she doesn't know and leave with a hundred new friends. I'm no wallflower, but I can't work a room the way Kaye can.

As we stepped through the open double doors of the barn, it seemed more to me like a small airplane hangar. There were no animal stalls, just a wide expanse of wood plank flooring that was free of any traces of straw; huge, churning fans and bright lights hung from the beams in the ceiling. Along the very back of the room, a stage had been built on which Zeke's music equipment now sat. The round drum at the rear of the stage displayed the name of the band: Cash and Bones. It was written in what reminded me of an old western wanted poster script – all caps and bolded.

It struck me suddenly that before now I hadn't a clue what they called the band. I couldn't remember Zeke mentioning it, apparently I had never asked. I thought it was an awesome name and told Zeke as much.

"Cash's idea. I guess I'll never escape that *Dry Bones* ditty from Sunday school...which was his first suggestion."

"Dry Bones? Hmmm. Sounds more like a doggie snack. George might enjoy it."

Zeke's eyes were dancing. "I'm not sure if even George would take to that. Might be too fancy for him, he's accustomed to the big bag of kibble from the feed store."

"Your loyal, loving companion and all he gets is food from the farm supply store? Poor, George."

"Loyal, loving companions do deserve better than that, don't they?" Zeke reached out to touch my hand; his fingers barely grazed mine before remembering our company. Jerking his hand back, Zeke ran it through his hair instead. "Yeah, you're right. I'll try to do better by George next time."

Sneaking a peek at Will, I wondered if he had caught the almost public display of affection, but he and Kaye stood staring at us as if we were speaking in a foreign language.

"Who is George, one of the band members?" Kaye put her hand on her hips in mock frustration, "So, do we get to meet the rest of the guys, or do we have to stand here all night listening while you two chat it up?"

She gave me a deliberate wide eye, a signal of sorts that she wasn't very pleased with my acting abilities. Fortunately, Will was taking in his surroundings and not paying a bit of attention to Kaye.

"I don't think I've ever been in a barn before," Will commented as he checked the place out. "I was expecting a lot more hay and the smell of manure."

Zeke laughed as he started guiding us toward the stage. "It's a bank barn. The top level – which is what we're on – would have been used for storing hay and grain. The animals would have been kept downstairs. Cy, my buddy Cash's dad, remodeled this place and holds jam sessions here on a regular basis. Occasionally he lets us hold one of our own – it's good practice for us. Cy rents it out too for private parties and stuff; we've even played a few weddings."

Kaye wrinkled her nose in disgust. "A wedding... in here? Ewww."

"Don't be so uppity, Miss Fancypants, barns can be *very* romantic," Zeke smiled his wicked little grin which I knew was just for me.

"Whatever." Kaye was certainly not convinced.

Of course, she'd never had the good fortune to be in a hay loft with Zeke during a sunset.

We approached three guys sitting on the edge of the stage. I recognized one of them as Cash; tonight his hair was loose from its pony tail and hung in waves past his shoulders. His shorts and Birkenstocks had been replaced by jeans and boots – he sported the Grateful Dead shirt I'd given him from the store.

Cash jumped up when he saw us. "Hey, Sallie! Thanks again for the shirt."

"It's good on you." I complimented. The colors of the shirt emphasized his eyes. I hadn't noticed before what a beautiful shade of pale green they are.

The two other guys stood up to greet us, as well.

"Josh, Ryan," Zeke was making the introductions, "this is Sallie," he laid his hand on my shoulder, "and Kaye and Will, Sallie's friends from northern Virginia."

The two waved their hands as they said hello.

Josh was tall and thin with light blonde hair cut short in the back but with long bangs that hung across what might be blue eyes – it was hard to see them beneath the fringe. Ryan was slightly shorter with broad shoulders and some seriously muscular arms; tiny gold hoops dangled from each ear, his jet black hair was styled almost in a Mohawk – except the top wasn't long and the sides weren't completely shaved. Ryan's eyes matched the color of his hair and his skin was the color of copper. Apparently they all got the memo for tonight's dress code: jeans, boots, t-shirts.

"Josh plays bass, Ryan is our drummer," Zeke clarified.

Kaye's face was aglow like she had stepped straight into heaven. She immediately struck up a conversation with the guys about how excited she was to hear them play. They'd be busy listening to her chatter for a little while. None of them seemed to mind though, especially Cash, who hadn't taken his eyes off of her since speaking to me.

I decided I needed to find the ladies room before the show

started.

"Hey, Will." He turned to face me with a broad smile. It made me hate this character I was playing tonight, but for what I thought was Will's sake, I was planning on performing at an Academy Award winning level. "Do you mind if run to the restroom real quick?"

"Sure, go right ahead. Do you want me to walk with you?"

"No. That's okay. I'll ask Zeke where it is. You can stay here and hold our spot." The barn was starting to fill up; I did not want to lose my prime place on the front row.

Zeke instructed me to go back behind the stage and take the staircase downstairs; the bathroom doors would be marked.

The lower half of the barn still resembled a stable and was comprised of several stalls. The last two on each side had been turned into enclosed restrooms. The doors were decorated with half-moon cutouts like you'd see on an old outhouse. One was marked "Ma,' the other "Pa". It was cute. My own Ma would get a kick out of this place.

I did my business, fluffed my hair in the mirror, and rubbed on some flavored lip gloss. I glanced at my watch and saw that it was eight-fifty. I needed to get back upstairs.

I had barely stepped outside the bathroom when I was grabbed by the waist and pulled into the nearest stall; the door slammed shut with a loud bang.

"I have been dying to do this since I spotted you outside," Zeke breathed as he gently pushed me against the wall and began kissing me hard. We were all lips and hands in hair for a while before the kiss ended. Zeke raised an eyebrow, "I'm half-tempted to scoop you up and get us both out of here."

"Judging by the crowd here tonight, I think you'd have a lot of disappointed fans."

He shrugged his shoulders. "Maybe so, but I'm not sure I'll be able to concentrate onstage knowing Will is standing next to you thinking that you're *his* girlfriend."

"I'm sorry about that. But, like I told *you* earlier, Kaye and I thought it would be for his benefit not to know about the two of us for one more night."

Zeke moved his head in opposition. "And, like I told *you* earlier, I disagree and it's not just because I want every guy out there to know that you're with me. I don't think this is fair to Will. If I were in his shoes, I would much rather know the truth than be protected."

I sighed – his opinion made sense.

Zeke caressed my arms and smiled in sympathy. "I know you're doing what you think is best – but don't be surprised tomorrow to find that he's not only unhappy with you about being dumped, but also about the way it was handled." Then he grinned. "But don't worry, you can come cry on my shoulder."

I groaned and good-naturedly punched him on said shoulder. "We better get back upstairs before someone comes searching for us."

Zeke's lips brushed teasingly across mine. "If we must."

He let me go first, following behind a few minutes later. It seemed no one was the wiser about our tryst, and Will had dutifully held my spot. Zeke was right; it was such a girly thing for me to do this to Will, pretending that everything was normal tonight.

As the band took the stage, I heard someone let out a loud, irritated gust behind me. I turned and found myself in a face-off with Adrienne. She must not have been wearing her stilettos tonight, but she certainly hadn't left the low-cut blouse at home - and she was flanked by a couple of wannabes with bleached hair and push up bras.

"Hello, *Adrienne*."

"Oh. It *is* you."

Her disdainful tone caused Will to turn around to see what was going on. When she caught a glimpse of him, Adrienne's demeanor changed. Suddenly she was my best friend.

"Lucky me! I thought I might run into you here, Sallie. Who's this?" Her smile was faker than the red acrylic nails on her fingers.

"My friend, Will." He was taken aback by my introduction – he must have been expecting me to say *boyfriend*.

The exchange wasn't lost on Adrienne. "Nice to meet you, *Will*."

His lips lifted in a wary smile before replying, "You too."

Adrienne shot me a smug glare before she moved her mouth close to Will's ear. "Hope you enjoy the performance."

Then Ryan kicked in with the drums; his smashing, clanging cymbals signaled the start of the show.

Moonshine Serenade

Chapter Eleven
Sally Goodin

I had heard Zeke play his guitar a few times, but had never heard him sing until tonight.

I stood between Will and Kaye, mesmerized by the sound. Zeke's singing voice left me as spellbound as his speaking one. The tone was warm - husky but more like suede than sandpaper. I wanted to reach out, take hold of it and wrap it around me like a cloak.

The first couple of songs were fast. The crowd clapped and whistled; girls leered up at the band from beneath eyelashes laden with layers of thick black mascara, biting their glossy lower lips in invitation. I half expected one of them to toss a bra onto the stage.

It didn't take me long to assess that band was really good. Not that I'm a professional talent scout or anything, but they totally impressed me. If I heard a Cash and Bones song on a playlist, it would definitely be something that I would download. Though every song they had performed so far was a cover, the sound was unique and not necessarily arranged the same as the original. A country ballad might be revved up with heavy guitar work, or a rock song mellowed out by a jazzy rhythm.

Zeke sang lead and Cash backed him up. Their voices complemented each other well. Cash's had a higher pitch – a sort of nasally twang, but the blend between the two was like sugar and spice. Josh chimed in occasionally with a harmony, but Ryan just rocked the drums with his pumped up arms, nodding his head in time with the beat.

And Zeke rocked that stage… the kind of front man that teenage girls would plaster posters of all over their bedroom walls…and for good reason. The way the cords of muscle stood out on his forearms as he gripped the guitar in his hands, the shake of his tousled head when he tossed his hat and launched into a guitar solo, and the caress of his lips against the microphone, even made me almost want to scream out like a frenzied fan girl.

On the fourth number, Zeke exchanged his guitar for a banjo, the floor vibrated with the sound of the crowd stomping and cheering. They must have known what was coming.

"Here we go now," Zeke called out.

His fingers started flying across the banjo strings; the skill completely blew me away. I wondered why his parents hadn't packed him up and sent him straight to Austin or Nashville. There was no doubt in my mind that with his talent Zeke could play music professionally.

So engrossed in watching him pick the banjo, I paid no attention to the song he was singing until I was surprised to hear my name in the lyrics.

Had a piece of pie an` I had a piece of pudding'
An' I give it all away just to see my Sally Goodin

Well, I looked down the road an' I see my Sally comin'
An' I thought to my soul that I'd kill myself a-runnin'

I jerked my head up. Zeke caught my eye and winked.

Love a `tater pie an' I love an apple puddin'
An' I love a little gal that they call Sally Goodin

An' I dropped the 'tater pie an' I left the apple pudding'
But I went across the mountain to see my Sally Goodin

It was fast-moving music; most of the people around us were dancing.

Well, flat-footing to be exact.

Mom and Samantha are pretty good at it.

Me - not so much.

Maybe it's their overactive Irish genes because flat-footing reminds me of some of the Lord of the Dance steps – like a marionette on a string with arms and legs that move up and down.

Kaye was even into it tonight. A cute guy standing next to her grabbed her hand, she jigged with him as if she'd lived in Franklin County all her life.

I glanced over at Will and held out my hand in a request for a dance partner. I was willing to give it a try if he was, but Will crossed his arms against his chest. I couldn't tell if it was because he didn't care to dance or because he wasn't thrilled about the words flowing from Zeke's mouth.

Sally is my doxy an' Sally is my daisy
When Sally says she hates me I think I'm goin' crazy

I'm goin' up the mountain an' marry little Sally
Raise corn on the hillside an' the devil in the valley

With a flourish of fingers across the strings, Zeke finished up the song. Kaye bounced back next to me breathing a little heavy.

"That was fun," she said excitedly, "different…but fun."

The next number was *I Wanna Be Sedated* accompanied by the banjo. Zeke had talked about playing a Ramones tune. I loved it. I wasn't the only one. The crowd bobbed in place and thrashed around like they were at a real punk show.

Though, I'm pretty sure the guy standing in the corner wearing bibs, a John Deere hat, and holding a tobacco spit cup had probably never heard of The Ramones. Too bad for him, I considered and then rethought my judgment. I'm sure whatever he listened to on a regular basis made him happy, and after all, isn't that what music's all about?

I shouldn't be such a snob.

The band played on and on. The only breaks were when Zeke would stop to gulp water from a bottle propped up near the drum stand and to chat with the crowd, taking a few requests and responding good-naturedly to a drunken female fan that had sloppily charged the stage and wrapped herself around Zeke. He slow-danced with her for a minute and then kindly helped her down into the waiting arms of what appeared to be her equally as smashed date. I hoped they had a designated driver or planned to camp out here for the night.

It was approaching two hours when Zeke walked over to the nearest amplifier and from a stand behind it pulled out a toffee-colored mandolin. Returning to the microphone, Zeke announced the last song would be a new one he had written. As his fingers gracefully stroked the strings, the soft twang of the melody was instantly familiar as the one he had played for me at the lakefront cottage.

The rest of the band seemed to fade into the background as Zeke faced me and began to sing.

New meeting
A journey home
Past in pictures

Moonshine Serenade

Innocence roams
And in your dreams
Is a moonshine serenade

Summer night
An electric touch
Moving shadows
Supernatural clutch
And in your dreams
Sings a moonshine serenade

Do you see that we're intertwined?
Cord unbroken
Tied by a hand divine
And gives us dreams
Of a moonshine serenade

The stream of energy flowing between Zeke and me had now flooded the room with the force of a tsunami. I could feel Will growing increasingly edgy beside me as Zeke continued his serenade. This was not how I had wanted Will to find out, but there was no mistaking the relationship now.

I stayed focused on Zeke, partially because I was too much of a chicken to face Will; but mostly because Zeke's ballad wasn't yet done and his eyes had never left mine.

All secrets
They melt away
Bones ignited
Resurrection day
And brings you dreams
With a moonshine serenade

Floating fearless
Sky turns gray
Thunder rumbles
A chance to play
For your dreams
My moonshine serenade

Zeke strummed through the ending and gently laid the mandolin at his feet.

The silent crowd stood stunned for a moment and then began

to slowly scatter. Except for one guy sporting a scraggly goatee, who, not realizing the show was over, called out in a slur of words, "Come on, dudes, play some Skynyrd!" A fist pump into the air and a chant of *Freebird, Freebird* didn't help to rally the band.

I turned to meet Will's gaze. He was wearing an expression that in all of my years of knowing him, I had never seen.

"Will, I..." But before I could finish, Will bowed his head and walked away. Adrienne, whom I had completely forgotten was even there, shot me a triumphant smirk and then strode off after him.

I felt Kaye's hand lightly touch my shoulder. "You did the best you could, Sallie. I'll go find him."

"Better get there before Adrienne does," I mumbled at the back of Kaye's head.

The band was resting on the stage behind me, gulping water and chatting about the set.

I balled my hands into a fist and turned to confront Zeke. "I don't know whether to kiss you or to punch you," I lashed out.

"I'm sorry, Sallie," Zeke apologized softly as he stepped down from the stage. "It was never my intention to upset Will. I wanted to surprise you. I finished the song this week in West Virginia and had arranged with the guys to perform it tonight before I even knew Will would be here. But I will not apologize for doing it anyway because it meant so much for me to sing it to you." Zeke laid his right hand across his heart, "I don't play games, Sallie, and I don't hide my feelings...not that it would do me much good to try to hide the way I feel about you anyway. I *love* you. And, though you may not be, I'm ready for the whole world to know."

"Zeke," I stepped closer to him. "It isn't that I'm not ready for the whole world to know." My voice was imploring. "I wanted to give Will a little more time...to explain how things happened between me and you. I feel I owe him that much. Maybe I went about it the wrong way, but my intention was good." Wrapping my arms around his waist, I laid my head on his chest. "I love you too, Zeke - enough to risk the friendships of my two oldest friends."

"I don't want you to lose your friends." Zeke's arms encircled me, giving me a tender squeeze. "Let me talk to them. I'll say it was my fault, that I coerced you, brainwashed you, and subjected you to alien torture." Though I couldn't see his face, I knew that Zeke was smiling. He ruffled the back of my head and then whispered into my ear. "Did you like the song even a little bit?"

My response came easy. "You could sing it to me every day for the rest of my life, and I would never once grow weary of hearing your voice."

That was all the encouragement Zeke needed to plant one smoldering kiss right on my lips. Cash, Josh and Ryan whooped it up in the background.

Zeke rolled his eyes. "Just ignore them. I do it all the time."

"Hey, you two," Kaye's voice called from behind me, "Who was the bleach blonde chick that followed Will out?"

I turned toward the person who I hoped was still my best friend. "Her name's Adrienne. Why?"

Kaye's eyes were angry slits. "Because Will left with her, that's why."

"Did you try calling him?" I asked Kaye from the front seat of my mom's car.

Zeke was driving. It was dark out, and these curvy country roads were difficult enough to maneuver in the daylight. He had asked the guys in the band to finish breaking down and load his equipment into the Jeep while he helped us hunt for Will. Josh and Ryan were left to do the work alone because Cash was sitting in the back seat with Kaye.

"Of course I've tried calling him; I've left him four voice mails and three text messages!"

Cash patted Kaye's hand. "It's okay. Adrienne's not *that* bad."

The daggers whizzing from Kaye's eyes prompted Cash to remove his hand. And quick.

"If I knew Adrienne's cell phone number, I'd try getting in touch with her." Zeke offered.

Great. The one time I actually wished Zeke had her number.

"You don't happen to have it do you, Cash?" Zeke asked.

"No." Cash acted shocked that Zeke would even ask such a question.

"Are you sure?" Zeke wasn't convinced.

"Yes, I'm sure."

And I'm sure that I overheard Cash mumble something like *she won't give it to me.*

With the exception of Kaye drumming her fingernails against the glass as she peered out the window, it was quiet in the car for a couple minutes before Zeke broke the silence.

"I think I know where she may have taken him."

Kaye practically pounced over the seat onto Zeke's shoulders. "Where?"

"Her parents have a condo at the lake. It will take a little while to get there from here, so, Gimpy, you may want to call your mom and let her know you'll be later than expected."

I followed Zeke's suggestion, explaining to Mom that Kaye and I were with Zeke and that we were conducting a search party for Will who had left with someone else. Mom seemed confused about that tidbit of information, but I didn't want to get into too much detail at the moment. She seemed pleased that Zeke was heading up the hunt and told me to stay out as late as I needed to find Will.

Adrienne's condo was in a different direction from where Zeke had taken me on Monday. Because it was dark, the scenery seemed to blur past us until we hit an area of the lake that was lit up like a beachfront boardwalk in the middle of cow country. To my right, I could see movie-goers exiting a theatre and a few cars lined up at a nearby fast food establishment. Zeke made a right-hand turn at a stoplight, and soon after, our view became bathed in darkness once again.

No one talked much on the drive; even Kaye was eerily quiet. Zeke drove mostly left-handed, as his right one was clasping mine. He would occasionally give me a smile of encouragement as if to say that everything would be alright.

After wrangling some sharp curves, Zeke pulled into a development with a few more twists and turns, then slid the sedan into a parking space in front of a set of cedar-sided buildings.

"That's Adrienne's car," he pointed his thumb at the vehicle next to us, "her place is straight ahead."

Kaye jumped out, sprinted to the front door and started banging on it. The rest of us exited the car and stood nearby as she continued to knock in frustration. The lights were on, but no one was home.

"Let's try around back," Zeke suggested.

We walked around the edge of the building. The patio was empty, but a glance toward the lake revealed two people sitting on the grass by the water's edge.

"Wait here," Kaye ordered before she stormed off. I ignored her demand and followed behind. This was entirely my fault after all. I should be with her to deal with Will.

Kaye's strides were fast and furious. "Will!" She yelled.

His head jerked around toward us. Jumping up from his seated position, he stormed angrily in our direction. "What are you doing here?"

Kaye punched him as hard as she could muster in his shoulder. The impact knocked her to the ground, but it barely moved him backwards.

"What were you thinking, running off with someone you don't even know?" Kaye snapped as she stood back up.

Will smirked, "What makes you think I haven't done that before?"

Kaye groaned in aggravation. I walked up and stood beside her. "I think this is really about me and Will, Kaye. Let me talk to him."

"I have nothing to say to you," Will's reply came through gritted teeth. "I'd rather get back to Adrienne."

Will turned to leave, I grabbed his arm. "Please, Will."

I don't know which it was – the pleading in my voice, the tears in my eyes, or just the simple fact that he was behaving completely out of character; but Will realized it in that moment too, and his face softened.

"Okay, Sallie. Let's talk." He brushed that stray lock of hair that I was so fond of away from his eyes. "You're up."

I wasn't keen on the fact that Adrienne was within earshot. "How about we go somewhere more private?" I suggested.

I inspected our surroundings. Zeke and Cash were standing on the patio; Adrienne was waiting by the shoreline for Will to come back to her. Fortunately, a gazebo with a bench stood on a nearby dock.

I motioned with my head, "Let's go over there."

We walked silently side by side. I tried to quickly review what I planned to say to Will, having practiced a speech in my head earlier in the day; but it was as if the words had evaporated from my brain.

Ugh! I was going to have to wing it. I hoped I wouldn't turn into a blubbering idiot.

Sheltered from the lights surrounding the homes, it was dark inside the gazebo. As we sat down, Will's face became obscured by the shadows. The casual splash of waves against the pillars beneath us was a sharp contrast to the tense mood.

"So," I was fidgeting nervously with the fringe on my cut-off shorts, still unsure of exactly how to start the conversation. "I guess you know about me and Zeke."

"Do you think I'm stuck on stupid, Sallie? Yeah, of course I know."

"Will, I am *so* sorry. I never meant to hurt you or for you to find out any other way except directly from me."

He let out a loud sigh. "I thought a little about this last night because I noticed yesterday the way you two could hardly take your eyes off each other, but I blew it off thinking that surely you would have told me about another guy, or even Kaye for that matter, and she seemed clueless too. So I thought that today I'd be more affectionate and attentive – maybe that's all it was...that we needed to spend some time together because mostly we have been apart since we started trying out this whole relationship thing. Then today you seemed distant, like my attempts at affection were pushing you away instead of drawing you closer. I was confused because you're not that way...the kind of girl who plays games."

I could tell that Will was studying me, but I found it difficult to read whatever emotion was playing across *his* face. So I looked back down and kept playing with the fringe.

"So tonight when Zeke sang that song to you, I was less upset about the fact that you had obviously met another guy, but more hurt because you hadn't told me. I mean, we talked about that exact thing the night before you left. Don't get me wrong. I do really want to be with you, and that hurts too because after tonight I realize that's not possible." From the corner of my eye, I saw Will shake his head side to side. "I guess it was dumb to think we could pull off a long distance relationship anyway."

"Can I talk now? Try to explain?" My voice sounded as squeaky as a scared mouse.

I gave him a modified version of the story I had told Kaye. It was tempting to tell Will about the ghosts, but I was afraid it would make it seem as if this was more about me. I wanted it to be clear to Will that this conversation was about *him* and *his* feelings.

What I didn't leave out was the plan to tell him about Zeke tomorrow, in a good-faith effort to make sure he had a good time tonight. We both laughed about what a sucky idea that turned out to be.

"Just think," Will said quietly, "if you hadn't moved, we wouldn't be having this little chat."

I thought about that for a moment and realized it wasn't true. "Maybe not now, maybe not tonight, but it would have happened eventually, Will, because I would have run into Zeke at some point on a visit to my grandparents. And isn't it much better to be doing this now than in six months or in a year when we would have had so much more invested? I wouldn't be able to stop Zeke and me from happening regardless of the time or place. And it has nothing to do with you. You are a great guy, and I always want us to be friends."

Will snorted. "Great, I'm getting the very meaningful *it's me, not you and let's be friends* speech."

"Well, I really mean it."

"I don't get it, Sallie. You've only known him for a couple of weeks."

How could I explain it to Will when I'm not really sure that I get it either?

What I did know is that I would honestly feel bad for any of my friends who didn't get to experience this sort of love in their lifetime - all-consuming and absolute, as if it really was ordained by a higher power.

"I hope you do *get* it someday, Will, because I want it to happen for you too, and I'll be the first person standing on the sidelines to cheer you on."

We sat there in silence for a moment. Now each wave that splashed beneath us seemed to draw some of our tension away with it, the ebb and flow was soothing enough to rock a fitful child to sleep.

"Kaye's going to be so disappointed," Will said with a grin in his voice. "I think she was planning our wedding."

"I know. She's already given me some grief about that." I touched Will's hand and tried to examine his eyes. "So, are we good?"

I couldn't quite tell, but it seemed as if a smile played across his lips. "I think so."

We walked back toward the group which had now converged on the patio. Everyone was sitting except for Zeke. He stood with his back up against the wall and his arms across his chest, almost as if he was worried about how all this would go down.

Just before we got within hearing distance, Will jerked his head toward Zeke. "It's too bad that after talking with Adrienne, I can't even be mad at him."

I was about to ask him to clarify that statement when Kaye jumped both of us.

"Hallelujah! You two made up!"

In an attempt not to rub the relationship in Will's face, I rode in the backseat with him and Kaye while Zeke drove us all the way back to the barn to pick up his Jeep. We left Cash there (apparently, he and his dad live in a cabin on the property), I followed Zeke back to my house in the sedan.

Zeke pulled in the driveway briefly only to tell us all goodnight and that he'd see us in church. I had forgotten we had worship service in the morning; this would end up being a short night for all of us.

On our way from brushing teeth and washing faces in the bathroom, Kaye and I stopped by to say goodnight. Will was already curled up under the covers but still awake. After Kaye left the room, I stayed on the edge of the bed.

"Will, can I ask you a question?"

"Go ahead." He let out a big, loud yawn.

It was contagious, I yawned too. "What did you mean when you said that after talking with Adrienne, you couldn't be mad at Zeke either?"

He rearranged his pillow to face me better. "She told me that if it was any consolation that Zeke would never steal anyone's girlfriend intentionally and that he will be really good to you. And something about how she wishes she hadn't let things get so messed up between the two of them because she misses his friendship. That's about it. She was really nice."

"Adrienne was nice?" I couldn't hide the surprise in my voice.

"Yeah. Why else do you think I would have left with her?"

Oh, I could think of a couple of prominent reasons why he might have left with her.

"I needed somebody to talk to. She said she'd bring me back here later."

Hmm. It seemed that Will had caught a glimpse of the Adrienne that Zeke used to know... and maybe more than know in a casual sense. I'd have to ponder that one.

I stood up to make my exit, "If you say so. `Night, Will."

"Goodnight, *FRIEND!*"

I grabbed the pillow from the other side of the bed and threw it at his head.

We were definitely good.

Chapter Twelve
His Eye Is On The Sparrow

Sunday turned out to be a pretty decent day. I split my time between worship service and dinner with my grandparents. Will and Kaye had been invited, as well as Zeke who pleasantly declined saying he'd already made plans with his family. I knew the real reason - Zeke was giving Will some space. He would be here for a short time, and there was no point in making it an uncomfortable visit – at least not any more uncomfortable than it had already been. So the rest of us ate Grandma Ellen's pot roast and peach cobbler, played horse shoes, petted Daisy (clarification: Will did – Kaye wouldn't get near her). We crashed around midnight after touring our property, excluding the cemetery. Though Kaye had begged, I was too afraid we'd run into Mr. Super Scary Straw Hat dude. After that, we piled up in my room to discuss general nothingness.

Will and Kaye left around noon on Monday, both basically in good spirits about what had occurred over the weekend. I wasn't quite sure I deserved how well they had taken it all, but I guess somehow they understood this connection I had with Zeke – especially Kaye who also knew about the ghosts. So, the two of them weren't interested in locking our friendship behind bars and throwing away the key. We hugged, Kaye and I cried, and Will smiled at me with those gem-colored eyes. It crossed my mind that I might miss Kaye and Will even more now that we had survived our first major friendship challenge and seemed to have walked away more bonded because of it.

They had dropped me off at the shop before leaving town. Kaye was dying to see the place and, upon her inspection, very much approved. I spent the afternoon helping Mom shift racks around and changing the display window until she finally felt satisfied with how it looked. Zeke was booked with evening guitar lessons, so I did something that I hadn't done much of since we had moved from Springfield – just chilled at the house with my family. We ate popcorn, watched a movie on the plasma television (good going Dad because it was seriously sweet). After catching up with Zeke on the phone, I hit the sack relatively early.

It was another night free from weird dreams and strange noises. A bizarre sort of calm – but I was happy to have it.

Today, I had asked Mom for the day off to spend some alone time with Zeke. We hadn't really been without some sort of company since Friday night, and I wanted to be able to simply hold his hand without it being a potential issue for anyone within our general proximity. She was fine with that since this week we were having what she referred to as a soft opening. She felt the customers would mostly dribble in, and she wouldn't need me as much. She hoped that after the planned "Grand Opening" on Saturday set to coincide with the Fourth of July holiday (and my seventeenth birthday), they would begin to pour through the door and my services would be more necessary.

However, a phone call from Zeke this morning reminded me that it was Tuesday, which meant our alone time would have to wait until this afternoon since it was his day to entertain at the nursing home. Just needing to be near him, I offered to tag-along, he thought it was great idea. So now we were headed into Rocky Mount, and I was eager to witness another aspect of Zeke's life. As I fastened my seat belt, I hoped that the sundress and sandals I was wearing wouldn't seem too dressy next to Zeke's standard jeans and t-shirt.

Having not spent much time in nursing homes, I was surprised at how welcoming it appeared from the outside. I had expected the place to resemble an institution: somber gray building with barred dark windows, but instead it was a quaint one story brick building adorned with window boxes that overflowed with bright flowers, a covered cobblestone porch with wicker chairs, and a decorative grapevine wreath on the front door.

The lobby was no less homey. A cushy sofa and arm chairs flanked a white fireplace. Oriental rugs warmed the tile floor, and lamps glowed throughout the room. Zeke placed his hand in the small of my back and guided me toward a desk in the corner near large wooden double doors.

"Hey, Chandra," Zeke called as we neared the desk.

The receptionist smiled, she seemed to be about the same age as me and was exotically beautiful with skin the color of creamed coffee and a cap of tight, shiny black curls that accentuated her dark chocolate eyes and full crimson lips.

"Hi, Zeke," she answered familiarly, "how was your trip?"

"It was great, thanks. Glad to be back. How's the summer job going?"

Chandra's face lit up. "I am loving it! It's nice to be able to check in on my great-grandma from time to time."

Her smiling eyes switched over to me.

"Chandra, this is my girlfriend, Sallie."

It was the first time Zeke had introduced me by that title, and it surprised me as much as it evidently did Chandra because she jumped out of her seat and practically stomped to the front of the desk.

"This is your girlfriend?" She placed her hands on her hips and shook her head. "Some of the ladies around here are going to be mighty jealous." She added with a wink in Zeke's direction, "It's nice to meet you, Sallie."

I held my hand out to shake hers, but instead she grabbed me exuberantly in a friendly hug. Then she stepped back, eyeing me up and down. "I don't think I've seen you before at the high school."

"Oh, you wouldn't have. I moved here this summer, but I've visited Franklin County since birth. My grandparents live here."

"Well, welcome," Chandra said firmly. "Break it to them gently," she said to Zeke as she nodded toward the door, "those sweet old cougars."

The cougars to which Chandra referred were waiting excitedly for Zeke with their wheelchairs and walkers in what appeared to be the cafeteria/activity room. The aroma of freshly baked bread wafted from the kitchen as Zeke made his way around the fifteen or so ladies (and a few men) engaging each of them in a short greeting. I watched as he bent to gently pat the hands of the elderly women and clasp those of the men in handshakes.

Not wanting to divert the attention from his fans, I slipped to the back of the room and sat on a cushioned bench placed against the wall far from the purview of the audience members who sat entranced by Zeke who was perched on a stool playing his guitar.

The songs today were a quiet calm compared to the concert Saturday night, or even the praise choruses from Sunday morning. These were traditional hymns with stanzas of words rarely used today in contemporary worship music.

Many of the residents sang along with Zeke, some of them held up their hands in praise, a few bowed their heads. I recognized Grandma Ellen's favorite, *The Old Rugged Cross,* and watched as a tiny lady with fuzzy white hair wiped a finger across her cheek.

Struggling to stand, a man with a walker slowly pushed his

way to Zeke as he started the chords to the next song. Laying a shaky hand upon Zeke's shoulder the old man began to sing in a voice so strained I could barely hear.

> *Why should I feel discouraged?*
> *Why should the shadows come?*
> *Why should my heart be lonely,*
> *And long for heaven and home?*
> *When Jesus is my portion*
> *My constant friend is he:*
> *His eye is on the sparrow,*
> *And I know he watches me;*
> *His eye is on the sparrow,*
> *And I know he watches me.*

As my own eyes grew misty, I began to understand why this time was important to Zeke and what it meant to the men and women who shared it with him.

I once heard a minister preaching the funeral of a great-great Aunt who had made it to one hundred years say that most people dream of living a long life, but the reality is that the longer you live the more people you lose, until sometimes at the end, you're almost the only person you know or love who is still alive.

I didn't get it at the time, thinking I was going to squeeze out every bit of this life that I could and that living to a ripe old age would be a blessing. But today, surveying these people it made sense. They had lost parents, spouses, siblings and children; now at this time in their lives the only thing they had to live for was death.

The old man continued to sing; his withered body leaned closer now to Zeke who tried to hold him up with one shoulder while not missing a single chord.

> *Whenever I am tempted,*
> *Whenever clouds arise,*
> *When song gives place to sighing,*
> *When hope within me dies,*
> *I draw the closer to Him,*
> *From care He sets me free;*
> *His eye is on the sparrow,*
> *And I know He watches me,*
> *His eye is on the sparrow,*

And I know He watches me.

As the song ended, Zeke laid down his guitar and taking him by the elbow helped the man back to his seat. The man grasped Zeke's hand for a moment. I could see the man whisper thank you, but Zeke replied, "No, thank *you*."

"Wasn't that touching? I adore that song."

I nearly jumped out of my skin. So intently had I been observing the scene before me that I had paid no attention to the elderly woman who had sat down beside me.

I rubbed my hands across my cheeks and then wiped them on my skirt before I turned to my seatmate. "Yes, it was."

She was a frail lady with gray hair pulled back into a loose bun. There was something familiar about her eyes, although I couldn't place why.

"Oh, my," The woman exclaimed. "You are the spitting image of someone I knew a long time ago!"

Maybe that was why she seemed familiar to me as well; perhaps I had met her on one of my many visits to see my grandparents. "I thought I knew you too."

"Oh no, honey. I knew the person to whom I am referring when I was about your age. My name is Letitia Wray, but way back then, I was known as Letitia Holley."

My stomach lurched into my throat, plunging down the hill in the front seat of a roller coaster would have caused a lesser reaction. "No way!"

She eyed me quizzically. "Yes, way. Is that how I'm supposed to answer?" She giggled girlishly.

I was completely stupefied, unable able to form the words that were stumbling on the tip of my tongue.

"But I live in your house. I found your diary in a closet there. You were sixteen and…"

"How embarrassing," Letitia blurted before I could go any further, "I can't imagine what I may have written at sixteen years old. Something silly about a boy, I'm sure."

I sat forward in my chair a little too eagerly. "No, it wasn't silly at all! In fact, it was really serious. You wrote about witnessing a mur-"

She placed a hand colder than a block of ice on my arm, stilling my voice. Spiderish blue veins bulged from the paper thin skin; her fingers were skeletal in their grip. "Let's not talk about that now. Why don't you bring the diary by here tomorrow, honey, and we'll look through it together." Her warm voice was a soothing contrast to the coolness of her touch. It settled me down.

"Okay. I can do that. Just any time of the day?"

Letitia raised up both her spindly forearms. "Any time is fine with me. I've got all the time in the world."

Laying her arms gracefully in her lap she remarked without hesitation, "I believe someone's calling you over to him."

I dragged my eyes from Letitia to see Zeke waving an arm in my direction. "I guess you're right." I faced her hesitantly. "So, I'll see you tomorrow?"

"Just ask for me at the front desk." She reached out and took my hand. Her tiny one appeared so fragile in mine; I was afraid that even the most gentle of my squeezes would cause her bones to crumble like a piece of fine china. "Goodbye, honey."

I walked slowly away, looking back a couple times to make sure that she was still sitting on the bench and not some figment of my imagination. But she was there and shooed me along encouragingly with the wave of her hand.

Zeke introduced me to everyone; it seemed I was the intermission entertainment. The ladies patted my arm as they praised Zeke. A man named Mr. Brubaker was acquainted with Grandpa Jesse and shared the story of the night my fresh out of vet school grandpa helped him deliver a stubborn calf in a snowstorm – all four of them (the cows included) practically freezing as a heavy snow piled up around them. Mr. Brubaker had carried the slippery calf back to the barn in his numb arms while Grandpa Jesse managed to guide the wailing mother cow back with a rope and a lot of tugging. Both men had slept in the barn that night with the cows; the calf survived, and my Grandpa had earned a great deal of respect. I could see it in the old man's bleary eyes – he missed that life – frostbitten fingers and all.

Zeke insisted that I join him on the next song, thanks to my mom who had informed him (that in her opinion) I have the voice of an angel. But I am strictly a shower singer, and the thought of singing in public terrifies me.

I refused at first, but Zeke got the old folks involved. After much prodding, prompting, and one toothless man who said with assurance, "Come on, sugar, we can't bite," I found myself standing nervously beside Zeke as he started into *I'll Fly Away;* an apparent favorite as our audience clapped and sang with us.

But my nerves melted away as our voices blended in a perfect harmony - this was not as awful as I had imagined it to be. I enjoyed singing with Zeke and the response we received from our small crowd.

Zeke, unable to hide his enthusiasm as we ended the song, threw the guitar onto his back, lifted me off the floor, and twirled me around. The claps grew louder, I'm fairly certain that I heard someone let out a long whistle.

I dropped into a curtsy when Zeke set me down, plopped into the nearest empty chair, and glanced expectantly in Letitia's direction hoping, for some reason, to see an approval of the performance on her face. The bench we had shared was empty.

"You sounded great!" Zeke grabbed me around the waist and planted a kiss on the top of my head as we walked through the parking lot. "A natural talent."

I gave him my evil eye. "You're just saying that."

"No, I really mean it. An angel," Zeke snickered, "like your mom said."

We had reached the Jeep, I turned to face him. "Oh, pa-lease!"

"I'm serious, Sallie. Didn't you hear the natural harmony of our voices?" Zeke stopped to open the car door for me. "Like Johnny Cash and June Carter, Stevie Nicks and Lindsey Buckingham, Robert Plant and Allison Krauss or," he shot me teasing glance, "Darryl Hall and John Oates."

"Who's growing the `stache? You or me?"

"Somehow I don't think doing this would be as much fun if you were sporting a mustache." Placing his hand on the back of my head, he bent down to give me a slow, lingering kiss. "Anyway, the two of us making beautiful music together is no surprise to me because we are simply made for each other." Zeke touched my nose with the tip of his finger.

"Just don't be asking me to join the band. I'm happy to be the groupie."

"Aw, come on now, Linda - you could shake the tambourine and sing backup," Zeke joked as he dropped the guitar case behind my seat.

"I don't think so." I climbed into the Jeep and reached for my handbag. "And I'm no Yoko Ono either."

Zeke chuckled as he shut my door. Two Beatles references in one conversation and each of us actually knew what the heck the other one was talking about.

Zeke was right. We are made for each other.

I was digging in my bag, searching for my phone, as he climbed into the driver's seat. "I told Mom I'd check in with her when we finished up here."

Zeke started up the engine, "If she hasn't had any, we can take her some lunch."

I was about to reply what a great idea that was when I turned the phone over in my palm. "Whoa! I have a bunch of voice mails. What's up with that?"

"I hope everyone's okay."

I mouthed *me too* as I punched in my voice mail code and listened for the first message. It was from Kaye. In fact, they all were from Kaye, an identical quintuplet of messages.

"You have got to call me as soon as possible, Sallie. Will is not happy!"

I turned to Zeke. "Good news and bad news. All the messages are from Kaye. But she says to call back as soon as possible because Will is upset about something. I don't get it because he seemed really good when they left yesterday."

The Jeep was idling; we hadn't moved an inch as Zeke had waited to find out if there was an emergency. He turned the engine off. "I know you're worried. Go ahead, call her back now."

I punched Kaye's speed dial number. She answered as if she had been staring at the phone willing it to ring.

"What have you been doing? Solving the national debt?" She screeched into my ear. Zeke grimaced. Even he could hear her.

"Sorry. Yes, Kaye, I was busy. What's wrong?"

"Are you sitting down? Because you will *not* believe what I'm about to tell you."

"Yes, I'm sitting."

"Good. Here it goes." Kaye inhaled sharply. "We. Are. Moving. Dad accepted a job offer at a hospital in Roanoke that he – and I quote –couldn't turn down. He dropped the bomb on us this morning."

It was my turn for screeching. "What? When?"

With my reaction, a wrinkle of curiosity stretched across Zeke's brow.

"We'll be there before school starts. I begged Daddy to buy a house in Franklin County, so that, if he's going to do this to me and Will, at least we can be at the same school as you."

I could hear Kaye's fingernails clacking on her computer

keys – no doubt announcing her upcoming move via social media now that she had broken the news to me. I could picture her with both perfectly manicured hands on the keyboard as she clutched the phone between her ear and shoulder.

"Believe me, Kaye, I know better than anyone that this will be a huge adjustment for you. But the good news is that we'll be together again." Zeke's eyebrows shot up with that comment. "But poor Will. He's a senior this year."

"No kidding. He's livid, although he did say to me that if the two of you were still together, it would be less of a big deal for him."

I looked over at Zeke who still hadn't a clue what Kaye was saying on her end, but he had placed a reassuring hand on my thigh.

"Kaye…"

"I know, I know. True love…blah,blah,blah."

"Kaye!"

"I'm sorry, Sal. I'm really happy for you and Zeke – just still in shock here."

I sighed empathetically, "Been there. Done that."

The call ended with a promise to keep me posted on all new developments. A quick recall of the conversation to Zeke produced a whistle and a "Wow!"

"It's a good thing that Miss Fancypants will be here for you. I'll be a senior too, so, if he'll let me, maybe I can help Will out in some way. I know it will be difficult for him especially."

My heart really ached for Will. Senior year was such a huge deal anyway, but to be torn away from friends you have known for years – some since elementary school, and to be thrust into an unfamiliar environment (especially a high school environment!) would be brutal. Even if you were someone like Will who was handsome, friendly and athletic, it would still be tough. I hoped he would be open to a friendship with Zeke and not stay focused on what had happened between the two of us – I guess the three of us, really, if I was technical about the whole situation.

Breaking into my reverie, Zeke reminded me to call my mom and ask her about lunch. But she had already picked up a sandwich from Edible Vibe, the great little cafe near the store whose offerings we had become addicted to last week. So Zeke and I decided on an afternoon at the lake house.

Being alone with Zeke was a rest stop for my soul which was weary from bad ghosts, bad dreams, and a bad breakup with someone whom I was never technically dating. We grabbed hot dogs, chips and sodas from a convenience store on the way down and ate them on the dock. Because it was an unplanned visit, we didn't have swimming suits – though with the big yellow sun shining down on us, it was the perfect day for lounging at the lake. Zeke teasingly suggested skinny dipping which was both a terribly exciting and terrifying thought for me. I knew he was kidding, so I didn't waste any brain cells worrying over the possibility of me seeing him or him seeing me naked, however tempting it might be. Zeke talked me into harmonizing on a few more songs with him. I was much less nervous this time; it helped that we weren't surrounded by an audience – except for the leafy trees whose long branches clapped with the breeze blowing off the lake water.

We were sitting fact-to-face, our crossed legs touching at the knees when Zeke dropped his guitar, jumped up and started stomping around in what could have been a Cherokee rain dance.

"What's the matter, you don't like the weather?" Zeke either couldn't hear me or didn't get my attempt at humor, and kept jumping up and down. I clambered up from my seated position and spoke louder this time. "Why are hopping around like you've got ants in your pants?"

"Bee. Down my shirt. I *hate* bees!"

I stifled a giggle at the sight of him dancing around, swatting at his back because he was afraid of a bee.

"Ow!" Zeke yelped.

"Did it sting you?"

He had stopped the crazy foot moves and was rubbing the back of his left shoulder. "Yeah. Dang, that hurts."

That's what you get for swatting at it, goofball – I decided not to say that out loud, but my heart started racing when I realized there might be a reason Zeke behaved like a little girl around bees.

"You're not allergic are you?"

Zeke shook his head no.

Well, that was a relief. I'd have to drive him to the hospital, and my handling of a stick shift might end up killing him before the allergic reaction did.

"I'm a big wuss; have been ever since I got into a yellow jackets' nest as a kid and had the fire stung out of me. My buddies rib me about my bee phobia all the time."

"Be still, I'll take a look."

I placed my hands on either side of his waist and started pulling up his shirt. I heard his sharp intake of breath as my palms came in contact with his bare abdomen. With trembling fingers, I forced Zeke's arms over his head and by standing on my tiptoes was able to pull the shirt off his body. Zeke stood as still as a statue while I ran my hand across his chest, then moved so that I was standing behind him. My fingers searched the muscles of his back until I found a red welt where the bee had stung him.

"It's not that bad," I assured him as I rubbed the spot with my thumb and placed a light kiss there. "All better now."

Zeke spun around, crushed me to his chest, locked his lips on mine. Heat surged from the tips of my toes to the top of my head. I wound my arms around his neck and kissed him back with a new freedom that had emerged since what I felt for him was no longer a secret to my friends, and my guilty conscience had been absolved.

I felt one of Zeke's hands brush my hair, then he sighed, placed a finger under my chin and tilted my eyes toward his. "What brought that on?" He was smiling.

"I love you. And, well – you're sort of irresistible."

"Oh, *I'm* irresistible?" Zeke's eyes sparkled. "I love you too, Sallie." His lips moved tenderly against my hair as he whispered the words. He started singing my song as we slow danced, swaying back and forth in the warm summer breeze that blew off the lake and tickled my hair.

The sound of a doorbell ringing in Zeke's pants pocket interrupted the mood. Holding onto me with one arm, he retrieved his phone and then frowned. "It's a text from Adrienne. She's in some kind of trouble and needs my help."

Zeke let go of me and began punching the keys in reply.

My body temperature seemed to drop sixty degrees as fury stronger than a winter storm swirled inside me, it felt as if razor-sharp pellets of ice were jabbing into my heart. Once again, the intensity of this jealousy astonished me. How dare Adrienne interrupt my time with Zeke!

"Are you going?" It was practically a growl.

Zeke's eyes were apologetic. "I have to go, Sallie. It's the right thing to do."

"So you're going to choose Adrienne over me?" The question spewed out of my mouth with a poisonous plume.

What was it that enraged me the most? The fact there was a past between the two of them which seemed to continually affect my present? Or was it that Zeke was so eager to drop me to rush off and rescue poor Adrienne in distress.

He reached out and tried to grab my hands, but I wouldn't let him, gripping them firmly to my sides. Zeke settled for holding my shoulders.

"No, I'm not choosing her over you. You can come with me if you want to."

"She hates me, Zeke, because you're with me, and you know it!"

Sympathy surfaced in Zeke's eyes. "That's not true, Sallie. Adrienne has some issues, but you're right. It might be better if you don't come."

So now he was taking up for her. I was beyond discussing this topic any further at the moment. Anger had hindered my ability to hold a rational conversation. I was even past crying. I needed time to think before I said something that I would regret.

I turned away from him and stormed off the dock, shouting words over my shoulder. "Just take me back to my house, Zeke."

Chapter Thirteen
Already Gone

The ride was long from the lake to my house.
Quietly endured.
No music to soften the silence between us.
The roof was open; allowing the wind to whisper in my ear –
chiding me for my foolish behavior.
Forget it.
You're being silly.
He loves you.
You love him.
Nothing can change that.
The words whirled and twirled a flourish of tendrils through my
mind.
Occasionally I would lay surreptitious eyes on Zeke; his face like a
stone – there was no attempt to interrupt my thoughts.
His one endeavor came as we pulled into the drive.
A hand reaching for mine; a question asked in a low voice.
May I call you later?
I was already gone.

Chapter Fourtee
Breakdown

The slap-slap sound of my flip-flops echoed against the tile floor. It was quieter here than a funeral home, the clamor from my footsteps was embarrassingly loud. The receptionist greeted me with a smile. She wasn't Chandra. This lady was closer to my mom's age and slender with stylish short brown hair. I was somewhat relieved – surely Chandra would have asked me about Zeke.

I wouldn't have much time to spend with Letitia. I promised Mom that I would be at the store by ten o'clock, it was already nine-thirty; but I could always come back to the nursing home later and visit for longer.

The receptionist peered over her dark rectangular glasses. "Hello, may I help you?"

"Yes. I'm Sallie Songer. I'm here to visit Mrs. Letitia Wray."

She removed her glasses, narrowing her eyes at me. "Letitia Wray? Are you sure?"

Her reaction startled me. I had been here yesterday and was positive Letitia had said her married name was Wray.

"Yes, I'm sure. Mrs. Letitia *Holley* Wray."

The receptionist set down the pencil she had been using to work the half-finished crossword puzzle that lay across the desk. "I'm sorry to be the bearer of bad news, but Mrs. Wray died several months ago."

I clutched the edge of the desk for support. "What? But I saw her here ..." I let my voice trail off. No need to alarm this poor lady. There were too many medical personnel nearby and I had managed to avoid the psych ward for this long.

"Okay, then. Thank you for your help." I turned to walk away. The sound of my flopping shoes was even more obnoxious as I tried to get out the front door quickly. I could allow myself lose my composure outside.

"Wait a minute," she called after me. "What did you say your name is?"

I reluctantly turned back to face her with tears brimming in my eyes. At least she would be under the impression they were tears of grief, but those *were* there too.

I gulped them all down. "Sallie. Sallie Songer."

"Mrs. Wray did leave a box that none of her family members claimed. Your first name was written across the lid. Do you think it could be you?"

"Was the name spelled S-A-L-L-I-E?"

She stood up and pushed her chair back. "Please, stay right there. I'll go get it and see."

As she left the room, I felt my legs begin to wobble; so I dropped down into the nearest armchair, clutching Letitia's diary to my chest.

This is insane!

My thoughts had become a gushing downspout of question marks. Had I seen other dead people during my lifetime not realizing they weren't alive?

I bent over, holding my head in my hands. I couldn't seem to wrap my mind around what was happening to me. Was this spirit sighting flair of late going to continue for the rest of my life? If so, I really needed to figure out a way to determine who was dead and who was alive because otherwise I'd start second guessing everyone I came into contact with. In fact, I was already coming up with a list of people with whom I should check back.

The receptionist emerged through the swaying double doors carrying what resembled an old fashioned hat box. "Yes, it's written the way you asked."

"Then it must be for me." I felt the need to explain why I felt with some certainty the box was meant for me. "Most of the time you see the name ending with a Y - my great-grandmother and I are the only Sallie's I've ever known to spell it with an IE."

She handed the box over to me. "It's yours then. I'm glad we finally found the owner. We couldn't bear to throw this away. Mrs. Wray was such a sweet little lady; she certainly had some great stories to tell. We've really missed her around here."

I nodded my head. "Thank you so much for your help."

I made it safely to the car before I leaned my head against the steering wheel and burst into tears.

Crying.

Appeared to be the thing for me lately – I did a whole heck of a lot of it last night.

Once Zeke dropped me off, I had gone directly to my room, wrenched off my sundress, ripping one of the thin shoulder straps in my haste, and pulled on my running clothes and shoes. It was late afternoon and still hot, but I didn't care. I needed the sound of my rhythmic footsteps to drown out the erratic beating of my injured heart. I avoided the route that included the Marlow's driveway, opting instead for the path I had carved out my first night of running here.

I had been running for about a mile when the bubble that had been expanding inside my chest exploded, a torrent of tears streamed down my face, blurring my vision and affecting my ability to breathe as my nose became stopped up from the whole gooey mess.

Snorting almost as loud as one of the horses grazing in a nearby pasture, I stumbled off the road and up a small incline, dropping onto the edge of a field. The dry grass prickled the backs of my thighs, so I pulled my knees up to my chest, wrapped my arms around them, buried my head and let the tears flow unheeded. There was no one here that I needed to hide them from.

I don't know how long I sat there. It could have been minutes or hours. My mind was completely lost in its own misery when I felt the soft brush of a hand. The touch was gentle upon my shoulder – almost as if a leaf had drifted in the breeze and delicately landed there; then it was gone before I barely had time to register the sensation. I jerked around – half expecting to see that Zeke had not gone to Adrienne after all and had found me here bawling harder than a bunch of hungry babies in a hospital nursery.

But I was alone.

Stupid imagination.

Stupid me.

Despite my desire to really *not* want to see Zeke at the moment, I was disappointed. With the back of my hands, I wiped my wet cheeks and stood up to begin my slow journey back home.

Dad was surprised to see me when I trudged into the kitchen, apologizing for only having made sandwiches for him and Samantha.

"Mom must be working late again," I said as I grabbed a glass to fill with water.

"Yep, she's working on something alright." Dad replied as he hopped up from the table and headed toward the fridge. "Let me fix you something to eat."

I gulped some water. "No thanks. I'm not hungry. I think I'll hang out in my room for a while."

Samantha, who had previously been absorbed in her latest

Nancy Drew, peered at me from over the edge of the hardback cover titled *The Hidden Staircase*. "I thought you were with Zeke."

"I was earlier today." I attempted to keep my voice even.

Her eyes narrowed skeptically; then she shrugged her shoulders. "Whatever."

Samantha resumed her position of book worm. I wasn't sure if she was being nosy, perceptive or playing detective. Either way, I was out of the kitchen and up the stairs before Samantha could be any more of any one of them.

Without even kicking off my shoes, I lay across my bed and stared up at the ceiling; its stark white plaster was painted in a stucco pattern with sharp peaks and deep valleys that mimicked the day I had experienced. Singing with Zeke, meeting Letitia, and hearing Kaye's news – those were all major peaks. Having Zeke choose Adrienne over me was a major low - mostly because of my ridiculous reaction. He was simply being a nice guy. I blew it all out of proportion.

What must he think of my being such a big, jealous monster? But regardless of how hard I tried, I couldn't shake the *Psycho* knife attack against my heart each time I allowed myself even a miniscule moment of considering what Zeke's connection to Adrienne might be. Unfortunately, in some ways, I guess I'm not as mature or grown up as I have prided myself to be. My humility brought on a fresh set of stinging tears.

Rolling onto my stomach, I searched the room for something, *anything* that could change my focus. My eyes stopped on the photo of Kaye, Will and me sitting on my nightstand. The fissure was still open between my face and Will's. I had never replaced that cracked frame. The drawer of the stand was slightly ajar; I must not have shut it completely when I had shown Letitia's diary to Kaye.

The diary.

I was going to give it back to Letitia tomorrow but hadn't thumbed through the book in days. Would it be a bad thing to peruse a passage or two now since I had actually met her, and she was no longer only an old photo and a young girl's words written on a page? She hadn't appeared bothered by it this morning. Maybe if I read a bit more I could somehow link the whole ghost-diary connection before I returned it to Letitia and lost the opportunity. Plus, I could confess to her tomorrow that I had looked through her diary a bit more tonight.

I propped myself up with pillows and turned to the entry

after the last one I had read.

June 16

There hasn't been much to write about lately. It's been raining here, and I've been cooped up like a chicken for over a week. It was sunny today, so I asked Mama if I could go for a walk. She agreed - probably to get me out of her hair more than anything since she was busy cooking and putting up a mess of greens we pulled from the garden this morning. Mama tells me sometimes I'm more of a hindrance than a help to her in the kitchen.

With Daddy away from the house and Mama busy in the kitchen, I decided to try my luck and search for more clues, provided that all this rain had not washed away anything I had missed the last time I was there. But I didn't even make it to the tree line before I saw the same woman standing in the cemetery that I had seen there before. She noticed me before I could sneak around her and seemed so sad I felt that I had to say something. I waved a timid hello as I moved closer. She responded the same. I noticed that she wasn't really a woman, but a girl who couldn't be too much older than me. She was wearing a green cotton dress with her hair tucked beneath a wide brimmed floppy hat and her eyes were covered by dark glasses.

I read the headstone of the grave she was visiting. I felt as if someone had socked me in the chest. It was Beauregard Jones, my friend Mary's older brother. The girl must have heard me gasp because she asked me if I knew this man. I told her yes and how.

Then she turned to me and asked if I'd do her a favor. Without even knowing what that favor would be, I responded that I would. From out of a pocket in her dress, she drew a crumpled envelope and handed it to me. She pulled off her hat. Long hair fell down around her shoulders, and she slipped the glasses off her face.

"Don't ever read this," She told me with teary eyes, "but keep it in a safe place. Promise me that one day you'll give it to someone in Beau's family."

I agreed to do it. She thanked me and, without even telling me her name, tucked her hair back under the hat, slid the dark glasses back up her nose, and walked away from the cemetery.

I rushed back home, placed the letter in the back of this diary, and wondered if the pretty girl knew that the remaining members of Beau's family had left town yesterday.

I sat up faster than a rocket lifting off for outer space. I flipped to the back of the diary, but nothing was there. I shook it upside down a little harsher than I probably should have hoping the envelope holding the letter would fall out.

Still nothing.

Maybe it was stuck somewhere, so I thumbed through the rest of the pages.

Again…nothing.

Letitia must have found someone in Beau's family after all. I guess that was a good thing.

A rap on my bedroom door broke my concentration. I shoved the diary up under a pillow before I answered, "Come in!"

Both of my parents strolled through the door with weird grins on their faces. Right away I was leery of what might be about to happen, seriously hoping it was not one of those you need to save yourself for marriage kinds of conversations. That would be so embarrassing with one, let alone both of them, in the room.

"Umm. What's up with you two?"

Dad was the first to respond. "Well, we know your birthday isn't until Saturday."

"But we have an early present for you." Mom clapped her hands as she hopped into the air, unable to hide her enthusiasm any longer - not that she was doing a good job of it before. "And it's a surprise! So we need you to wrap this scarf around your eyes, and we'll help you down the stairs."

It couldn't possibly be what I was thinking….in Springfield they'd insisted there was no money in the budget for that. So, there was no need to allow myself to get overly excited. Whatever it might be though, I was definitely game for this little surprise of theirs.

I leapt off the bed and turned my back to my mother so she could put the blinders over my eyes. With each one holding an elbow, my parents guided me down the stairs to what I thought could possibly be out the front door. I felt Mom's hands fumbling with the knot she had tied at the back of my head.

"Darn it. I'm so bad at this," I heard her grumble. "Kevin." And then it was my dad's fingers poking and prodding in my hair.

"Ouch!" I complained. "I appreciate the gift and suspense, but can you go easier on the head?"

"Sorry, honey," Dad apologized as the scarf floated away

from my face.

I opened my eyes, and there it was.

Parked in the driveway with a big white bow on the hood and my grandparents standing by the driver's side door was a Volkswagen Beetle that could have been an enormous red M&M perched on four wheels.

"Happy Birthday, Sallie Beth," Mom and Dad exclaimed in unison.

My reaction sequence occurred in this exact order: I squealed, jumped up and down, burst into tears, and grabbed each of my parents in a hug before I raced toward the best seventeenth birthday present imaginable.

This was definitely another peak in my roller coaster of a day.

I was already in love before I even got behind the wheel. And after giving my grandparents a ride back home, I couldn't imagine a mother having more love for her newborn baby than I did for my shiny new car.

So here I was the very next morning sitting in the driver's seat of my surprise gift, head bent over the steering wheel sobbing tears of sorrow over another gift I didn't ask for and was much less excited about receiving.

How had I become the ghost girl?

Was it something in my genetic makeup? Grandma Ellen sure did have fun sharing ghost stories, but I don't recall her ever saying that she had actually been granted ghost sighting status herself.

Or is it that something is seriously wrong with me? Like a mental problem, or a chemical imbalance in my brain. Did Mom drop me on my head when I was a baby?

But then there was Zeke who seemed sane enough to me and had seen an apparition for as long as he could remember.

Only one, though.

He hadn't mentioned any others.

Time was ticking away as I pondered. I needed to get to the shop. Mom would certainly expect me to make a good effort to be on time since I had a car of my own now. She hadn't found sharing one with me to be working out very well. And being that Grandpa Jesse has a friend who owns a used car lot and gave them a sweet deal on this red hot little number, it was easy for them to purchase it together as a seriously cool birthday gift for me.

I had to pay for the gas though. So off to work I must go.

After laying Letitia's diary and box in the passenger's seat, I pulled down the sun visor and glanced in the mirror; relieved that I had brought a makeup bag with me. I touched up the mascara, powdered my nose, and reapplied some lip gloss. I shifted the car into drive (thank goodness it was an automatic) and headed off to the shop which was less than ten minutes down the road.

As I watched the nursing home fade away in my rear view mirror, a question occurred to me.

How did Letitia know who *I* was when I saw her yesterday?

I had never told her my name.

The thought sat in a corner of my mind as I wound my way through the downtown Rocky Mount streets. I passed the music studio and my brain shifted direction so fast it was like I had developed acute ADD when I saw Zeke's Jeep sitting in the parking lot.

My heart tumbled – he was *so* close, yet I had pushed him what might as well be a million miles away.

I wondered what had happened with Adrienne. I was up most of the night thinking about it. That, plus the excitement of the birthday gift, had created a serious bout of insomnia.

I slid into the lot behind our building. There was a good chance that if he happened to be watching out the window he'd see me. But Zeke didn't know about this car and wouldn't be on the lookout for it. I hopped out and ran around the building.

The doorbell jingle-jangled as I walked into our store; it was empty except for Mom who was standing at the counter sipping from a mug of what was probably hot tea and munching on a scone.

She shuffled some papers as I walked in. "Hey, baby! I got you a muffin and some orange juice from the coffee shop."

"Thanks, Mom!" I noticed that without meaning to do so we had dressed similar today in khaki skirts and light blue shirts. I ran my hand over my outfit. "Check it out, we're almost twins."

"Great minds, right?"

I sat on the stool next to the counter and grabbed my muffin. I picked some crumbly pieces off the top and ate them first - those were my favorite. The muffin was chock full of blueberries and tasty.

"So," Mom began once she noticed my mouth was conveniently full of muffin top, "Zeke stopped by here a little while ago. I got the impression that you two might have had an argument yesterday. He's pretty upset."

"Did he give you any details?" I asked innocently after sipping from my juice.

"No, he said to tell you that he was wrong and that you were right."

"Okay."

My mom was surprised. "Just...okay?"

I shrugged my shoulders. "Yeah, that about sums it up."

"Don't you want to run around the corner and talk to him?"

That was so typical of my mom, trying to run interference for me.

I pointed to the antique clock hanging on the wall behind her head. "No, maybe I will later. You told me to be here by ten o'clock, it is now officially five after."

Mom narrowed her eyes and surveyed the empty store. "I think I can manage for a few minutes without you."

I realized I was going to need to change the subject and soon. "Hey, guess what! In all the excitement last night, I forgot to tell you that the Landry's are moving here too."

That did it.

Mom was all ears.

Chapter Fifteen
Edge of Seventeen

By one o'clock in the afternoon, we'd had all of two customers: a retired couple following The Crooked Road with an Airstream trailer and a tiny, yippy dog that the woman carried around in a picnic basket as if he was Toto from *The Wizard of Oz*.

It took them some major effort to maneuver a parallel park position which occupied three of the few spots available in front of the building. They were friendly and asked a lot of questions but didn't buy a single thing. I sent them to the music studio, hoping they'd ask Mr. Nice Guy Zeke Marlow a million and one questions; sort of my silly act of revenge. My tactic must have worked because I had seen them pull away in their giant tin can only a few minutes ago.

The store was in pristine condition. I had dusted, swept, shined, rearranged and was now seriously wishing I had thought to bring something to read. I needed a break and had gathered enough courage to see if Zeke was still at the studio. I found myself wanting to talk to him about Letitia almost as much as I was dying to find out exactly what had happened last night.

Plus, I missed him like crazy and wanted things to be back to normal – whatever normal happened to be around here.

I walked back to Mom's office and poked my head in the door. Red reading glasses were perched on the end of her nose, her hair was pulled up in a knot held together with a pencil and she was concentrating on some computerized inventory program.

"Mom, do you mind if I go out for a little while?"

Without even moving her gaze from the screen she replied, "Are you going to see Zeke?"

"Maybe."

"Good. But remember if you can't say something nice…"

"Don't say anything at all. Blah, blah, blah. Whatever."

As I turned to walk out the door, she spun around in her chair and playfully swatted me on my behind.

"Be nice."

"I'll try," I called back, making my way to the front door.

Heat smacked me right in the face as I stepped outside. It was one heck of a hot day, the kind where you could fry an egg on the pavement. Waves of heat were pulsating off the tar on

Franklin Street. As I rounded the corner, I could see the Jeep sitting outside and heard music escaping from the studio. It was a fast tune – bluegrass – I recognized the song, Grandpa Jesse played the cassette on a regular basis.

I straightened my skirt and took a deep breath before I opened the door. Parked on chairs in a corner were Zeke, Cash, and an older man I didn't recognize, but who could only be Cash's dad. He was lanky like Cash with a long thin nose, a full beard, and hair that made me think of white and brown sugar mixed up together. Zeke was picking the banjo, Cash was sawing on the fiddle, and his dad was strumming a guitar.

They were so consumed by their jam session that no one even realized I was there. I watched Zeke with his head bent over the banjo, foot tapping on the floor. He was in heaven. There was no other way to describe the pure elation that shone on his face. They wound up the song with laughter; Zeke's fingers were flying so swiftly across the banjo strings that the other two clapped and hooted in amazement.

It was then that they noticed me.

Cash was the first to jump up, "Hey, Sallie! How long have you been standing there?"

"Long enough to enjoy a little *Foggy Mountain Breakdown*."

Zeke shot a boastful eye at the two other guys. "I told you she's a know it all."

Nodding my head in Zeke's direction, I spoke directly to Cash and his dad.

"Ignore him much?"

They answered together, "Oh, very much."

Zeke sat back in the chair, crossed his arms, and gave me one of his broad, toothy grins.

Doggone him.

It made me break out in a goofy grin too.

"Now, don't you have a smile that could light up this whole town?" Cash's dad loped toward me with an outstretched arm and a voice coarse from a lifetime of puffing on cigarettes and downing pots of hot coffee, "Hi there, Sallie. I'm Cyrus Palmer, but most folks around here call me Cy, including my son."

I shook his hand; the fingers were lined with calluses from his many years of playing strings. An aromatic mix of tobacco and peppermint floated on the air around him.

Zeke strolled up behind him. "You better watch out, Sallie. Cy is one smooth talker."

Cash was putting up some instruments on a shelf but called over his shoulder. "Yep, he's working on wife number four, and they get younger each time. My next step mama will probably be a grade under me."

Cy shook a teasing finger at Cash. "I won't be taking no lip from you boy. I may have been married three times, but I've practically raised you on my own."

Cash walked over and good-naturedly punched his dad on the arm. "We've lived the ultimate country music song, haven't we, Cy? The wives ran off, the truck broke down, and the dog has done died." He emphasized his normal southern tone with even more of a countrified flair.

Cy let out a sound that was more of a cough than the chuckle that it was. "Laugh all you want to, but I *am* gonna write a song about my life one day; you boys can make a hit out of it for me. I'll be rich, you'll be famous." He playfully slapped Cash on the back. "Getting girls won't be a problem for you anymore, son." He shot a thumb in Zeke's direction. "Of course, this one here's never had an issue with that."

Cy!" Zeke and Cash both expressed their particular displeasure with those last comments at the same time.

Patting my hand, the jovial man offered his apology. "Oh, excuse *me*, Miss Sallie."

Zeke rolled his eyes and led me gently by the arm. "Let's get out of here."

I waved goodbye to both Cy and Cash as Zeke guided me out the front door. I regretted leaving my shades back at the store and raised a hand to shield my eyes from the blinding sun. Zeke reached into the pocket of his short sleeved buttoned-down shirt, pulled out his sunglasses, and offered them to me.

"Thanks." I ducked my head as I slid them on, embarrassed to raise my face directly to his.

Shoving his hands down in the pockets of his cargo shorts, Zeke asked where I wanted to go. "I'm not giving any lessons until three o'clock."

Having thought earlier today about the best place to have our discussion, I answered him quickly, "How about the cafe? I could use a Coke, and I'm kind of hungry."

Hopefully, it wouldn't be too busy at this time of the afternoon; plus it would be indoors, which would be a must on a day like today that had to be hitting close to the one hundred degrees mark.

Zeke agreed. Our strides were side-by-side; keeping pace

with each other but not speaking any words on our short walk. We had successfully missed the lunch crowd, and the restaurant was blissfully cool. The waitress greeted Zeke familiarly and, at his request, placed us at a corner table near the window. We ordered Cokes and some gourmet grilled cheese sandwiches; then with the menus gone we had to finally face each other.

I crossed my arms on the table, turned my head toward the window, and chewed on my lip. Apparently, I had given more thought about where to go to talk then I did about what I had to say.

"Did your mom tell you I stopped by?" Zeke's voice was soft.

Without even turning my head in his direction, I gave a short answer, "Yes."

"I really am sorry, Sallie."

"So, what was the big emergency?" I was careful to keep my tone neutral as I faced Zeke, not wanting him to be under the impression that I was planning some sort of attack.

Our drinks arrived, Zeke waited until the waitress left before he responded.

"She needed a ride."

I scoffed a reply. "Didn't that happen another time recently?"

"Yeah, but the circumstances were a bit different."

Zeke sipped on his soda before he continued, "This time Adrienne needed a ride from her house down to the condo at the lake."

By the furrow in my brow, Zeke could see that answer didn't make much sense to me. "They put up a good appearance in public, but Adrienne's dad is an alcoholic. Her mom goes out of town," he crooked his fingers in quotation marks, "on shopping trips to get away from him. Mrs. Brock acts as if they're both the loves of her life around other people, but really the only person she cares about is herself – Adrienne's just a prop. Yesterday, Adrienne's dad left work early, came home, and tied one on. He got pretty obnoxious – called her a slut like her mom and hid the car keys so she couldn't leave the house. She was scared, desperate to get away from there, so she crawled out of her bedroom window and met me at the end of her driveway. I drove her to the condo, stayed a little while to make sure she was alright. Then I went home and thought the whole night through about how to get things right with you." Zeke laid his hand on mine, "I shouldn't have done it, Sallie, made you feel like I was choosing another girl over you. I could have called Cash; or even my dad, for that matter, because he knows all about that family's situation – he's been their minister for years. But Adrienne's ashamed of the truth about her family, and she trusts me."

Well, that was not what I had expected to hear.

My version went something more along these lines: Adrienne made up some pathetic story to earn Zeke's pity and to wrench him away from me. Zeke drove furiously to her side where she was waiting in a transparent negligee and fuzzy high-heeled slippers. After seducing him, she convinced Zeke that I was boring, bland, and boob challenged; so he was here today to break it to me gently and send me crying back to my mama.

So, maybe that's not exactly how I really expected it to play out...well, the Zeke dumping me part anyway. But I seriously thought that Adrienne would do everything in her incredible amount of physical prowess to try to make that happen (sexy lingerie included). Yet I found it was me that felt sorry for the girl that had everything on the outside but was miserable on the inside. And I was reminded that, although I'm not entirely blessed with the physical attributes of the stunning Adrienne, my life was beautiful in the areas where it really mattered: family, friends and having people around who really love me. Including the amazing guy sitting across from me whom I now adored all the more for what he had done to help Adrienne yesterday.

"No, you did the right thing." I intertwined my fingers with his, "She really did need you. I'm the one who should apologize to you for behaving like a spoiled brat - which I can explain if you'll let me."

Raising our joined fingers to his lips, Zeke placed a soft kiss on the back of my hand. "I wish that you would."

My words flew out in an unrehearsed rush. "All of this," I waved my free hand between the two of us, "is new to me - falling in love with you so quickly...well, falling in love at all, really - and the emotional intensity, like jealousy, that has come with it." I glanced back out the window again. "I've heard it described this way in stories and songs, but it's been quite overwhelming for me to experience firsthand." I returned my eyes to Zeke's. "I think the major contributor to my unreasonable performance yesterday is this impression I get that there's more to your friendship with Adrienne than you've told me about...that unknown factor is pretty scary to me."

Zeke reared back in his seat and raised his palms in the air. "I haven't intentionally been secretive, so let's get it all out in the open. What do you want to know? I don't want you to be scared anymore."

What didn't I want to know? I guess I could start with the question that had plagued me the most. "Have the two of you ever dated?"

He must have been expecting that one because Zeke didn't appear fazed by the words as they emerged from my mouth. "I guess you could call it that. We went out a few times last year. But I've never called her my girlfriend."

That went well - on to then next one.

"Have you kissed her?"

"Yes."

Crap. She was probably a really good kisser.

It seemed that Zeke was intent on being honest, so I asked the scariest question of all - the one where you're really not sure if you want to know the answer but can't keep yourself from asking it anyway.

"Have you done more than kiss her?"

Zeke's eyes met mine firmly. "Absolutely not."

I felt relieved enough to take a bite of my sandwich that had been sitting on the table untouched for the last couple of minutes. Zeke did the same.

I'm tasted delicious, but I couldn't properly enjoy anything until I was finished with my interrogation.

"One more question."

"Okay, shoot."

"Will said that Adrienne told him she had messed everything up with you. What did she mean by that?"

This question did surprise Zeke. He toyed with the chips on his plate and chewed on his lower lip while he thought about the answer. "She tried to make the relationship more than what it was. When I didn't show the same sort of interest for her that Adrienne did for me, she started acting possessive - texting all day, leaving voice mails, and being a total... well you know...to any girl who came within a ten foot radius of me. After I sat her down and explained that I would only ever see her as a friend, she seemed to cool it a little; but her previous behavior made me uncomfortable even attempting to be friends with her anymore. I was afraid she'd get the wrong idea if I showed her any kind of attention, so I tried to maintain some distance." Zeke paused for a moment and fiddled with his chips again. "The thought crossed my mind yesterday before I went to help her – what will Adrienne read into this if I come? But I've seen Mr. Brock when he's drunk. I know how he can be." Zeke shook his head as if recalling a particular occasion. "I talked to Adrienne about you last night. She knows how I feel about you and swears not to interfere with that anymore."

My shoulders relaxed. Zeke noticed, "Still scared?"

"No."

That was an honest answer, too.

"Just so you know," Zeke squeezed my hand, "I'm no stranger to jealousy, either. When I came back from West Virginia and saw Will with his mouth on yours, I about lost all the good manners my mama has taught me." He gave me a half-grin, "I wasn't sure if I'd be able to calm myself down, so I prayed to the Good Lord to keep an arm around my shoulder and a hand over my fist."

"I've never taken you for the fighting kind."

Zeke leaned forward, his eyes serious. "I'm not." He settled back into his chair. "So what were you doing at the nursing home this morning?" Zeke popped a potato chip into his mouth.

For a second, I wondered how he knew about that and then realized Mom must have told him where I'd gone this morning.

"I meant to tell you about this yesterday, but with the whole Adrienne thing…" My voice trailed off.

"So, tell me now."

I explained to Zeke about meeting Letitia yesterday and my promise to return her diary today.

"Wow, Sallie!" He exclaimed as I finished the story. "What are the chances of something like that happening?"

"That's nothing, Zeke. Wait until you hear the rest of the story."

The expression on his face changed from simple interest to complete astonishment as I relayed the events from this morning.

"That's three ghosts I've seen in a matter of days, Zeke. And this one – this one actually talked to me, and she looked real, and she sounded normal." My voice started to quiver, "She even touched me!"

Zeke shuffled his chair next to mine and wrapped an arm around my shoulders. "Hey, darlin'," he soothed, "it'll be alright."

"But do you think it's normal to be in contact with so many dead people? How many of them have you seen? You've only mentioned the one to me."

Zeke patted my back. "I don't know, Sallie, maybe you're special. I don't know for certain that I've only seen that one guy. Who knows? I may have seen something else and, like you, didn't realize it at the time. If it helps any, I did see you sitting with that lady yesterday."

That did help, but it also helped to have him next to me. Zeke's very presence had a calming effect.

"Did you go through the box she left you?"

I tucked strand of hair behind my ear. "No. I didn't have time. I told Mom I'd be at the shop by ten o'clock."

"In your new car?" It was an obvious attempt by Zeke to change the subject. It worked. He got a smile out of me.

Then his sly look made me suddenly suspicious.

My eyes narrowed. "Did you know about it before I did?"

Zeke's face broke out in a wild grin. "Yep. You have no idea how hard it was for me not to let that slip yesterday. I was *supposed* to keep you out long enough for them to get the car to the house before you got home - which is another reason I stopped by your shop this morning. I needed to apologize to your mom for screwing up the one responsibility I was given for your birthday surprise. It's a good thing for me that the Songer women are doling out forgiveness today. "

He planted a kiss on the top of my head. "Let's finish up here so you can show me the new ride."

This time our journey down the sidewalk was hand-in-hand. I took Zeke for a spin around the block – he was appropriately complimentary of the vehicle, though to fit his frame comfortably he did have to scoot the front seat so that it practically touched the back one.

After that, Zeke dropped me off at the store and waved a hello to my very happy mother through the window. "I've got a late night of teaching lessons. I'll call you when I'm done."

"That sounds great to me."

I received a chaste peck on the cheek – Mom was watching after all - and Zeke strolled away, blowing me a kiss before he turned the corner and was out of sight.

Most of my time was spent with an elbow and chin propped up on the countertop – eyes glazed over from staring out the window, but a few customers breezed through as the afternoon wore on.

An affable, gray-bearded trucker with the name Larry embroidered in white letters across the pocket of his blue work shirt stopped in to hunt for a birthday present for a daughter who loves antiques. I helped him pick out a bracelet with a mother-of-pearl inlay and offered to gift wrap it for him when he told me his wife had died from cancer and that he wasn't very good at doing that sort of thing himself. After telling me all about his nine grandchildren and thanking me for the wrapping job, Larry wished us good luck with the store as he lumbered out the door. He had been so pleasant that I found myself hoping Larry would be back another time.

We locked up at six o'clock; it was still hot as blue blazes outside. A piece of gum that had been dropped on the pavement outside our door had oozed into a pink amoeba-like shape from the heat. As I neared my car, I watched a little tow headed boy carrying a guitar case being led by his mother into the music studio. I wondered if he was one of Zeke's students.

I bet Zeke is great with kids.

I shoved that thought right out the other side of my brain.

No need to be thinking about what Zeke is like with kids when I'm sitting on the edge of seventeen.

Dad and Samantha were walking in the front door when I pulled into the driveway. Mom was not far behind; she had stopped by Kroger for milk, bread and ice cream - staples in our house. She'd put pork chops with gravy in the crock pot that morning, I helped her finish up dinner with some rice and jarred veggies from the grandparents' garden.

We chatted about our day around the supper table. I had to edit my part about the nursing home visit, but Samantha did most of the talking anyway. Mom declared she must be in hog heaven staying with my grandparents during the day because Samantha had plenty of stories to share about the goat, the chickens, and the creatures she'd discovered in the creek. I glanced over at Samantha in the middle of one of her stories, noticing how her cheeks were rosier and that tiny brown freckles had popped out across her nose.

I wasn't the only one who had blossomed in the few weeks we had spent in this place. I could only imagine how Samantha would react if I confessed that ghosts are indeed real, that this house is sort of haunted, and that a real murder mystery had occurred nearby.

By the time we'd finished eating and cleaned up, it was pushing seven-thirty. I went for a run, the heat and humidity left

Moonshine Serenade

my hair and clothes drenched as if I had been dunked in one of those carnival booths. I showered, dried my hair, and donned a tank top and jean shorts; deciding to sit on my bed and rummage through the box Letitia had left while I waited for Zeke to call.

Round and decorated with tiny purple flowers, the box was a size that may have once held a woman's Sunday bonnet. My name was scrolled in blue ink across the top; the script was the same as I had become accustomed to seeing in her diary.

I removed the lid, the aroma of lavender wafted into the room like petals in the wind. Inside was one crumpled envelope. My name was written across it as well, but the handwriting was different.

Cupping the envelope in both hands, I lifted it gently. The corners were yellowed and upturned, and it was creased down the middle where it had been folded in half at one time. I turned it over and ran my finger beneath the seal which hadn't been opened in ages, but came apart easily without any tearing or force. I tenderly tugged the letter out. It was written on ivory parchment.

I unfolded it slowly and laid it on the bed before me. Though addressed to my same name, it was obvious this letter had been written long before my birth.

Dearest Sallie,

My deepest regret is that I'm not there to explain this to you in person, or deeper still, that I am writing this letter at all. Yet given the circumstances that encouraged our flight, it should truly come as no surprise to you. If I had waited to tell you this news after you had awakened from your sweet slumber you would have insisted on coming with me and it is simply not safe for you to be seen with me, my darling. How I wish I had never brought you into this terrible situation! You could have lived a life without secrecy and deceit. I suppose our love was too strong, for you said it yourself the day we were wed: "I'd rather live one day with you than an entire lifetime without."

I had hoped the day would never come when I would need to return from where we fled, but unfortunately, my love, that day is upon us. I wish nothing more than to stay by your side as you sleep so peacefully with our child growing inside you. But we need money to survive, and I haven't been able to come by much here.

It's my fervent hope that I'll return soon to watch you blossom into motherhood and to nurture the child God has given us. But should I not, you must follow these instructions carefully, my dear Sallie, as your life and the life of our child may depend upon it.

Please give me one week, a full seven days upon which to return to you. If this should not occur, take the money I've left for you inside of this envelope and buy yourself a ticket for home. Please do this, Sallie, so that your family can help you raise our child. You will need them.

If I have not returned to you, it will only mean one thing – my death – because my death is the only thing that would keep me away.

You must be careful, dear one. Please tell no one about me. Say your husband left you pregnant and destitute. Tell them that is why you refuse to use my last name as your own. Say whatever you must to protect yourself and our child! You know more than I ever should have confessed to you, and because of me, your life could be in danger.

Be strong my love. Regardless of what happens, I will always be with you, and I will always love you.

Your husband,

Beauregard

Sallie – Flight – Wed – Pregnancy – Return home – Tell no one about me – Beauregard – Letitia.

These words twirled in my brain like a tilt-a-whirl – faster, faster, faster; and when the ride was over, I stumbled out dizzy but delighted from the experience.

There was no doubt in my giddy mind - this was a letter from my great-grandfather to my great-grandmother.

Letitia had been the key all along.

Had she not just mentioned a man named Beauregard in the last diary entry I read? Had she not written about receiving what had to be this exact note from a young woman crying over his grave who could only have been my Great-Grandma Sallie?

Hastily, I reached for the diary. It fell open to the first page I had read last night as if I had placed a bookmark there. Cradled in the crease of the binding was a black and white photo that I had not seen before. The image of three young people in shades of gray gripped me at once – two girls, one boy. Letitia was in the middle - a genuine smile on her face in this picture, to her right was a pretty girl with long, curly black hair, and to Letitia's left was the young man whom I had come to know as Zeke's ghost.A coaxing voice from inside my head urged me to look at the back of the photograph; without hesitation, I flipped

Moonshine Serenade

it over. By Letitia's own hand these words had been scripted:
Me, Mary and Beau
February 1939

Chapter Sixteen
Two Places At Once

Poised like a bullet, I flew down the stairs with car keys in hand. Just before shooting out the front door, I poked my head into the living room to inform my parents that I was headed to Zeke's house. I didn't wait for a reply. I was in too big of a hurry – plus Mom had made it no secret to me how much she approves of the relationship.

There were no cars in front of the Marlow's home as I slid into park. I assumed that because it was Wednesday night his parents must be doing some church related activities. Zeke himself was apparently not home from work yet. It didn't really matter because I wasn't there to see him anyway.

George greeted me with a wagging tail and wobbling tongue. I patted him on the head; he dutifully fell in beside me as I started up the gravel road toward the barn. I had no exact idea what my plan would be once I got there.

Thankfully, there was enough light to guide my way; but with little sunlight to filter through its slatted beams, the interior of the barn proved to be much darker than the outside. George plopped down inside the front doors, laying his head upon his paws.

Maybe I had become less sensitive to the smells of country life because the scent of the barn seemed more muted to me than the last time I was here. Remembering where Zeke had grabbed the flashlight from before, I pulled it from the wall and pointed in the direction of the ladder. I was no less nervous than the last time I climbed those rungs, but this time it was for an entirely different matter.

I had never actually sought out a ghost before.

I climbed the ladder slowly, carefully; I didn't have Zeke behind me this time to prevent my rubbery legs from pitching me backward into the darkness. With only one rung left, I took a calming breath and then launched myself forward into the loft.

Straightening to a standing position, I flashed the light around the hayloft, aiming it like a spotlight into each of its corners.

"Hello," I called out softly, "Anyone here?"

Seeing nothing and receiving no answer, I made my way across the boards to the loft window and, after struggling with the latch, was able to throw the door open. The moon hung in the sky like a pumpkin pie from which someone had served a couple of slices; in a few more days, it would be full. Holding my gaze were wisps of clouds that drifted forlornly across the face of the moon. I couldn't have imagined a truer reflection of my sudden glum mood; apprehension had withered into bitter disappointment and sadness. Maybe my last encounter in this loft had been a one-shot deal, maybe Zeke needed to be with me – maybe this wasn't a special ability at all, as Zeke had remarked, but some sort of curse that I would never be able to control or use to help others.

"Sallie." The name was spoken as a hand flitted across my sunken shoulder.

My spinning heels were rooted to the wooden floor as I faced the man positioned before me - my great-grandfather, Beauregard Jones.

"Sallie, I've been waiting for you for so long." His voice carried the familiar country twang of some of the older folks I had met on the day that I had visited the nursing home. It sounded like pinto beans and cornbread, square dances, apple cider, and back breaking work.

He held out his hand; reaching for me with long fingers that waved in a welcome invitation. "Come here, my sweet Sallie Beth."

Feeling no fear, I ran into his arms; they encircled me with a hold that was not ethereal as I had imagined hugging a ghost would be. I could have been wrapping my arms around any living person.

Beauregard placed my face in his hands and smiled. "Ahh. You are the spitting image of your great-grandmother. And yet, you are so similar to my mother - attuned to the spirit world."

Words wouldn't form in my mouth; I didn't know what to say to this man who had been an enigma to my family for so long. He let go of my face and I backed up, slid down the wall, and sat with a thud on the floor. My great-grandfather gracefully sat down beside me.

"I tried to contact my mother, Jeanette, after my death – to let her know who was responsible and to ask her to protect my sweet, sweet Sallie. But in her grief it was as if she blocked me. When my parents joined my sister in Louisiana, my spirit wasn't able to travel in that way and it wasn't until my mother's death that she was able to visit me in her own spirit form – to hear me tell of my daughter, Ellen. She died just before your own mother was born. How thrilled she would have been to know of a great-granddaughter, and then – *oh my* – you and your darling sister. What a beautiful heritage."

As my great-grandfather talked, I noticed his resemblance to my mom…not so much in his features – because, after all, she is so Irish she's practically a Leprechaun – but in his mannerisms… the way his lips curved in a smile, the soft crinkles around his brown eyes.

"I watched my Sallie until her death – trying to make my presence known to her as a comfort. I held her hand as she passed." Beauregard shook his head, "She was so young. I stayed with Ellen and was witness to both her and Beth's growth into womanhood." He chuckled, "Little Beth, a red-headed spitfire as a child."

"Sounds like Samantha," I interrupted – my brain beginning to function.

My grandfather's eyes scrunched in a smile. "Oh, yes. I was so sad when Beth married and moved away. But then she would visit. And one day, she brought you - a squirming bundle of beauty. I heard them call you Sallie Beth and observed with each visit how you blossomed into the very visage of your namesake."

"I've seen her," I started slowly. Beauregard's eyes widened, almost horrified. "But just in pictures," I added quickly.

His face recomposed itself, relief evident. "I'm glad that she's not here, that she really has moved on to a better place; I long to be with her."

"Why are you still here?"

"I'm still here because I want Ellen to know who I am…to know that I did not intentionally abandon her. Sallie was so very good at keeping the secret about *who* she had married. She endured so much for that, and after she died the truth went with her. I kept waiting for one of you," he touched the tip of my nose, "to show the skills of my own mother - someone who could communicate with the nonliving. But no one – no one at all until…"

"Zeke?"

"Yes, Zeke. I've tried to talk to him, but I've never had enough strength to get the words out. I used so much of it to stay close to your grandmother – to know her and protect her; until your family moved back here, and then *you* could see me, and my strength, my abilities doubled. It was as if you and Zeke needed to be near each other for *you* to be able to open your gift; Zeke's had been unwrapped for quite some time."

Some gift; but Zeke's suggestion of a spiritual connection between the two of us did hold a new meaning for me now.

"But Grandfather," It felt odd calling him grandfather considering that in appearance he wasn't much older than Zeke. He sensed my quandary.

"You don't have to address me as grandfather, Sallie. It sounds so formal. Please call me Beau."

"Well, *Beau*. But Zeke and I have been together before – as kids."

Puzzled, Beau shrugged his shoulders. "Something must have happened between then and now that alerted your subconscious. Do you recall any contact with the spirit world before now, before me – *before*..." his voice fumed and his bottom lip quivered, "before that day you saw *him* in the cemetery?" His eyes were full of pain as he searched mine.

I racked my brain trying to think of a time when I may have encountered something otherworldly. No sightings to recall – none of the things Grandma Ellen had ever described in the scary stories that I relished. I did have weird dreams from time-to-time, but Kaye had been able to explain them away with her dream interpretation book.

Wait a minute! Kaye...the Ouija board.

I jerked up my head. "Yes!" I conveyed the story of the day the Ouija board had told me not to go to sleep because it would kill me.

"That vile – I can't call him a man because he's not now nor was he ever much of a man in my opinion."

"What *man*?"

"The *man* you observed in the cemetery, the *man* from whom I've been protecting you, your mother, and your grandmother... the wretched *man* who violated my sister and murdered me here in this barn."

I sucked in my breath sharply. I was both surprised and confused because Letitia had seen Beau murdered in the woods.

"I thought you were killed in the woods behind my house."

Beau gawked at me as if he wondered where in the world I got that idea. "No, I was attacked in the woods, knocked unconscious and then I must have been carted to this place. It's here that I was hanged, my body discovered and declared a suicide."

And then in the quiet of the hayloft as the orange moon rose higher in the inky sky, Beau told me the story of his life.

He had been born to Daniel and Jeanette Jones in 1920. Jeanette Honore was raised in New Orleans on Chartres Street in the lower French Quarter near the Ursuline Convent and the Beauregard House, the former residence of a well-known Confederate General.

"Can you imagine where she took my name from?" Beau said with a smile.

It was a home that she had passed almost every day of her life until she had met and fallen in love with Daniel Jones, a carpenter from Virginia. After a whirlwind romance, he married and whisked Jeanette away to the little town from where he had been brought up in Virginia.

"A place that you know as Boones Mill," Beau added as if to clarify.

Her family was not happy. She had been well educated and was expected to marry above her station, not below it – which was her parents' opinion of Daniel.

Theirs was a simple but sweet life. Beau's sister, Mary, was born two years after him and their mother enhanced the two siblings' school lessons at home: they read the works of Shakespeare, Homer and Dante, they were taught to speak simple French and learned to play classical music on a beat-up piano that had been passed down in Daniel's family.

"Mary and I would perform dramas for our parents. The death scene from Romeo and Juliet was our favorite..." He twisted is lips as if he had sipped something nasty, "though we didn't dare include the kissing part."

Daniel worked when work was available. Jeanette learned to grow a small garden and put up her wares for the winter. When the Great Depression hit in 1929, Daniel found fewer and fewer jobs. Beau did what he could to help the family – dairy farms, apple harvesting; and by the time he had reached his teenage years, he was introduced to a way of life that was more profitable than anything he could have ever imagined: running moonshine.

It didn't take Beau long to pick up the tricks of the trade, even learning the bootleg turn, a driving maneuver where he'd skid the car 180 degrees...though mostly for fun because, by the time he had started hauling, revenuer raids and chases were fewer than they had been during the prohibition years.

But it was still a dangerous enterprise. Beau kept it a secret from his parents who never really questioned where the money came from as long as it kept coming.

"Don't judge them for that," Beau's eyes implored me. "Those were some tough times."

He met Sallie Hodges at a harvest dance. Her strawberry blonde hair and green eyes dazzled him. It was love at first sight for both of them. In her, Beau had found a confidante, someone with whom he could share his secrets – including his real source of wages. She squeezed his hand and vowed her love regardless. Fearing Sallie's family wouldn't allow it, the relationship was kept hidden from everyone they knew; the two met in secret whenever, wherever they could.

But Beau's method of earning a living hit too close to home when his sister was attacked by a man drunk off the stuff that had helped put food on their table – the very man who had convinced Beau to transport the moonshine he made. His name was Theo Wicke.

Enraged, Beau beat Theo almost to death. Mary was sent to Jeanette's family in New Orleans while Beau eloped to Eden, North Carolina with Sallie.

They rented a room in a boarding house and within a month Sallie was pregnant. Jobs were scarce, money tight, and Theo Wicke owed Beau money, a great deal of money – enough for Sallie and Beau to live off for months.

With a child on the way, Beau felt his only option was to confront the man who had assaulted his sister, the man whom he had almost killed, and the man who could put food on his table once again.

Beau mailed a letter to Theo Wicke that gave him instructions for a meeting place, date and time. It was a place where they had exchanged money and sometimes goods – at the large oak tree in the woods behind the cemetery. The dirt road leading there provided an easy access for vehicles and foot traffic, which is how Beau had arrived that day – by bumming rides from Eden to a point where he could walk the remaining few miles.

But Theo had developed his own plan; hiding his truck in an even more desolate and rugged spot. He had planned to kill Beau all along – for the money, for the beating, for pure meanness.

"I never regained consciousness until I woke up dead. I helplessly watched when my distraught father discovered me."

"Wait a minute. Your father found you?"

"Yes. This was our home place. My dad built this barn with his own hands, and the house in which we lived."

"Zeke's house?"

"Yes, though it has lived through a few renovations since that time."

I bowed my head – astounded and struggling to make sense of it all as I stared at the swirling patterns of wood grain beneath my feet.

"My parents moved to New Orleans not long after my burial. They were fortunate that my father had a friend with a little money who had been begging to buy this place for years."

"What happened to your sister, Mary?"

"She survived the delivery, the baby did not. But from what my mother told me in her spirit form, Mary ended up with a good life in Louisiana, married to a man much the same as my father."

Beau's eyes were wistful as he looked out the open loft window. "Mother pleaded with me to come with her before she walked into that glorious radiance." He turned his gaze upon me, "You can't imagine how desperately I wanted to go on that journey with her, but my priority was here with the family I had created…even if it meant I could only watch over them as a ghost."

"Why is Theo Wicke's spirit still around? And harassing me?" I explained to Beau about the occasions when I had been subjected to his grim ghostly encounters.

Beau replied solemnly, "I'm not sure. He tortured me in life, so he's torturing me in death? Maybe he blames me for his downfall – his spirit showed up not long after my murder and has been a threatening presence ever since. Even though he cannot harm me, he has tried to reach my family."

My pocket began to buzz, interrupting our conversation. I pulled my phone out and glanced at the number displayed. It was Zeke.

"Hi, Zeke."

"Hey, there!" Zeke's voice was jovial. "When I saw this giant ladybug parked in my driveway, I knew you must be around here somewhere; but I can't seem to find you."

"I'm in the barn."

"The barn?" Zeke's playful tone switched to one of surprise. "What are you doing there?"

I asked for Beau's permission without uttering one word. He nodded his head in approval.

"I'll explain when you get here."

"Okay," he replied warily. "I'll be there in a few."

While we waited for Zeke to arrive, I told Beau the story about finding Letitia's diary and her role in helping me to figure out our relationship.

Beau's eyes crinkled in a smile. "Letitia was a very good friend to Mary, now she has proven to be a dear friend to me as well. I think she may have fancied me once, but I was so in love with my Sallie it was as if I was blind to any other women from the day I met her. I'm thankful Letitia didn't realize it was me that day in the forest. She might have tried to intercede. I cannot fathom the idea of what might have happened to her if she had done so."

A happy bark alerted us that Zeke was nearby. I walked to the edge of the hayloft and shined the flashlight towards the door. Zeke knelt by George as he entered, patting him on the head.

"Good boy," he praised. "Thanks for taking care of my girl."

"I'm up here," I called down to Zeke.

He gave me a wave. "I can see that."

Zeke was up the ladder in half the time it took me; when he reached out for an embrace, I pointed the flashlight toward Beau.

"Um, we have a guest."

"Hello, Zeke." The words rolled off Beau's tongue as if he'd been waiting for years to say them.

I grabbed Zeke's arm as he stepped backwards.

"I'd like to introduce you to my great-grandfather, Beauregard Jones."

Chapter Seventeen
White Lightning

There was a sizzle in the damp air; it pulsated like an electric wire plunged beneath a stream of water. My hair was beyond manageable, so I clipped it into a messy coil on the back of my head as I walked from the parking lot to the shop.

The official grand opening of our store was planned for tomorrow, but Mom was expecting the place to be in pristine condition by the end of today. Her hope was that after advertising in both local papers and placing a sign on the sidewalk outside the door that we'd get a decent crowd considering that a lot of places would be closed for the Fourth of July holiday.

I was not thrilled to be working tomorrow on the Saturday that also coincided with my seventeenth birthday; but we'd be closing by six o'clock and I'd have the rest of the evening to spend with Zeke - he had promised fireworks, after all.

My bigger concern was today. I had made a decision that was to be followed through with tonight. I had hemmed and hawed over it a bit; but once my mind was made up, it was generally on one track, and I'd be anxious to go through with my choice. I was crossing my fingers that Zeke would agree to do it since his life would be affected as well.

It came to me yesterday. The impetus: having told my entire family about Beau immediately after supper. Thankfully, Mom had already made plans with my grandparents to join us for the evening meal, and a slow day at the shop had given me plenty of opportunity to develop my story. Still uncomfortable with the thought of anyone other than Zeke and Kaye being privy to my strange ability, I wasn't entirely honest with them on how I had fit the puzzle pieces together; but the diary, the letter, and the photo were enough to convince Grandma Ellen. So along with my mother and Samantha, we visited the cemetery that evening before the sun had time to set.

Though Zeke had joined us for supper, he had felt the journey to Beau's gravesite should be a private exchange and left for home as the rest of us set out on our walk. I understood Zeke's reasoning for wanting to give my family some solitude under the circumstances; but as he pulled out of the drive with a couple of beeps from his horn, I realized how much Zeke had already become a part of our family - not just because of how we felt about each other, but also because of the kinship he had formed with my great-grandfather through the years of their silent association.

It was a silence that had come to an end Wednesday night amidst the rafters and wood planks of the barn loft. Zeke had been astonished to learn of our relationship, and was even more so when he heard Beau speak. The explanation of the energy the two of us created together much less of a surprise; *I told you so* had flashed from the corner of his eye.

I yearned for Zeke's presence as the four of us followed the same path Samantha and I had taken our eventful fourth day here. It was the first day I had realized I could see ghosts – the first day I had seen Zeke since we had been children, and the first day of the proverbial rest of my life which up until now I had thought was the goofiest adage I had ever heard – one of those you might see posted on bank signs and church billboards. But it was true that my life had been altered that day in ways that I would never be able to modify; and I had come to realize that everyone reaches that day at some point in their life. Whether you were young, old, or middle-aged, it was bound to happen; your choice was either to find your feet or hobble around.

It may have taken me a little while, but I had found my feet.

Since my last visit, the meadow had sprouted stalks of tiny blue flowers and long stems of stiff, yellowed grass, some bowed over with fuzzy plumes. Honeybees and butterflies buzzed around in the softness of the waning sunlight.

One particular butterfly had captured Samantha's attention during the walk; a chase had ensued as we crested the hill which dropped to the cemetery below. I saw movement amongst the headstones as I had before, but this time there was no sixth-sense of apprehension. I could make out clearly that it was Beau, our protector from that other foreboding spirit who apparently still had some bone to pick - for what reason I had yet to figure out.

Beau beckoned as we walked toward him. So infectious was his greeting I had to brace my arms against my sides to keep from returning the gesture. But I knew that he knew, so I just smiled. That certainly wouldn't raise any eyebrows amongst my company in the way that it would have if I had suddenly began waving wildly at nothing in particular.

I was the third one through the twisted gate. Beau casually

appeared by my side. We watched as Mom and Grandma Ellen maneuvered amongst the stones, commenting as they approached each one and read the names out loud. Samantha was still focused on trying to catch that butterfly; its bright yellow wings flitted gracefully from flower to flower with her following stealthily behind.

"My body is over there," Beau said in a low voice - almost as if he thought the others could hear him. But, no, I was the only ghost freak present and accounted for.

I pointed an arm toward the spot and called out, "I think its right there."

With hands clasped together, the two hesitantly walked over to the marker; wrapping arms around each other's waists, as they stopped to look at the name etched crudely across the simple stone.

Mom read the words in a voice laced with tears, "Beauregard Jones. He died on May 30, 1939." She tilted her head to the side. "Hmm, May 30. That's my wedding day."

A smile broke across Beau's face. "At least we know something good also happened on that date."

My grandmother knelt down before the stone, "So I'm a Jones." She ran her fingers over the name. "I know so little about my father or his family, but at least now I know where to begin."

I felt Beau's light touch upon my elbow, "Will you talk to her for me?"

I nodded my head. Of course I would; it was something they both needed. The difficulty would be doing so without giving away my secret.

"Will you tell her how much I love her? And that it was the pleasure of my short life to know that she was coming into the world. I would have given anything to have spent a lifetime as her father, walk her down the aisle, and be a grandfather to her child."

Kneeling beside my grandmother, I placed an arm across her shoulder and gave her a gentle squeeze. "Grandma, you know Beauregard must have loved you more than life itself to have died to protect you. I'm certain that he would have wanted nothing more than to be with you as you grew up – to give your hand in marriage to Grandpa and hold Mom on the day she was born."

Her lashes were wet as she turned to me. "I'm sure you're right, Sallie Beth, but I guess we'll never know the entire truth."

I centered my face on hers – unwavering. "Oh, I do know the truth. And let me tell you something, Grandma, family meant everything to this man."

She gazed at me for a moment – her glance thoughtful - then I saw understanding in her eyes. Grandma Ellen patted my cheek, "You're right. You are absolutely right."

Beau smiled and then knelt down beside her, placing a hand upon the small of her back. Grandma Ellen's head jerked around as if she was expecting something or someone to be there. "What was that?"

A squeal of delight diverted our attention; it was Samantha. She was facing us with arms outstretched; the yellow butterfly alighted in the palms of her hands.

The blast of cool air that greeted me as I stepped inside the store was refreshing. Mom was standing with her back to me hands on hips critiquing a display of patriotic themed merchandise. In an effort to attract customers tomorrow, she had jokingly suggested that I dress up as the Statue of Liberty and stand out on the sidewalk holding a placard. At least, I thought she was joking. It's hard to tell with her sometimes.

I dropped my bag onto the counter. "It's perfect, Mom."

She shrugged her shoulders and turned to face me. "Well, it's going to have to do because I'm all out of ideas."

I know her better than that, she'd change that display at least twenty more times today.

"Don't worry, Mom; tomorrow's going to be fine." Speaking of fine… "Have you talked with Grandma this morning? How's she doing?"

Mom fiddled with the display some more as she replied. "You know, she's doing incredibly well, considering it all. In fact, I think she's finally found some peace. She says that when she imagines her mother and father being together in heaven, she now can visualize two faces."

What I didn't have the guts or heart to tell either of them was that scenario was exactly NOT the case and that it was a change I planned to make as soon as possible.

Our ribbon-cutting ceremony was scheduled for noon, and it made us feel like a big deal in this small town. The mayor was there, the heads of the Chamber of Commerce and the Retail Merchants Association, a shaggy-bearded photographer from the local newspaper, and a bunch of our fellow store owners –

including the ever charming Cy Palmer to whom the ladies seemed drawn with his gravelly voice and quick wit.

Mom and I would be front and center in the newspaper photo, clutching a pair of industrial-sized scissors aimed at the bright red ribbon that had been strung outside our front door. We hosted a simple reception inside; Grandma Ellen and Grandpa Jesse were our caterers of homemade goodies, coffee, and lemonade. Samantha walked the room with silver platter in hand, serving our guests slices of lemon pound cake while I carted my own laden with jam thumbprint cookies and snicker doodles.

Zeke stopped by for a few minutes before it was his turn to head to work. He followed me around as I delivered sweets to the good townsfolk which elicited a puppy dog remark from Cy. Zeke shrugged him off and shot back with some good natured insult about how to treat women.

Seeing a break in the number of visitors, I left my plate on the nearest table and pulled Zeke to Mom's office. He obviously thought something else was on my mind as he pulled me close and leaned in for a kiss, though I obliged – seriously, who wouldn't – my real agenda was to fill him in on my plan.

The plan to send Beau home.

Into the light, up to heaven – whatever it is generally called.

I had given it a lot of thought last night after the cemetery visit as I lay in my bed waiting for the sandman to show up. A few words of the song the old man had sung in a whisper at the nursing home played like a scratched-up recording over and over in my head.

Why should my heart be lonely,
And long for heaven and home?

Beau missed my great-grandma, Sallie. That was for certain. I saw it in his eyes every time he mentioned her name.

I thought about how it would be for me if I had to live more than fifty years without seeing Zeke's face, hearing his voice, feeling his touch.

It was time Beau knew that he could go home, that we would be fine without him. Grandma Ellen had learned his identity. Beau had the opportunity to talk to her through me. Now he could live his eternal life with the woman he loved.

I wasn't sure how to do it.

If it would even work.

Or if Beau would be willing.

I knew, and without any doubt, that if we were successful,

my namesake would be standing on the other side with arms wide open to greet Beau.

In a way, I kind of wished I could be there to see it.

I sat on the edge of Mom's desk as I explained my decision to Zeke. He agreed to help, suggesting that if we freed Beau's soul, so to speak, the homecoming would happen on its own.

With Zeke on board, we pulled our plan together. I was to leave him a message when we closed up shop. With an evening free of lessons, he'd be able to meet up with me and we'd call out for Beau in the cemetery.

Our logic: that the ground where his bones are interred might give us the best vibe, juju, mojo, or whatever it is that we needed. Zeke and I are both new to this whole spirit releasing ritual, and we didn't have Kaye around to give us any advice – be it from her many books or not. We were mainly crossing our fingers that the location would enhance our endeavor in helping Beau to get to the place he really needs to be.

The second half of the day was less busy in terms of visitors than the first half, which was good per Mom's instructions to make this place shine. She let me go an hour earlier than I expected, so at five o'clock I packed it up and left with a warning from her to be careful because one doozy of a storm was rolling in.

I left Zeke a message to meet me at my house around six o'clock. After changing into jean shorts, tank top, and sneakers, I paced around my bedroom. By seven he still hadn't showed, so I considered three options: Zeke must not have picked up my voice mail yet, was stuck late at work or in route here.

A peek out my window revealed an army of clouds marching through the dark sky. The storm Mom had warned me about was advancing quickly; I needed to get the cemetery sooner rather than later and couldn't wait for Zeke any longer. I sent a text message asking him to meet me there and set in that direction. Just my luck, the clouds rained heavy artillery down on me before I was even half-way across the field.

And though I had remembered a flashlight, I didn't even think to bring an umbrella, so I was drenched by the time I walked through the gate. My tank top clung to me as if I was about to enter a wet t-shirt contest at the beach, albeit I didn't have the right sorts of goods to actually participate in one of those. A few wet tendrils had escaped the hair clip and hung like slick slithering snakes down my neck and across my face. I pushed them aside, calling out for Beau as I made my way to his gravesite, surprised that he didn't immediately appear.

What was the deal with these men tonight? Usually it's the girl who keeps the guys waiting.

I aimed the flashlight around the cemetery; revealing nothing but shadows - it was much darker than it should be this time of day, if I didn't know better I would have thought that a solar eclipse had occurred.

It wasn't long before I saw the distant crackle of a lightning bolt and heard the sonic boom of thunder that followed; I suddenly realized that my love of summer storms was predicated upon the scenario of my being sheltered from and not stuck out in the middle of one. I tried to recall the old wives tale of counting the seconds between lightning seen and thunder heard to determine approximately how far away the storm is before converging right over you. Or was it thunder first, and then lightning? And it seems like I needed to divide the number of seconds by yet another number, or maybe I was confusing the calculation with something else. Whatever the equation may be, it wasn't adding up right now in my distressed brain.

With another bolt of lightning and reverberating thunder close behind, I made the quick decision that maybe tonight wasn't the best night after all.

Beau's spirit had been around for more than seventy years - this could wait a few more days, right?

If I hurried, maybe I could reach the protection of my house before things got too dangerous and catch Zeke before he ventured out into this nasty mess.

In my haste to seek shelter from the storm, I turned too quickly and tripped over a grave marker. I reached out with both my hands to block the fall, but instead of moving forward my head was viciously jerked backward, the clip ripped from my hair which then tumbled down wildly around my face. My shoulder smashed hard against a stone as I landed on my back, sending a jolt of pain down my right arm while my body sank into the sodden grass.

Dazed, I lay silent and still against the dank earth. The storm churned overhead, rivulets of water were streaming down my face.

What happened?

Had I been struck by lightning?

My metal flashlight could have acted as the conduit. But my hair didn't smell fried, and I could still wiggle my fingers and toes so apparently there was no lasting damage. Just in case, I threw the flashlight away from me, now contemplating how I'd manage to find my way back in this odd darkness.

I sat up on my elbows and shook my head, an attempt to get my bearings back before standing up. Just as I felt lucid enough to get on my two feet and make my way back to the house, a raspy cackle sent a shiver of fear down my spine. Dreading what I instinctively knew was there, my eyes flashed upward nevertheless and into the snarling face of Theo Wicke, his bloodshot eyes merely inches from mine, his lips curled back to reveal rotted teeth in a menacing grin. This monster had completely slipped my mind in my quest to arrange Beau's reunion with Great-Grandma Sallie.

"Well, well. Looky who we have here, an' without yer grandpappy 'round ta protect ya." His voice slurred with a thick, backwoods drawl.

Theo leaned his scruffy face closer to mine; the scorching stench of pure alcohol burned my nose. I knew somehow it must be moonshine; he seemed to be bathed in it. With a grimy hand, he reached out to stroke my hair.

"An' so purty."

I wondered if this was how it had been for my great-aunt Mary – this disgusting man - drunk, dirty, and disheveled descending upon her.

I dug my elbows into the ground, scuttling as fast as I could like a crab searching for the safety of its hole in the sand. "Get away from me!" I screeched.

"An' miss out on all this? I been waitin' a long time, honey. Finally, one a Beau Jones' lil' girls is a Seer." He ran a tongue over his grimy lips, "It sure has been fun playing with ya, but tonight I's a gonna make it real fun."

"You...Can't...Hurt...Me..." The words came out in broken gasps.

He threw his head back and laughed. It was a sickening sound. "I can do whateva I want."

Panic set in as he crouched over me, it was hard to think clearly - everything seemed to be happening in fast forward, but with a rush of adrenaline, I realized my only option was to fight back.

As hard as I could.

Raising my knees to my chest and with all the force I could muster, I kicked him in the center of his chest. "You can go to hell!"

His body lurched backwards; I was shocked by my own

strength.

Wasting no time, I jumped up and started to run for it. The grass was wet and slippery; I slipped and slid as I struggled to get a foothold. The heavy, raspy breathing of Theo Wicke was not far behind me.

"You heard the little lady." That voice was music to my ears.

Beau was here at last.

I spun around. The two of them were circling each other like boxers ready to rumble.

"I've warned to you keep away from my family."

Theo snarled. "Warned me? Shoot. What do ya think ya can do about it? I wouldn' be messin' with them iffn' it wasn' fer ya – beatin' me was one thang, but then a stickin' yer nose in where it didn' belong."

"You deserved that beating. You deserved far more than that for violating my sister."

"Well, ya got yer wish didn' ya? Too chick'n to do it yerself, so ya had someone take care a it fer ya."

They had stopped circling now and stood glaring at each other.

"What are you talking about?" Beau sounded genuinely confused.

"Look at ya, tryn' ta act all inn'cent in front of yer granddaughter. I ain't stupid. I knowed it was ya who tipped off that revenuer when ya came back ta town. The crookedes' revenuer 'round these parts." Theo shot a glance over at me, as if I'd have any sympathy for the scoundrel. "It took him a few months ta catch up ta me, but affn' he did, that coward shot me right in the back so he could steal my liquor an' make a killin' off it hisself. He knew no one would ask nary a question or even care 'bout my death. Just before he poured a jar a my own shine over my body an' lit me on fire, he said it was ta bad ya were already dead because he owed ya good. Then he dumped my body in an unmarked grave right over yonder next ta yers. I jes stood nearby, a haint, an' watched while he hooted an' hollered like it was the funniest thing he eva laid eyes on. I vowed right then an' there that I wouldn' rest til ya paid fer what ya did ta me."

Beau's dark eyes were enraged. "It seems to me that I have already paid for it, and my sister, my parents, my wife, and my child.

At that moment a bolt of lightning struck close enough for

me to see it, so hot it burned bright white like the tip of a branding iron - its acrid smell searing the air. I fell to my knees, wrapping trembling arms around my head. My vision was blurred as if my head had been shoved beneath murky lake water. I couldn't discern between the tears and the drops of rain plummeting down my cheeks.

"Sallie, Sallie! Where are you?" Zeke's voice cried out in the darkness.

Like the rain pouring down, relief washed over my body and then in the same second, concern for his wellbeing. I screamed a reply, "Run, Zeke! Go back! It's not safe here!" My voice sounded hysterical, even to me.

The next jolt of lightning rocked the ground like an earthquake, splitting the earth open next to Beau's grave. Bones protruded through the dirt. I watched as a skull rolled out onto the unbroken ground; its mouth lay open like a puppet in a soundless cackle.

I began to scurry on hands and knees toward the sound of Zeke's voice but was jerked up from behind before I'd made it far. The combined stench of alcohol and body odor alerted me that I was not being held by one of my rescuers.

"I wouldn' dream a going ta hell excepn' with yer purty lil face." Theo hissed into my ear.

Holding me tight against his chest, he stepped back into the open unmarked grave; the red mud was dense and began to pull us down like sinking sand. I clawed desperately at the ground, ripping up chunks of grass and dark, wet earth.

"You're not going anywhere with him, Sallie." Zeke had reached the graveside just as my thighs began to submerge. He grabbed me beneath the shoulders, pulling with all his might. Theo's arms tightened about me, I struggled – straining towards Zeke.

Theo snarled at Zeke, "Get on outta here boy, this ain't none a yer bizness."

"Let me go, Zeke." The words came from a place deep within me, a place I didn't realize even existed. "Let me do this. He'll go away, and everyone else will be safe."

Zeke's eyes were pained as he stared into mine.

"Don't you let her go, Zeke," I heard Beau command from behind me, "and when I say so, yank her out with everything that you have."

Zeke's jaw was rigid with tension. "I'm not planning to let Sallie go. Ever." He spat the words in my assailant's face.

In that moment, time seemed to stand still.

I studied Zeke – sopping hair matted to his head, face wrenched, eyes a steely gray that matched the thunderclouds overhead. I'd never see those eyes again, and it was my fault for bringing him to this place. We were up against a foe we couldn't beat. Theo Wicke was stronger than us. Beau knew it. That's why he had stayed earthbound for so long.

But it was all going to end.

Tonight.

With me.

I wondered how it would feel to drown in dirt, suffocating slowly as my nostrils filled with muck; and how Zeke would explain to my family about what had happened to me. I hurt for him, for what he would have to endure, for what he had already endured.

I felt myself slipping further and further, the last few grains gliding through an hourglass.

"NOW!" The word flew loud and furious from Beau's mouth.

Zeke's face contorted as he used every bit of strength within him to drag me from the pit; it was a struggle as Theo's hands grasped for whatever part of me they could – legs, ankles, feet. For a moment, it was a tug-of-war with my body as the rope. Finally, with one massive heave, I was slammed against Zeke's chest. As we tumbled to the ground, I whipped my head around in time to see Beau give Theo a heavy stomp on the head, his arms wavered in the air, and with a loud sucking sound what was left of that evil man was gobbled up by the ground. He shrieked as he went down, a painful wail reminding me of nails across a chalkboard. I covered my ears and buried my face in Zeke's chest.

We lay there tightly wound together, sheltered within our own cocoon. Zeke kissed my hair, my face, and my lips as I lay sobbing up against him. "It's okay, you're okay. I won't ever let you go," he murmured against my ear.

"What in the name of …" Beau exclaimed beside us.

Still wrapped around each other, Zeke and I sat up in unison to see the cause of Beau's strange tone.

It was easy to spot.

The bones that lay scattered around Theo Wicke's grave were rattling; like jumping beans, they hopped across the ground.

I watched open-mouthed as they shot up from the earth and

came together one by one like a three dimensional puzzle to form a skeleton of the former man. It danced a gruesome jig. Arms and legs were dangling as if they were exposed, broken limbs, the skull wobbled grotesquely atop a spindly neck. Then it seemed as if the skeleton took a bow – tipping an invisible hat in our direction before the bones collapsed into a heap and burst into flames. The blaze shot into the air burning brightly like a bonfire, and then, as quickly as it had ignited, the fire burnt out leaving a pile of ashes that were promptly pummeled into the earth by the downpour.

With the show over, Zeke helped me to my feet and I rushed to embrace Beau. The first words from his mouth were an apology of which I was having none of and I told him so.

"But if it were not for me..." He began.

I knew what he was going to say – if not for me none of this would have happened. That was probably true, but if not for him a lot more wouldn't have happened either.

"If it were not for you, Beau, I wouldn't exist – neither would my sister, or my mom or my grandmother." It seemed to me that Beau had spent the last few months of his life and the many years of this spiritual non-life in a quest for atonement. I explained to him that no one held him accountable for the events that had occurred in the past or present. Life is life. Bad things happen. But good things happen too. Because of Beau's life, a lot of good things had happened in the lives of other people.

Zeke pulled me close, "She's right Beau. If you had not married your Sallie, I would never have mine. And that would make it one lonely life for me because I can't imagine my world without her in it."

Beau laid a hand on Zeke's shoulder, "I know what you mean. I know exactly what you mean."

The plan Zeke and I had made for Beau was clearly an epic failure, so the three of us began making our way out of the cemetery. I was moving slowly, already sore from the struggle and covered waist down in red mud.

The rain had ended, but clouds resembling tattered lace lingered in the inky sky. As they parted, a shaft of light from the almost full moon pierced the night like a shooting star; alighting on Beau's face and illuminating him from head to toe. He stopped abruptly.

"No, it can't be." Beau held out his palm. I watched awestruck as a petite hand appeared out of the darkness to grasp

Beau's and then as a woman's entire body stepped into the circle of light. When she faced me, I could have been gazing into a mirror reflecting a different era version of me. Her strawberry blonde hair was styled in big loose curls that reached past her collar; she wore a green short-sleeved dress with a cinched waist and a full, calf-length skirt. Her tiny feet were shod in a pair of black pumps.

I jumped forward, my feet moved by their own compulsion. "Grandma Sallie?"

"Yes, sugar. It's me." Her voice lilted in a southern belle peal.

I rushed toward her then, wrapping my arms about her waist and laying my head upon her shoulder. In return, Grandma Sallie enveloped me in a familiar squeeze so like my own mother's. The aroma of lavender perfumed the air.

We stood there for several minutes, holding onto each other as if we were making up for all the hugs that she had missed over the years with Grandma Ellen, my mom, and me.

With a sigh, I stepped away from her, holding on to her left hand as I reached for Beau's right. "You've come to take him home, haven't you?"

Grandma Sallie nodded, "It's time." She turned to Beau with a smile, "Are you ready?"

Beau pulled me into his arms and kissed the top of my head. "Thank you." He spoke softly into my ear, "Use your gift well."

Letting me go, Beau waved to Zeke who in one swift step was standing by my side. "You take care of her," Beau advised, his young face suddenly very much that of a grandfather.

Zeke gave him a salute, "Yes, sir."

Beau reached for his wife's hand, "I'm ready now."

"I love you both," I blurted, anxious to get the words out before they disappeared.

Standing hand-in-hand, they replied together, "And we love you." The beam began to fade, and as if they were actors standing on a stage beneath a dimming spotlight, they were gone.

"I guess it worked after all," Zeke sounded amazed. "Are you alright?"

"Yeah, I am. I really am." I grabbed his hand. "Walk me home, Zeke."

Chapter Eighteen
Shelter

"**Q**uit fiddling," Mom fussed as she put the finishing touches on my costume.

"I can*not* believe that you are actually making me do this!" I practically growled back at her. "Isn't there an abuse law that prevents this sort of child labor?"

"Come on, Ladybug," Zeke chuckled. "You're the *sweetest* looking Statue of Liberty I've ever laid eyes on." I had informed Zeke that it was time to stick a fork in Gimpy, his endearment since the deer-in-headlights incident. I assume Ladybug is its replacement.

I mouthed an exaggerated *whatever* in his direction as Mom stepped back to give me the once over.

"Zeke's right. And you only have to wear it this morning before it gets too hot."

I threw my hands into the air, forgetting the soreness of my bruised shoulder for a moment – a subtle reminder of last night. "You have got to be kidding me. You are honestly going to make me parade around outside in this get-up?"

Zeke held a hand over his mouth - an attempt I am sure to hold back the loud guffaws that were about to erupt with the force of a volcano. "Think of it this way," his voice trembled with impending laughter, "you still don't know a lot of people in this town, so your mortification level should be at a minimum."

Mom pointed a finger at Zeke, "Now that right there – was *not* helpful."

"Sorry, Mrs. Songer," Zeke replied, appearing duly chastised. Then he gave me a wink and a peck on the cheek before he strolled out the door shouting, "Have fun!" He was headed back home after a quick visit with his mom to the farmers market; I was doomed to a morning of misery.

What a way to spend my seventeenth birthday, I contemplated as I paced back and forth on the sidewalk, holding a flaming torch sign that read *Grand Opening*. Something Mom had done to advertise our store must have worked because we *did* have people coming in – a decent crowd of them, and for that I could tell that my mom was pretty stinking happy.

I eventually decided that her happiness made my supreme

humiliation worthwhile – until Adrienne showed up with her mother, her snotty little nose stuck so high up in the air as she passed me by that if it were raining today, she most definitely would have drowned by now.

With that, I came to the conclusion that nobody's joy was worth my standing here wrapped in a poor man's toga looking like a religious freak announcing the end of the world.

It was close to lunchtime.

I was hot.

And my feet hurt.

My poor performance as Lady Liberty was officially over.

Once inside I rushed to the bathroom, changed into a t-shirt and skirt, repaired my melted makeup, and pulled out the French braid Mom had put in my hair.

In the midst of chatting with Carla Brock over a crystal vase, Mom shot me a grateful glance as I headed to the cash register to ring up a dark headed lady who was waiting patiently.

I could see Adrienne studying me from behind the rack of t-shirts.

"This is a very nice place," the lady complimented while laying a bicentennial plate that bore an eagle and the American flag onto the counter. "I will definitely be coming back and bringing my sister with me."

Was Adrienne trying to figure out what Zeke sees in me?

"Thank you so much." I replied, wrapping the plate in brown craft paper before placing it in a bag. "Have a nice Fourth of July," I added as I gave her the change. She smiled and replied that I do the same.

I caught Adrienne's eye. She promptly ducked her head into the clothes hangers, pretending to be studying one of the designs.

Feeling bold, I walked over to her. "Do you need any help?" I asked in a genuinely gracious manner. I don't know if she understood what I was really offering, not just some assistance here in my little shop, but in her life – as a friend.

For one second, I thought I saw something in her eyes - a kinship…maybe even a peace offering. But she straightened up, stuck her chest out, and looked *down* her nose at me this time.

"No." She turned on her high heels and joined our mothers, her short, flouncy skirt swishing behind her.

I turned my attention instead to a gentleman who was very cordial in accepting my offer of assistance. This guy could be Cash in forty years. His gray, balding head was pulled into a low ponytail, and he wore a red, white and blue tie-dye shirt that smelled of patchouli. Less than three minutes into our chat, I found out that his name is Russell, that he lives in Floyd – a county neighboring Franklin, and that he had spent a few of his younger years as a fish taco peddler at Grateful Dead shows. Russell explained that he's a t-shirt collector himself, but was more interested in bringing some in to sell than he was in buying from our already ample supply. So I sent Russ over to deal with my mom.

We stayed busy through mid-afternoon. People rolled in and out like waves on the beach, but by five thirty, our number of customers had dwindled to zip.

"I guess everyone is at home firing up their grills right now." Mom commented as we leaned against the counter and surveyed the empty store. "But we did good today, honey. There is definitely a lot of stuff missing from that holiday display."

"A lot of customers told me today that they'll be coming back. If they actually do, then you should be in business for quite a while, Mom."

"Oh, I hope so!" She grinned from ear-to-ear and gave me one of her giant hugs. "I'm so glad to be home, it feels right. You know what I mean?"

I squeezed her back. "Yeah, I know."

Mom swatted me on the bottom, "Get outta here. Go hang out with Zeke. Have a happy birthday. We'll do a cake and ice cream tomorrow after church."

One more hug from her, then I grabbed my things and was out the door.

Zeke was planning to pick me up around seven o'clock which would give me only about an hours wait once I got home. He wouldn't tell me what was on the agenda for the evening. The only thing I knew for certain was that food and fireworks would be involved.

My cell began ringing barely before I had time to walk through the front door of my home. "Happy birthday to you!" Kaye sang into the phone when I answered. "I really miss you!"

This was the first time in a long while that we had not spent my birthday together.

"Aw, I miss you too. Are you packing for the big move yet?"

Kaye let out an exasperated sigh. "Not really. Mom's been bugging me about that. They found a few houses that seem good on the internet so we may be coming down next weekend to check it out."

"Really! Can you stay here?"

"I guess," She said in a drawn out, teasing tone, "as long as you're sure that I won't be interfering too much with your love life."

"Oh, maybe I could squeeze in a little time for you."

Kaye ignored my comment and chatted on, conveying both anticipation and nervousness regarding the big change that was about to take place in her life. And she claimed that Will seemed to be doing better, though he wasn't planning on coming with the rest of them to explore the possible new home citing indifference since it wasn't his choice to move from the one in which they were currently residing.

I mentioned Zeke's offer to befriend him if Will would allow it.

"We'll see," Kaye's reply was less than enthusiastic.

I was still holding out hope that my two favorite guys will eventually be friends.

Fifteen minutes later, the conversation had ended and I was sprawled out on my bed. I should never have allowed myself to lay there. The need to freshen up and change clothes was more of a priority, but I couldn't control my eyelids which were growing heavier with each breath. I guess parading around in the heat and assisting the constant flow of customers that we'd had today must have tired me out more than I realized. Or it could be that the events from last night had finally taken their toll on me physically. After the little white lie I told my parents (they were under the impression I had taken a tumble in the mud), I had taken a long, hot shower but still had a hard time settling down to sleep.

I was happy that Beau had transcended in a sweet reunion with my great-grandmother and could handle everything that had occurred to get him there, but the face of Theo Wicke was a burnt image in my head; the feral snarl of his voice and the smell of his rancid breath was a reoccurring invader of my mind. I had watched as he had descended into what I hoped was the deepest pit of Hell where he belonged. It was all over with him. I needed to move on.

But he had called me a Seer, and, other than the obvious connotation, I wasn't exactly sure what that implied.

Right now, I wasn't about to let myself reflect for one second about anything that had occurred last night. I was too tired. "Twenty minutes." I mumbled drowsily against the pillow. Twenty minutes was all that I needed for a little catnap and still have enough time to quickly prepare myself before Zeke arrived.

After concentrating my memory on the contours of Zeke's face and holding my nose to the bandana that still carried his scent (even though I had slept with it every night for almost the last two weeks), I was finally able to rest for a little while before it was time to get up and start my seventeenth year.

Sleep would come easy – the soft hum of the air conditioner blowing up through the vent and ruffling the curtains was soothing. Combine that with the coolness of the room and the faint light of the late afternoon sun, and it was as though someone had slipped me a sleep aid. I reached for the quilt I kept wrapped around the post at the end of my bed, snuggled beneath it and was transported within minutes.

I stood with bare feet amidst cool, curling ferns beneath a waterfall that cascaded gently over rocks and small boulders, carving a serpentine path into a forest hillside. Streams of sunlight filtered through the green canopy that spanned overhead, as if the golden gates of heaven had been flung open to shine down onto the world below. I was dressed in a frothy white dress that flowed to my knees. I felt the urge to twirl on tiptoe, the skirt fanned out around me like the crinoline frocks I was forced to wear on special occasions as a little girl. A friendly chuckle halted my flouncing about – it was Zeke strolling shoeless across a carpet of moss in a white buttoned-down shirt with rolled-up sleeves and khaki pants. With a tender smile, he reached for me, drawing me to his chest; as Zeke pressed his lips to mine, a soft shower of petals rained down around us.

I awoke with a start; the culprit was a thump near my head. Perhaps Samantha had been dropped off and was preparing her own birthday surprise for me. Frustrated, because that had been one amazing dream, I sat up ready to pounce on my little sister. Lucky for her, she was nowhere to be seen, so I dropped my head back onto the pillow and was met with something hard instead of the fluffiness I was expecting. I rolled to my side and saw Letitia's diary resting where my head should have been.

I had not left it there, specifically recalling that I had placed it inside my nightstand drawer the last time I had it out; plus I hadn't seen or felt it there before I crashed. Perplexed, I picked it up to move it out of my way when I noticed that a piece of stationery was folded and protruding from the top. I sat up and pulled out the note, unfolded it and began to read.

Dear Sallie,

My diary belongs to you now. Read more, if you'd like, of my thoughts and musings; but you will find that I only confided in this journal for about a year, and then I graduated from high school, got married, and started a family of my own. It was at that time that I moved from this house, the only home I had ever known. But I soon learned that home is not bricks and mortar or even a singular location. Home is a place that you create – wherever that may be.

My earthly journey is complete. And so I wish many blessings to you, my friend, as you embark upon yours. Do not fret your ability; instead, savor it, for there are those out there who will need you and your darling Zeke just as I did.

Yours truly,

Letitia

"Letitia, are you still here?" I called out hoping that she was still around and had not yet passed on. I paused, waiting for an answer. The room was silent, still. The only sound was the hum of the air conditioning and the swish of the curtains against the window panes.

There were so many questions that last paragraph had created – questions that Letitia could possibly answer about this supposed ability of mine. The reality of it all hit me hard. Those answers would probably come in their own time, in their own way and I would have to simply wait.

I tucked the note back into the diary and secured it once again within my drawer. I wasn't sure if I would read Letitia's journal anymore, having already found out pretty much everything that I was probably intended to know.

Was it no accident that my mom had chosen this home and that I had found the diary beneath the floorboards? Something else I'd never know for certain, but somehow I think Letitia had been with me from the very moment I stepped through the front door of this place.

I decided that I would seek out her grave next week, hopefully, the nursing home would provide that information and I could leave a flower of thanks there…maybe a lady's slipper that she so adored - though she had mentioned how rare they are. I would make it a point to find out.

"Where are we going?" I asked Zeke warily as we trudged up a well-worn path through the woods behind my future venue of education - Franklin County High School. I stumbled over roots and rocks and wished that Zeke had provided me with more information about the evening's activities since my little black dress and wedge sandals were not exactly what I would consider appropriate hiking gear. Zeke was better attired. He could have stepped straight out of an LL Bean catalog with the cargo shorts, short-sleeved buttoned-front shirt, and leather shoes he was wearing.

He pulled me next to him, "Just stick close to me. I'll protect you."

"I'm not scared, wishing I had worn some sneakers, maybe." It was tempting to allow some irritation to enter into my voice, but I seriously did not want to ruin this evening. Thankfully, the sticky hot day had cooled considerably, and it was dark enough that pesky little gnats weren't busying themselves about my head.

All in all, it was a serene summer night about to explode in a sonic boom of colored lights.

Zeke stopped to eye me up and down, "Do you want me to carry you?"

I jerked off my sandals with my free hand, preferring a stubbed toe to another twisted ankle. "No thanks, I'm not a sack of potatoes. I'll be fine – slow – but fine."

"I promise it will be worth it. You are gonna love this."

We continued to climb for a few more minutes before reaching a summit comprised of enormous rocks that rose above the high school football stadium situated below. Zeke wasn't the only person with this idea, others were scattered amongst the stones looking out over the tops of trees to the hundreds of people who sat across the field beneath us on blankets and lawn chairs anticipating the fireworks display that was to begin. The strains of a band in the midst of a set filtered up to us. It was a pretty decent version of the Bob Seger's *Old Time Rock and Roll*.

"This is Bald Knob," Zeke commented as he moved forward with outstretched arms, "elevation fourteen hundred feet. You can see for miles across Rocky Mount. In fact, it's where the town got its name from."

Still holding my sandals in one hand, I stepped cautiously in a faltering sideways movement, peering reluctantly over the ledge. I felt the sudden woozy sensation of vertigo like I was spinning and falling at the same time though I was standing as still as a statue.

Zeke was too busy enjoying the view to notice that I stood frozen in place afraid to shift my position even the slightest inch, which was crazy because I needed to move back and quickly before the food we had enjoyed before the hike ended up splattered across these rocks.

"Um, Zeke."

"Yeah," he continued to gaze out across the tree tops.

My words were coming out rapid and shaky, "Do you recall me telling you before we climbed into the hayloft that some heights do bother me? Well, this is one of them."

Zeke was by my side in an instant, his arms wrapped protectively around me as he guided me carefully away from the edge. "I'm sorry, Sallie. I forgot." And then he chuckled, "Chatting with a dead person is no big deal, but this bothers you."

I was too queasy to comment. But when I sat down in a less frightening location, I began to feel less like I was about to throw up. It was private too, which was nice. I snuggled against Zeke; the nausea dissipated as quickly as it had come on.

"Will we still be able to see the fireworks from here?"

"Oh, yeah. " Zeke smile shined in the darkness. "This is perfect."

Zeke was right; the fireworks ignited brilliantly over our heads with a pop and a sizzle. Red, white, blue, gold and green, a sort of holiday tinsel in the sky. My favorite effect since I was a little girl is one my mom calls the spider mum, which I'm sure isn't the technical name, but fits the description. This firework explodes into the air, opening up like a chrysanthemum flower; then tendrils resembling glitter coated spider legs spiral toward the ground.

The show was good and included a few of my favorites, but the best part of all was sharing it with Zeke. The crackle in the air reminded me of the sensation I still get whenever we touch.

When the display was over, we made our way down the mountain path, a trickier endeavor this time since it was much darker than when we had climbed up. It seems that trekking through the dark has become a regular occurrence for me lately. Though my ankle should survive tonight's adventure, I was pretty certain that the bare feet would produce some scrapes and scratches which would be a lovely shade of scabbed by tomorrow morning.

Having made our way back inside the Jeep without incident, Zeke grabbed a cowboy style straw hat from the dashboard and stuck it on his head. It was the very same one that had halted my steps that first day when he had stood leaning up against this vehicle in my driveway. He shoved the stick shift into first gear, and the two of us took off toward yet another surprise for me, the birthday girl. Zeke said he was making good on a promise he had made on one of our first nights together. I wasn't sure what it could be even after we parked at his house, and he led me by flashlight to the barn; but once we climbed up the ladder, and Zeke threw open the big window, I knew exactly why he had brought me to this place.

The indigo sky was sprinkled with stars and lit up by a moon so big, bright and round it was as if the sun had decided to stay up and party the night away with the fireworks. A warm summer breeze sweetened by honeysuckle and serenaded by the call of a whippoorwill floated through the open window.

I leaned back against Zeke's chest and sighed with contentment. "I guess I've never told you this, but I used to sit on the front porch of my old house almost every night and make wishes on the moon."

"What are you wishing for now? It is your birthday after all."

"Not a thing. My wish has already come true. I can't think of a better way to end my birthday than right here...right now...with you."

Zeke laid his head atop mine. "Aren't you wondering why I haven't given you a gift?"

"No, I hadn't thought about it really. Is this it, the best full moon ever?"

He gave me a gentle squeeze. "Well, I did have to go through a heck of a lot of haggling with the man in the moon to arrange that gift for you - something to do with our first born child." He chuckled lightly, "But there's also this." Zeke dangled a square package tied with a silver bow in front of me.

I wiggled out of his arms and faced him. "You didn't have to."

Zeke lifted my chin with his finger, "Having to do it and wanting to do it are completely different circumstances. I wanted to because I love you." He dropped the gift into my hand.

I removed the delicate paper, glancing up at Zeke as I tentatively ran my finger along the top of the white box. Never before had a birthday gift meant so much to me, even more so than the car I'd received earlier this week from my family. I wanted to savor every second, make the surprise sweeter.

"Well, open it." Zeke was obviously anxious for me to see whatever the box held. His eyes were dancing an excited little jig. "I had this made especially for you."

With a gentle tug, I lifted the lid. Nestled inside the box was a wide leather cuff bracelet the color of caramel. It was embossed with an intricately scrolled black cross - a sort of miniature replica of the tattoo on Zeke's arm; but, instead of a skull and bones, the center of the cross held a ruby red heart with big white angels wings unfurled from behind.

"It's gorgeous, Zeke." I ran my fingers through his hair and pulled his head to mine. "Thank you," I murmured against his lips, "I love you, too."

"Thank *you,*" Zeke's voice was earnest as he pulled the bracelet from the box, slid it around my left wrist, and snapped it closed. "For doing this to my heart," he circled the design with his thumb, "embracing it with your angel wings. It's not forever etched onto your body," he remarked playfully, "but it's meant to be a new reminder that in each other's arms we will always find shelter from the storms that rage around us."

Zeke pulled me close and placed soft kisses up my neck to my ear, along the curve of my jaw to my waiting lips. I rested my cheek upon his shoulder as he drew me even tighter. He was right. We could weather the storms brewing along our horizon - more ghosts, my best friend's brother, Zeke's ex-girlfriend or whatever it was that Adrienne claimed herself to be.

And yes…even high school.

Zeke and I would survive them all as long as we stood strong together.

A smile rose sweeter than a summer morning across Zeke's face as I leaned back to look into his eyes. He slid the straw hat from his head, set it with a wink atop mine, and, while we danced in the light from the shining moon Zeke hummed our song.

Acknowledgements

This book came together with the assistance of so many people that their numbers might rival the population of a one stoplight town.

To my husband, Tim, and my sons, Luke, Ben, and Sam: Thank you for believing in me. You are my sweet things.

Thank you to my family members who allowed me to borrow your names: Ellen, Samantha, Jeanette, and Jesse. To the many of you whose names were not borrowed for *Moonshine Serenade*: Hold on, it's coming.

To my early readers: Denise, Wendy, Emily, Laura L., Laura S., Traci, Jordan, Ashley, Tresa, Jessica, Aunt Elaine and Aunt Petunia. Thank you for shaking your pom-poms on my sidelines!

To my friend and fellow writer, Dana Rose Bailey: Thank you for the companionship. I hope that your debut novel, *Firebird*, flies off the literal and virtual shelves.

To those of you who have supported the Kindle edition of *Moonshine Serenade* with your five-star-reviews and sharing it with friends and sending me personal messages and stopping me in the hallways to ask me when the next book is coming out: Thank you from the bottom of my Zeke-lovin' heart. I'm working on that next book.

To Reba McNeeley: This book simply would not have happened without you. I promise to never again describe Chuckie eyes. I can't promise that I won't ever, again, put a comma where it does not belong.

To my together-in-heaven parents, Letitia Sallie and Larry: Thank you for loving each other.

About The Author

Raised in the Moonshine Capital of The World; Amy Shelor Dye makes her home there with her husband and three sons.

She can't imagine that there's a more refreshing place to live.

www.facebook.com/amyshelordyeauthor

36176524R00127

Made in the USA
Charleston, SC
27 November 2014